A VOICE

Donald Henderson was an ac⸻ ⸻
novels as D. H. Landels, but with ⸻ ⸻
BBC in London during the Second World War, his fortunes finally
changed with *Mr Bowling Buys a Newspaper*, a darkly satirical portrayal
of a murderer that was to be promoted enthusiastically by Raymond
Chandler as his favourite detective novel. *A Voice Like Velvet* and *Goodbye
to Murder* followed, but Henderson's death in 1947 at age 41 resulted in
his books going out of print for more than 60 years until they were
reissued in 2018.

By the same author

Mr Bowling Buys a Newspaper
Goodbye to Murder

DONALD HENDERSON

A Voice Like Velvet

WITH AN INTRODUCTION
BY MARTIN EDWARDS

COLLINS
CRIME
CLUB

COLLINS CRIME CLUB

An imprint of HarperCollins*Publishers*
1 London Bridge Street
London SE1 9GF
www.harpercollins.co.uk

HarperCollins*Publishers*
1st Floor, Watermarque Building, Ringsend Road
Dublin 4, Ireland

This paperback edition 2021

1

First published in Great Britain as *The Announcer*
by Hurst and Blackett 1944
'The Alarm Bell' first published in *Ellery Queen's Mystery Magazine*
by Mercury Publications, Inc. 1945

Introduction © Martin Edwards 2018

Donald Henderson asserts his moral right
to be identified as the author of this work

This novel is entirely a work of fiction. It is presented in its original
form and may depict ethnic, racial and sexual prejudices
that were commonplace at the time it was written.

A catalogue record for this book is
available from the British Library

ISBN 978-0-00-844939-1

Typeset in Bulmer MT Std by
Palimpsest Book Production Ltd, Falkirk, Stirlingshire

Printed and bound in Great Britain by
CPI Group (UK) Ltd, Croydon CR0 4YY

MIX
Paper from
responsible sources
FSC™ C007454

This book is produced from independently certified FSC™ paper
to ensure responsible forest management.

For more information visit: www.harpercollins.co.uk/green

INTRODUCTION

A VOICE LIKE VELVET recounts the misadventures of Ernest Bisham, a middle-aged BBC radio announcer who just happens to be a highly accomplished cat-burglar. An unlikely premise? Perhaps, yet the author was careful to include a disclaimer making it clear that Ernest isn't based on anyone in real life, let alone at the BBC. The story is skilfully written and quietly suspenseful. Like the rest of Henderson's unusual, off-kilter crime fiction, however, it has suffered long and undeserved neglect.

So often, the fate of a novel—whatever its quality—depends upon how effectively it is first presented to the reading public. Hurst and Blackett published this book in October 1944 with the unexciting title *The Announcer*, and subtitled it simply 'a novel'. Certainly, Henderson offers an intriguing and perceptive study in character, but it would surely have been wise to market the story as a *crime* novel—which, unquestionably, it is. Yet it seems to have been regarded as belonging to a different category from the author's crime writing, and was therefore published under one of his pen-names, D. H. Landels, even though the previous year Constable had published *Mr Bowling Buys a Newspaper* under Henderson's own name, and that novel became the most successful of his short life.

When Random House published this book in the US in 1946, they changed the title to *A Voice Like Velvet* (a phrase which crops up in the narrative) and made no bones about the criminous nature of the story: 'People who have a weakness for stories about gentlemen crooks—and judging by the popularity of Raffles, Get-Rich-Quick Wallingford, etc., there are thousands of them—will be delighted to make the acquaintance of Ernest Bisham.' This time, the novel appeared under

Henderson's own name, and the blurb made the most of his earlier success: '*Mr Bowling Buys a Newspaper* caused something of a sensation in mystery circles two years ago. His new book is the kind that English writers, for some reason, do much more expertly than our own. You will be seeing it on the screen before long; we hope it will not be *too* different from this fourteen-karat original.' This was more like it in terms of exploiting the book's commercial potential, and the critics were impressed. *Kirkus Reviews*, for instance, appreciated the way Henderson 'combines a psychopathic study with [an] effective hare and hounds adventure'. But he was a writer forever dogged by bad luck. He died the very next year, and as far as I have been able to ascertain, no screen version of the novel was ever made. Not even (or perhaps especially not) by the BBC.

The crime story focusing on a criminal, rather than a detective, pre-dates Raffles, the 'amateur cracksman' created by Conan Doyle's brother-in-law E. W. Hornung towards the end of the nineteenth century; in fact it pre-dates the detective fiction genre. William Godwin's *Caleb Williams* (1794) was published almost half a century before Edgar Allan Poe's 'The Murders in the Rue Morgue', which is commonly regarded as the first detective story. Through the years, the criminal protagonist has maintained an appeal to readers, as witness the success of Patricia Highsmith's books about Tom Ripley and Jeff Lindsay's about Dexter Morgan. (Incidentally, British readers unfamiliar with Get-Rich-Quick Wallingford may like to know that he was a swindler created by George Randolph Chester early in the twentieth century.)

So Henderson was working in a long-established tradition, but *A Voice Like Velvet* has a distinctive flavour. Ernest's activities may remind us of Raffles, but Henderson explores his character's state of mind in a way that Hornung never attempted. He also teases his readers, who cannot be sure what fate has in store for Ernest. As a crime writer, Henderson belongs to that loose group of authors who were influenced, directly or indirectly, by the work of Anthony Berkeley's *alter ego* Francis Iles, author of two ground-breaking crime novels of the early Thirties, *Malice Aforethought* and *Before the Fact*. Richard Hull, Bruce Hamilton, C. E. Vulliamy and Henderson were among those whose mysteries, like Iles' masterpieces, brimmed with irony and an awareness of the fallibility and limitations of conventional systems of justice.

It would be a step too far to describe Ernest as a self-portrait, but certainly he and Henderson had much in common, including a failed first marriage. Both men worked for the BBC, and *A Voice Like Velvet* wittily portrays everyday life at Broadcasting House. Before the Second World War, Henderson had spent years as an actor, as well as writing novels and plays, but success in all these fields proved elusive and he was often desperately short of cash. In his unpublished and incomplete memoir *The Brink*, rescued from oblivion by Paul T. Harding in 2010, Henderson said: 'I offered my services to the BBC, feeling that my experience as a writer might be of some use in wartime . . . Knowing little or nothing of the BBC until this date, I was a bit surprised . . . to be offered a technical job in no way suited to a writer . . . I was an assistant in a department . . . called the Recorded Programmes Department, and my duties were twofold; I had to put on gramophone records whenever told to do so, by day or by night—and I had to give "ten second cues", in studios, when various programmes were to be recorded for transmission at later dates . . . The most restful of the transmissions I was called upon to do was undoubtedly The Morning Service, as this only involved one disc lasting the conventional three minutes. There was always a soothing hymn.'

Although Henderson resented the BBC's bureaucracy, the salary compensated for the need to battle with red tape. After years of poverty and struggle, a steady job 'meant marriage and starting a home at last . . . As I was getting on for forty, I got more money than much cleverer people, simply and solely because they were younger.' It was while Henderson was at the BBC that Constable accepted *Mr Bowling Buys a Newspaper*, and this boosted his confidence. He proceeded to write a light comedy called *A Man of Character*, and then wrote this book.

In *The Brink*, he said: 'By the time I was working on [*A Voice Like Velvet*] I had been appointed an "assistant" in the Home News Talks Department . . . Here I was in a splendid position to study "announcers", for they would come into the News Room—an enormous, noisy place filled with erudite and striking literary personalities—a quarter of an hour or so before each news bulletin was due to be read to the waiting world.'

For Henderson, Broadcasting House had 'none of the glamour or romance of the theatre. There seems to me to be a continual safety-first feeling in the air.' So far as the BBC was concerned, he was an outsider. A rather different picture of life in Portland Place is presented in *Death at Broadcasting House*, published in 1934 by Val Gielgud and (under the pen-name Holt Marvell) Eric Maschwitz, both of whom were senior and experienced Corporation men. Their novel, an entertaining if relatively orthodox whodunit, proved highly successful and was filmed, with Gielgud himself playing one of the suspects.

Restless by nature, Henderson wasn't suited to conventional working life. He moved to the Features & Drama Department, concentrating on the former rather than the latter. However, curiosity was apt to get the better of him. On one occasion, he was sent 'to visit a factory on the outskirts of London where they were making Rose Hip Syrup, as well as extracting certain properties from the glands of animals. Both the rose hips and the glands appeared to be stacked overnight in a vast refrigerator thick with artificial snow. I was so absorbed by this that I stayed in it far too long and nearly caught pneumonia.'

As his personal finances improved, Henderson felt he could afford to resign from the BBC staff. However, he continued to work for the Corporation on a freelance basis, which 'seemed more fitting for a writer, rather than continuing on the inside, posing as a producer'. He wrote occasional radio plays for the BBC, including *The Trial of Lizzie Borden* which, like several passing references in *A Voice Like Velvet*, illustrates his long-term interest in 'true crime'. He shared this fascination with the detective novelist John Dickson Carr, who also worked for the BBC during the Second World War, and who encouraged Henderson to tackle the story of Borden, sensationally acquitted in 1892 of murdering her parents with an axe in Fall River, Massachusetts.

The Trial of Lizzie Borden was first broadcast in July 1945, and a *Radio Times* article publicising the play noted that Henderson had spent seven months working as a scriptwriter on *Front Line Family*, 'the famous daily serial which BBC listeners overseas have been hearing throughout the war'. Paul Harding's researches in the BBC archives reveal that on one occasion, Henderson was called upon to write a special episode at a few minutes' notice. He completed the script within a couple of hours, earning praise from the BBC and an enhanced fee of twelve guineas. *Front Line Family*, later known as *The Robinson Family*, was the BBC's first venture into soap opera—much to the consternation of those, like Val Gielgud, who feared that it would lead to creeping Americanisation of the Corporation's output—and was a forerunner of *Mrs Dale's Diary* and *The Archers*. Henderson's predecessors as writers on the series included Alan Melville, who had published a handful of lively detective novels in the Thirties and later became a popular broadcaster, and Ted Willis, who went on to earn fame as the creator of *Dixon of Dock Green*, and ultimately received a life peerage. Like them, Henderson had a talent to entertain, but sadly enjoyed much worse fortune.

In 1945, Henderson discussed with Gielgud and Michael Sadleir the possibility of adapting Sadleir's popular novel *Fanny by Gaslight* for radio, but the project fizzled out, as did a proposal to write a light-hearted radio thriller in six parts called *The Haunted Wireless*. He considered that 'book writing is thoroughly odd', but kept working on novels and also adapted *Mr Bowling Buys a Newspaper* for the stage. Tragically, he died of lung cancer when he was only 41 years old, at a time when his work was finally beginning to achieve recognition after years of setbacks. *A Voice Like Velvet* was, he said sadly, 'perhaps the best reviewed of all my books, [but it] was only allowed one edition of three thousand copies.' Among those who heaped praise on it in Britain was the influential critic James Agate, whose laudatory notice in the *Daily Express* was headed: 'Ah, just the sort of book I like.'

Thanks to the Detective Story Club, this highly readable tale of a scoundrelly BBC presenter can finally enjoy the new lease of life it has merited for many years.

MARTIN EDWARDS
February 2018
www.martinedwardsbooks.com

CHAPTER I

MR ERNEST BISHAM kept as still as possible behind the green velvet curtains and listened to a clock ticking. Suddenly he slipped from behind the curtains and made for the door. He went unchallenged along a corridor and opened the first door he came to. Nobody was in it, it was a bedroom. He went to a window and softly opened it. A few minutes later he was hurrying along a side street and panting slightly. He was not so young as he had been, and he was not so slim as hitherto.

He couldn't find a taxi, so he got a bus and reached Waterloo Station a little before eleven. Comfortably, he caught the eleven-five for Woking and sat in a first-class carriage, lighting a cigar, and knowing: 'That porter recognized me again—he knows I'm Ernest Bisham, the Announcer!' He still got a kick out of it, in spite of much recent mental research. Then he sat back and relaxed, thinking: 'I promised myself I would never do it again. But I've failed myself again. It's worse than smoking.' He made a new promise to himself not to do it again, he really would get caught one day, and think of his position now! But he recognized that it meant giving up the biggest thrill of his life, not excluding that first time he had sat at the microphone and read: 'And this is Ernest Bisham reading it.' Deep in his overcoat pocket his fingers touched something hard.

Mr Bisham had recently arrived at one of those stages any intellectual man can arrive at during middle life, if he is honest: which stage was to take a day off and have a serious look at himself. So he spent a rather windy March day looking at himself, and in the evening asked Mrs Bisham to have a look at him too. Unfortunately, the evening was interrupted by the arrival of Mr Bisham's sister. Bess Bisham had the knack of interrupting things. She always brought a bit of an atmosphere with her and somehow or other induced a pause. Even before her brother had become the famous announcer, Bess had possessed a tremendous sort of family consciousness and now it seemed ideal for her to go about saying her brother was, 'the BBC announcer, you know'. But she was a good sort, and she made a good friend if anyone took the trouble to be patient with her and not laugh at her war efforts.

Mrs Bisham went in for a good deal of sewing in wartime, and she strained her eyes and her pink lips at it, looking genial and concentrative at the same time, with three little lines over the bridge of her large nose. She had a beautiful petal-like skin, it was really the skin of a young girl. Yet she was on the hefty side, in an elegant kind of way. She was called Marjorie, with a j, not a g, and she spent her time saying she must not get snobbish, in spite of the rather snobbish district, and in spite of the determination of the public that announcers must become, and remain, the very hallmark of English respectability. This was all very fine, in its way, but the public might surely be entitled to like its announcers human, in addition? They were human beings, weren't they? And she had quite a dread of Ernest becoming pompous and inhuman. He was already a borderline case. But both Marjorie and Bess knew that the Bisham family had 'arrived' when Ernest came home one night a year or two before and said, as he threw his hat on the hall table: 'Thank God—they're transferring me from the Overseas Service! I'm going to be at Broadcasting House! You'll hear my name on the air!' As a matter of fact, it was the day Rommel had used up all his best cards and the war, for us, seemed suddenly to have reached a happier turning point.

CHAPTER II

His new duties were more of a relief than an excitement to Ernest. It was a long time yet from the advent of the General Forces Programme and a long time before he was to say it was the So and So News and it was 'read by Ernest Bisham'. He liked broadcasting, and he knew quite a lot about it; the public knew, or thought it knew, all about the wonderfully glamorous life of an actor: but if it had ever been an actor it would know something about such snags as being out of work, or of being in a three years' run with matinees three times a week. But to Bess and Marjorie, who thought the radio full of glamour and romance—which it was, of course—it was as if Ernest had been made Lord Privy Seal. They joined hands and did an excited and rather ungainly sort of dance in the lounge, tilting over a small Chinese table with the silver cigarette-box on it, and only stopping because one of the servants happened to come in. You could not dance with BBC announcers in front of the servants, however closely connected. As the particular servant said (she was sacked for it later, when it came out): 'Blimey, it's like dancing with God!' She was sacked because of the religious implications, quite apart from anything else that might be read into it. Bess advising Marjorie: 'You owe it to Ernest to live very differently now, dear. And what about a bigger house?'

Ernest, however, had a particular affection for Tredgarth, The Ridgeway, Horsell, Woking. He often pleased Marjorie very much by saying he had never been happy anywhere else, and that Tredgarth, in spite of its frightful name, had brought him a happiness he had never known before.

'And by that, of course, I mean you have brought it, Marjorie! For it was your house!'

Ernest paid compliments in rather a stately manner. He was

3

a bit ponderous, rather as if he was reading it out to fifteen millions at six o'clock, or to twenty millions at nine o'clock. But although he said this and laughed, she usually blushed, for he was always sincere.

'It's nice of you to say so, Ernest.'

'I mean it.'

'I know you do.'

They had the habit of linking arms and wandering around the house or the garden. There were little stone toadstools, and carved garden imps called Rufus and Redbreast. A small, pale boy, in stone, called 'Norman' in gilt lettering, was standing beatifically under a fine tree with his hands extended as if measuring the air. There was a little garden shed for Shorter, the gardener, to have tea in. Being a BBC official, the question of alcohol, for Ernest Bisham, needed intensely delicate thought, yet it seemed reasonable to fill Tredgarth cellars as full as possible in case of weekend guests. They were not obliged to drink. There was always a pin of Best Bitter, and a thinning shelf of gin, whisky, brandy, port and sherry. The cigar department was so depleted that there remained only a box of a hundred Coronas from Throgmorton Street, and two boxes of fifty from Piccadilly. The garden was full of leeks and sprouts and celery dug into trenches, though in another part there were delphiniums, forget-me-nots, fuchsia and dahlias. Marjorie and Ernest were both rather vague about gardens and staff arrangements, leaving most of it to Bess, who more or less lived there with them. Bess disappeared at long intervals, but always turned up, usually in the morning after a tinny toll call which asked: 'I'm in Folkestone, is the bath water hot? I heard you at eight, Ernest, you sounded rather hoarse.' Within two hours she would arrive in very large boots and a tin helmet and, 'Oh, a hundred Churchman Number One, for Ernest, canteen prices—or are you saving your voice?'

Generally speaking, it was calmer when Bess was away, for the servants didn't worry about anything, least of all work, and when she came back, they did, and it was never long before one of them was being threatened with the sack, Marjorie privately protesting: 'Please, Bess, don't offend them, we only get servants at all because Ernest happens to be Ernest Bisham, the announcer. And even under these circumstances the servant problem is becoming increasingly difficult.' But Bess said that no young person ought to take a servant's job in these days unless they were pregnant. She saw women down coal mines, even, and applauded the Russian women fighting at the front. 'Why don't you look for an elderly couple? That's all you need for this place.'

At dinner, Bess often looked quite feminine, especially after her masculine and muddy arrival as an ATS sergeant. Her grey hair was a bit short, but that was regulations; she was fond of saying that her hair had at one time reached down to an unmentionable part of her back, but even now she went in for oddly feminine blouses with little tassels down the front. If there were guests to sherry or 'warish' dinner, she behaved formally and discussed the War Cabinet. If there weren't, the subjects she chose depended on whether Ernest was at home or at the BBC. If he was at his place at the head of the table, she discussed what she would like to do with one or two of the other announcers; if she was alone with Marjorie, she never failed to lower her voice and say: 'Well, my dear—is it a success?' For Bess had been more or less the cause of the marriage, or at any rate the instrument of it, and for a time there did seem to be a doubt of its success. But that applied to the early stages of any marriage, didn't it? Was it a success now? Marjorie was rather difficult to draw out. It was often difficult to know if she was merely reserved, or somewhat evasive.

Marjorie Bisham knew quite well what it was that Bess wanted to know. Bess had the forgivable curiosity possessed by some spinsters of her age. And if she sometimes felt a small irritation over Bess, she didn't remember it for long and had developed quite a deep affection for her. She often felt sorry that Bess had never married, and now never would, and she once told Ernest she thought Bess was happier in her present state; Bess made a sort of profession of being a snob. 'She enjoys the reflected glory you bring her, Ernest! You must never let her down,' she teased him. But it didn't matter being a snob if you enjoyed it and were one for a particular reason. She and Ernest both had to be rather snobbish now and then, even if they were only pretending. At times perhaps they did really feel above other people. Then, it was awful to catch yourself at it. Everyone lived in a particular little world—didn't they?—within the outer world, and they had to live according to those particular standards. The alternative was to get out and live in another one. Mrs Bisham now knew that this particular world was one which she had chosen deliberately—having got out of another which hadn't fitted her at all. She had confided the details to Bess just before she'd decided to marry Ernest. And perhaps because Ernest, too, had been living in a world which hadn't suited him at all, the new world he found with Marjorie succeeded instantly—in the outward and practical sense.

In the emotional sense, however, as Bess suspected, it had not succeeded at all. Ernest and Marjorie had married without really being in love with each other at all. It was one of those practical and smiling marriages and there evidently weren't going to be any children. Marjorie got sad-eyed and went for long walks in a large white mackintosh, returning to have tea by herself in her room. Bess had to have tea with Ernest in the drawing-room, when she would be at leisure to demand what on earth was the matter with him. Sometimes, even, guests would arrive, having been invited by Marjorie herself, but who now genuinely pleaded a headache. The elderly Wintles might come, bringing their brownish son called Jonas, who was said to have already had a tragic life, though not yet twenty-one, and, with his dead brothers, had been amongst the First of the Few. Poor Jonas seemed to admire Ernest, in a distant sort of way, and was always saying he was 'browned off' about this or that. He seemed to admire Marjorie, in a poodle-like way, and when she wasn't on view he would declare to Bess he was 'utterly browned off to hear it. Can I do anything, Miss Bisham?'

But there seemed to be nothing he could do, or anyone else.

There was one shadowy evening over muffins, when just such a situation caught her once more. Marjorie had pleaded a headache, though refusing a doctor, and the guests this time were a bunch of rather nice people called the de Freeces, three rather tall cousins, or some such relationship, who spent the days nodding their greying heads and saying that the war would first of all be over by the spring, and then by the summer, and then by the coming Christmas. Then they would have to start all over again from scratch. They came on this occasion because Marjorie wanted to go and do some local part-time work in a new factory. And they rang the rusty bell sharp at four, all ready to nod their heads and say it was all arranged about the factory, it was nuts, and it was two shillings an hour if it was Sundays. But of course Mrs Ernest Bisham wouldn't want to do it for the money, they knew *that*, dear. Famous announcers must be *very* rich, and hadn't Mrs Bisham a little money of her own, didn't they say? And no doubt *he* had? Anyhow, they had such a charming house, all wandery and sort of part of the scenery, like a gingerbread cake. They arrived full of everything, and were 'mortified' to hear that Mrs Bisham was 'indisposed', making her sound like a famous actress who has really had a row with the leading man, except, of course, that in this case the leading man was far too charming. His manners were enchanting and it was such a thrill seeing the actual person who read the news over your wireless. It was fascinating.

But Bess wasn't at all fascinated; at least, not when the de Freeces had twittered away again.

She said, about Marjorie:

'I'm beginning to wonder *why* you married her! It surely wasn't because *I* suggested it?' Though if it had been a glaring success, she would have claimed this at once. 'Much better if you'd stayed as you were, Ernest. Much better.' She sat with a leg thrown over a bony knee balancing a Coalport teacup. Her stockings never fitted her thin legs very tightly, and her spoon never fitted the Coalport saucer very well, because of the depth of curve there.

Ernest, looking rather fat in a blue pin-stripe, stood by the high brick mantelpiece, staring with some embarrassment down at the log fire. He told her he wished she'd mind her own business and concentrate on a marriage of her own. He didn't intend to hurt her; it was just a brotherly remark. She replied quite brightly that he couldn't hurt her feelings like that; he knew quite well who she would have married if she'd had the chance, but men had never looked at her 'like that', least of all *him*, and so that was that. Then she said she really liked Marjorie, and she declared that Marjorie was not the 'type' to shut herself up in her room like this, she was too kindly. It meant that Marjorie was really becoming ill. You could be emotionally ill as well as merely having the measles. 'But I suppose men can't be expected to realize that! I like Marjorie much better than I thought I did. She's all right. And you started off all right—what's gone wrong? The first gloss has worn off, I suppose! Well, you're very stupid. I hope you're not behaving as if either of you is young? She is just right for you if only you give her a chance, Ernest, and handle her properly. It's your fault if you're pulling in different ways. Remember, she's been married before. She knows something about men.'

'I've been married before too,' he remarked sombrely.

'I should think the least said about that the better! What I'm trying to say is, if you wanted to play the bachelor, why didn't you stay one? You're still much too married to your radio, I suppose that's it. All this success has gone to your head. You can't treat Marjorie like that and expect to get away with it. She doesn't look like a girl, but at heart she is one. Treat her like one.' She stared across at him.

He was large and he was certainly getting rather plump. His shoulders were extremely large. When he wandered to the piano and played some Chopin his backview looked massive and pompous. But he looked distinguished. His greying hair did.

'I know you always pretend to think I'm a bore,' she called through the music. 'But you do listen to me, even if you pretend you don't. Why don't you buy her a dog?'

The music stopped.

His large head turned slowly and he was grinning.

'Buy her a dog?' he exclaimed, amused.

She had the strange notion that now he was in profile he looked sleek and slim. The shadows, of course. He would make a magnificent cat burglar!

A quaint litle shudder ran down her spine. Imagine a scandal like that! *Their* family! And an important man like Ernest!

'You're getting inhuman and pompous,' she heard herself exclaiming. 'We all are, perhaps. We're so stuck up in our little world here. There's danger in it and it's time we grew out of it. So many important things are happening everywhere.' She heard herself talking about China and Russia, and the new world after the war, and saying how could it be a better world unless individuals, actual individuals, started to improve themselves, and to rid themselves of their own little weaknesses? She said she was just as guilty as anybody else.

But he was walking up and down with his cup and a piece of ginger cake and roaring with laughter about the idea of buying his wife a dog.

'I meant a puppy, of course,' she said crossly.

He suddenly put down his cup and his cake.

'She knows she can have everything she likes,' he said a little sharply, and left the room. He didn't bang the door. He seemed to slide through doors.

His movements were oddly stealthy, weren't they, for so large a man. Yet, for instance, you heard of huge men who could dance delightfully, whereas little men fell upon you like a ton of bricks. She supposed he had learned it in the studios. He would often talk about how you could leave the studio while somebody else was still on the air. He was often interesting about it at dinner. He would speak about 'suspended microphones' instead of 'table' ones. It was most interesting.

And then, one Saturday, he did buy Marjorie a puppy.

CHAPTER III

THE moment reminded Marjorie of an occasion when she was very little. Her father had bought her a puppy in almost identical circumstances. Here was new proof that the history of our lives repeated itself. She hadn't got on with her father, whose rather new title had gone to his head, and somebody had told him that the only way to win her love back was to buy her a pony or a puppy. As she already had two ponies, he bought her a puppy, and she felt at once that if he was capable of buying a little girl a puppy—somebody else had given her the ponies—he couldn't be as bad as the neighbours said his title indicated. And it was only a knighthood anyway. She hugged him and pretended to herself that she didn't a bit mind his full lips, and she pretended it was merely childish to think that love had anything to do with the shape of the mouth. She forced herself to kiss his mouth, and when his lips felt dry and hot and full against hers, she pretended it was only because he was old now that she didn't like the feel of him. He dribbled, but that didn't matter at all, he had bought her a Cocker spaniel, black. It was sweet. It writhed round, and yards of red tongue hung out, and shining white teeth flashed in the firelight. And although quite soon it was dead, and its donor too—they both met with a fatal accident in the farmyard via a new bull—the thought of them both returned, as such thoughts would.

Marjorie had been brought up in the country kind of way, with plenty of money—or, rather, no awareness of it at all as a subject—and with all the familiar country attributes such as hunting, or following the hunt in cars, and shooting pheasants and hares, and playing tennis with drearies, and motoring out to some glamorous country hotel in the hopes of meeting a rich man—Daddy said always marry someone who was rich—who

hadn't got full, dry lips. Nearly all of them had, with tedious
habits to match. There was something so dull about most men.
You didn't seem to meet one in ten who was worth talking to,
and there was said to be a statistical shortage of men in any
case, due to the Great War. So as for meeting one in a hundred
who was worth real consideration? Their conversation was one
long drawl, or else it was hearty and alcoholic fatuity. Was it
because they were English? Suddenly it dawned on her that
she was already bitter. Yet her function as a woman had
somehow to be fulfilled. She was aware that she wanted to have
children. She had never known her mother, who had died of
Bright's Disease when she was a very small child, and any
supplementary guidance seemed persistently lacking. She was
taught by strange governesses, none seeming to have the
maternal touch, and she lived through one or two little country
schools in a lost and dreamlike fashion. She needed individual
attention, and somehow never got it. It was probably her own
fault, she often thought. As for her father, he was a queerly
impersonal man, busy at the life of village squire, without
managing to impress very much. When the new bull trod on
the spaniel and got her father against the wall, he was ill for
quite a long time with his fractured pelvis. Then, certainly, he
did seem to become aware of his daughter, and he died
wondering why he hadn't married again, if only to give her
some brothers and sisters, and a set of uncles and aunts.

Not a month after his funeral, Marjorie rather desperately
lost her head and married the only possible man within range.
He was called, ridiculously, Captain Bud. To her secret shame,
she was to be called Mrs Bud. But she expected to lose herself
in motherhood. Captain Bud hadn't a penny, but he proceeded
to get through most of hers in no time. He was a dreadful
little man, and she knew it, but she was terrified of being
homeless after being so safe. Her home had had to go to some
unknown cousin under the entailed will, and to escape to
London with Captain Bud, and to be secretly married there,

seemed the only reasonable solution to her problem, and it passed for romance.

Captain Bud had lived down the lane in a council cottage. He had a certain way with him, and he had dandruff on his coat collar. He was short, and people cattily said he would need a pair of stilts to marry Marjorie in. He was in an insurance house and didn't say much about his title of captain. He was fifty-two. Marjorie had the notion that young men were bores, lots of girls didn't like men of their own age, and she met Captain Bud at a hunt ball in Maidstone. Captain Bud, though quite properly introduced through suitable friends, had arrived without his white gloves, if, indeed, he possessed any, and she often felt that she married him solely because of this and the crumpled look of his tails. Everyone present treated him like dirt, and pointed to his dandruff in a Countyish manner, and although she wanted to treat him like dirt, something seemingly pathetic in his pasty face made her feel fatally sorry for him. She defied everybody by dancing with him, and afterwards lost her party and let him motor her to Tonbridge to a teabarn, where there was cream and night dancing. To her astonishment she noticed herself seeing him to his council cottage, which was an inverted procedure for a man and a woman, surely, and she heard herself agreeing to do it again on the morrow. When he kissed her, she was quite surprised to find he was good at it and his lips were quite intriguing. In about a fortnight she was telling herself she could 'change him', and at any rate she could brush his coat collar for him and stop people talking about his dandruff. He was decidedly a bit short for her, but it was all right, and she suddenly thought they were made for each other, it was perfect nonsense saying you had to marry somebody of your own age and your own class. She asked many of her Kent friends what they thought, but when they seemed rather quiet she put it down to envy. Captain Bud moved out of his council cottage and they rented a thin, tall house in Belgrave Square. The captain declared it was the grandest day of his pretty variable life, and he proceeded to hit the high spots in no uncertain manner.

Thinking of him now, when she had to—for memories chose the queerest times to thrust themselves upon one—she often thought what a contrast there was between Mr Bisham and Captain Bud.

Ernest always inspired her and made her feel conscious of her increasing position in society. Bud had always made her feel conscious of having married beneath her, which was a horrible thing to think, let alone feel. She would think: 'Now I *know* I'm a born snob,' and she would turn from Bud in disgust. He was called Fred.

Fred Bud liked pubs. He liked to totter out of one and into another, and he liked to know the Christian names of the owners. He liked to know the Christian names of most of the customers too, and he liked saying, 'What'll y'have?' to all and sundry, though, if any of them failed to return in kind he was singularly quick on the uptake.

In a few short months Marjorie was filled with a kind of horror at herself for having even contemplated him.

And she fled.

And she very soon found that the position of a young girl who is stupid enough to flee even from Satan himself, unless it is legal, is a very acute one. As her solicitor told her, she should have come to him first. She should have come to him on the quiet, and together they would have set a trap to catch Captain Bud when he was up to one of his larks, which were inevitably a neat fusion of alcohol and other women. As things were, the captain, now on the alert, was also now the innocent party, in the eyes of the world, and he could rush round to all his friends and say his wife had run out on him after only a few months, and that he could but conclude there was a man involved somewhere. This he did, adding that he had spoilt her from the word Go, and been sorry for her, but that now he had no option but to divorce her for desertion whether he

managed to catch the co-respondent or not. He proceeded to
write her two carefully worded letters asking her to return to
him. But, as she knew, and her solicitor friend knew, Bud knew
quite well she would be too proud to do this even if she wanted
to. Marjorie made another mistake in being too thoroughly
embarrassed to tell her solicitor everything, but she just
couldn't, he was an old family friend of her father's. Had she
done so, she might have got a divorce from Bud, with a bit of
luck and a bit of added scandal. But she dodged this and the
next proceeding was to wait three years until Bud brought his
desertion case. As she heard from various sources, Bud spent
the interim using such of her money as he controlled, and in
telling his friends: 'Damn nuisance this three years wait, old
man, but it's useless to expect any new evidence. I thought
there was a man, but I doubt it now. Dear old Marjorie had
absolutely no sex appeal, absolutely none at all.'

Marjorie's solicitor had side whiskers. He was of the old school
of thought, as the saying went, and although his stern countenance had been shocked out of its composure by one or two
tasty cases, his mind had never really entered the wild arena
which made up the present decade. Even when the blitz shattered his famous office chandelier, under which, it was said,
Oscar Wilde had once passed—though on his way to a more
go-ahead solicitor—the dignity of the premises remained.
Pictures of other side-whiskered solicitors still lined the cracked
walls, and the frosted glass on the doors still bore the names
of the titled partners. Marjorie's solicitor still sat in his accus-
tomed swivel chair with the grey stuffing coming out of it,
surrounded by the dust of centuries, jewels from the chandelier,
bits of glass and a shattered book-shelf. And he sounded very
pained to have to tell Marjorie that her case was 'over yesterday.
You're a divorced woman, my dear,' he said throatily. He still
thought it was a dreadful thing to be, even though she was
entirely innocent and had never done anything in her life more

abandoned than have three brown sherries. To Marjorie, however, the news came like the announcement of a school whole holiday. She thought at once and, in fact, exclaimed: 'I'm a free woman again, then! It's all over and I'm free! It's all been a sordid and dreadful dream!' Her strange and immediate impulse was to dash to the nearest Lyons and have a cup of tea in the friendly din there. But she had to be polite and stay until her solicitor had made a pained and stately speech.

'My dear child, you mustn't mind my offering you a little advice. I'm sure this unhappy business will be an object lesson to you. Men are very unscrupulous, and this little . . . amateur gentleman belongs to a very common kind. I do most sincerely hope you will treat me as a friend, more of a friend, after this . . . distressing incident—if you can call a thing that has gone on for four years an incident? Please don't go hotheadedly into a marriage again without asking my advice, my dear! I'm old enough to be your grandfather, and I was a friend of your father's. And remember, you must marry some money next time. This man Bud has cost you most of your inheritance.'

This part of the sorry business pained him even more than the other part, and Marjorie noticed he could hardly bring himself to speak of it. But in the end it was just no good speaking of it, he said; they must speak of the present, and of course the future, not the past. The past was dead. When she thought of the past, she must think only of the happier memories, as we all had to. It was awful thinking about our mistakes. There was her father to think of, he pointed out, even though it was not very nice to think of that bull; he had always distrusted Shorthorns. She must not remember her tears. After that, he rang for some coffee, only to be told that all the firm's cups had been broken by blast, and that the firemen had sprayed their specially imported coffee with some eighty odd gallons of dirty river water. It was still all over the general office floor. His elderly clerk looked rather like a Walt Disney spaniel which had just picked itself up after falling nine hundred feet down a

lift shaft. He was permanently pale and panting. Marjorie's
solicitor dismissed him courteously and said it was no fault of
his about the cups or the coffee.

'No, Sir Tom,' the old man quivered, pleased, and he sham-
bled out with his trousers hanging.

'Well, I'll go,' Marjorie said, still thinking of the friendly din
in Lyons teashops. 'And I can't thank you nearly enough for
. . . well, everything.' She really meant for not charging her very
much, but it was difficult to say that.

On the way out, he asked her what her plans were. When
she sounded vague, he suggested that she should put the little
money remaining into a bit of property, such as a new house.
He said she wasn't getting any younger, if he might say so, and
the great thing was to have a roof over her head. And she had
to live somewhere. He said why didn't she live where he did,
amongst her own kind? He lived near Woking, in Surrey, and
there was golf and the pine trees were very healthy. He and his
wife would help her make some friends. 'And it's near to
London. But you're fond of London, perhaps, and want to live
there?'

'No,' she hesitated. 'There's the club. And I like theatres.
But I think I'm used to the country.'

Pleased, he said the country was the best idea. Why didn't
she come down for a weekend and have a look round? She
thought, well, he can't be too old fashioned, or he'd frown at
a divorced woman! Perhaps people weren't ever what they
seemed? Perhaps they just had to pretend? And times really
had changed, hadn't they? It really wasn't quite so monstrous
for a woman to have been divorced—even if she was guilty?
And she wasn't guilty. She was just silly.

In any case, if people were still so stupid as to mind if somebody
had played one or two bad cards in their day, well, good luck
to them.

She suddenly saw herself as a kind of Woking Merry Widow!

Yes, it would be rather amusing to buy a house down there, and make people wonder about her. She would make a few intimate friends, no doubt, and the rest could wonder about her to their hearts' content. She would do the garden with a sad expression in a brown, floppy hat. She would do any war work that cropped up. Nobody would guess her advanced age, and people would wonder why on earth she hadn't been called up; they'd probably put it down to her kidneys. If life was to be fun, you had to make it so; you had to create some situation whereby Life was inclined to have a go at you. It could surprise you. If you felt secretly lonely and often miserable, nobody need guess it. And who knew what might not happen?

In a burst of excitement she bought Tredgarth, a white mackintosh, a lawn-mower—and a radio. Before the furniture arrived she turned on the radio in the empty hall and tuned in to the Overseas Service. A resonant and attractive masculine voice said, quite untruthfully, that she had just been listening to excerpts from 'Peer Gynt'.

CHAPTER IV

BRIEF but repeated mental excursions into the past being the hobby and the habit of the many, Mr Bisham often forgave himself for indulging it. He was also of the variety who found singular fascination in revisiting scenes from his past, if circumstances made it reasonably easy and attractive. If he passed through Putney, his head always turned towards a particular road and a big house on the far corner. One day, he realized, he might be revisiting the house where he lived now, a solitary figure in a brown overcoat and long white beard, staring sadly at the past which was still safely Now. Mr Bisham liked to dream, and he was decidedly introspective. He never knew whether it was a good habit or a bad one. Perhaps, like most habits, it had its good and bad points. The subconscious mind made a fascinating study, didn't it? The mind had such depths, you could explore and explore, and it didn't matter much where you were or what you were doing. You could watch yourself. He was standing in his bedroom-cum-study upstairs at Tredgarth now, watching himself as he had been standing behind those strange velvet curtains in a strange house. There he had stood, with his heart thumping as it always did, and his senses aware of the exotic. As a matter of fact, under the tension, he had thought of quite ridiculous things, such as liking Saturday nights, and hating rugger, but liking soccer and his prep school. It was odd. And now, standing in his bedroom, and looking at the necklace in his hands, instead of concentrating on the rare beauty of it, and regretting that he dare not give it to Marjorie for their wedding anniversary, or for her birthday, or for Christmas, or for any other time, he suddenly started thinking about the two and sixpenny necklace he had given to Celia that time, and for just the same kind of reason. Locked up in their flat, he had had emeralds and turquoise

18

brooches and sapphire pins by the dozen; but they were dynamite.
He thought now, as he had often thought then: 'She doesn't
know, and she must never know.' And as he made no money out
of it, he had regretted not being able to buy a safe. Yet, he thought
now, was there any reason why he shouldn't buy a safe now? He
was Ernest Bisham, the famous announcer, and surely it would
not be odd for Ernest Bisham to own a safe? One of his most
distinguished colleagues owned a fruit farm! That was no more
curious than a safe? Besides, he surely owed it to Marjorie? She
must never be hurt. He owed it to Bess, and she must never be
hurt. Poor old Bess, who believed in him so, but who didn't
really know him at all. Marjorie didn't know him either. How
could she? A woman had to know all about a man—or feel that
she knew all about him. And he well knew that it was because
she didn't feel it that things were not quite right between them.

But where this was true of Marjorie, it was not true of Celia.
Celia had no brains, and very little perception. She was just a
sex machine. She would probably have been thrilled if she'd
ever tumbled upon the truth about him! She adored the pictures!
Indeed, it might have saved them! But, if Marjorie ever found
out? He often imagined her horrified expression, with Bess,
haggard, in the background. Old Marjorie would cry: 'Whatever
do you do it for, Ernest?' He would smile and say regretfully:
'I can tell you why I started it, Marjorie! And perhaps the reason
is still the same! I wanted to!' 'Wanted to!' they would cry in
horror. Then he might say there had never been any money in
it, but it had saved him a few times, financially, in a small and
sordid way. Now, he might say, he did it partly because he found
it irresistible, and partly because in his present exalted position
the thrill was so intense through the risk being so much greater;
moreover, opportunities for meeting the wealthy had never been
quite so splendid before he had become an announcer. He now
met rich eccentrics, and rich widows—well, too often. And
some of them were very talkative. This did not make it particularly easy, but it made it both attractive and possible.

He stood looking at the proceeds of his latest robbery, and thought how nice his wife would look in some of it. How thrilling it would be to see her face light up if he gave her the pearl necklace that might have cost him so dear. There was something to solve here, it was galling. This necklace would have been wasted on Celia. But Marjorie would be a perfect setting for it. She had height, and grace, and she had a really lovely throat.

Hearing someone moving in the house, he put the valuables back in a copy of the *Sunday Times* and locked it away in a deep drawer in his desk. He kept thinking how much he would like to give Marjorie the necklace. But it would be the act of a lunatic. The papers were full of it, not forgetting photographs. The worst must never happen, and he felt so sure it never would, providing he used his brains. Fate didn't suffer fools, and he had always conceded that. He thought of Marjorie when he had given her the puppy. He had suddenly seen that there could easily be love between them. Imagine giving her the product of the adventures that ran the risk of costing them both so dear! When he gave her the puppy, she had looked up with such a lovely expression, like an excited child. She was sensitive.

Locking the drawer and putting the key in his pocket, he sat down in his armchair and idly took up the newspaper. His latest adventure was spread about wherever there wasn't any war news. He sat frowning and wanting to think about Marjorie and the future, but his thoughts were flooded with memories of Celia—and the past.

Mr Bisham, amidst the stress of present problems, found it comfortable to tell himself he ought never to have met Celia. In the same way, it was comfortable to think that Marjorie ought never to have met that dreadful fellow Captain Bud. One of the first things she had suggested was that she and Ernest should tell each other everything they thought conducive to a successful second marriage. To this he had agreed; and whereas he had told her everything except the darkest secret in his life, she had told him absolutely everything. But if you were going to say that all couples who made dreadful marriages ought never to have met each other, it wasn't going to get you anywhere. So perhaps it was better to think how character forming it was, or how character damaging. It was a kind of fast trick pulled by Life, or Fate, which had a perverted sense of humour at times; it was rather like a man who knows you are sincere and so pulls a fast one. It was true that later on it could make it up to the victims, who lay flat on their beds feeling rather tired. Life was a great one at timing, too, better than the very best actor. These little jokes always happened at the psychological moment; either you were broke, or desperate in some other way; Fate waved a wand shaped like a devil's tail—and the trouble began. And the worst of it was it could go on and on; for, easy as it always was to get into trouble, it was perfectly frightful trying to get out of it. It was like trying to reland on a rocky coast when the storm was at its height. As a boy, Mr Bisham thought that his one and only bit of trouble was likely to be his father. He had much in common with Marjorie, for his mother had died before he had been old enough to know her, and for some hidden reason which even Bess didn't know, Mr Bisham Senior had kept no photographs of her and never spoke of her. Even more queerly, Bess had herself been banished the Putney house when still a girl, and sent to a relative in far away Norfolk. Ernest knew nothing of her existence until he was adult, so strange were the ways of fathers. He never even contemplated enquiring about his mother, for his father was a formidable kind of man who didn't go in for talking. He went in for silences. He was very high up in one of the Ministries, and his work in the Great War appeared to have been of a vital and secret nature. There were clues of various kinds that he had made the name of Bisham a very strong and reliable one, and perhaps it was the very knowledge of this that had perversely inspired Ernest to his unusual hobby, which he had first regarded, sinfully, indeed, as a profession. There were plenty of clues, too, that people were afraid of Mr Bisham Senior, and this also seemed to be a sort of challenge. Clerks would call at the Putney house, moving rather furtively, and they would timidly ask if they might be ushered into the Presence. And one of them always asked, pale, 'What kind of mood is he in this morning, young man?'

The house in Putney was square and formidable itself, cold through unnecessary coal economy, and all the doors seemed frightened to open. Where the Bisham relations hid, never came to light, and it was only later that he discovered Norfolk was the place. The only touch of humanity at all was old Mrs Clarkson and a series of charwomen who crept about with buckets to do the doorsteps. They stayed till they could stand the silences no longer and then fled from the place. Mrs Clarkson seemed to stand it; Ernest always supposed she was adaptable, like an old cat, and he grew very fond of her. She was always there all through his prep school days at Harrogate, and his public school days, and whenever he came back for holidays she looked after his clothes and tried hard to take the place of a mother or an aunt. She was a beady-eyed old thing with a witchlike chin, and he still remembered her frequent position, peeping at keyholes in his interest, to see how the latest silence was getting on within. Ernest got through unbelievable silences, usually with Havelock Ellis propped up against the water-jug, and now and again a spot of Meredith. It had long since dawned on him that life wasn't playing fair by him. What was the use of being taught the public school notion that you must always be a sportsman and a gentleman, if life didn't keep to the same rules? He was still at his public school when it occurred to him he might have to take the matter into his own hands sooner or later, but before he was quite ready to do so a schoolboyish incident set a strange train of thought seeping through his young mind. He was dared to climb through the Headmaster's study window one wintry night and steal his birch. His reaction to this challenge startled even himself. He at once accepted the challenge and with an outward air of complete calm proceeded to accomplish the unnerving feat. He still remembered the intensity of his feelings in the darkness of that awe-inspiring study; the speaking furniture and the distant footsteps in the quadrangle outside: his noiseless return, with the birch prized out of the locked cupboard with a bit of wire. Moreover, on a second challenge, he calmly took it back again. And he remembered being asked: 'But I say, man, weren't you dead scared of being caught? It would have meant six of the best!'

'I knew I wouldn't be caught,' he had answered, modestly but firmly.

'Burglars always get caught!'

'No! You only hear about the ones who get caught!'

He was still sure of this and applied it to every crime. He was quite satisfied that an intelligent person could go all through life and not be caught—providing he wasn't a fool and used his brains. He believed in the power of circumstances, and Fate, but not in this one direction. He believed a man could achieve anything he really wanted to achieve, if his mind was constantly applied to it. There was no question of getting caught. Yet this did not detract from the thrill—for he had no proof of his belief until life was over.

Arriving home with these newly forming beliefs after his last term at school, he decided it was time to take his life in his hands so far as his father was concerned. Ever inclined to be impulsive, he took it into his hands after a singularly long silence at breakfast, by hurling Havelock Ellis across the room. It landed with a report like a revolver shot up against the buff wall. Mr Bisham Senior, however, carefully counted four minutes by his gold watch before looking up and saying, economically:

'Well?'

It was rather bad luck on Ernest to achieve such a discouraging start, especially when he had planned it all so carefully through many agonized nights. But having launched his attack, so to speak, he made a brave attempt to push ahead with it, despite enemy resistance at once hardening. He pleaded, simply, that as his school days were now at an end, he felt he would now like to take his life into his own care and keeping. What he also meant was that he would like a bit of income to do it with, but his nerve went before he could get this out. Deeds didn't unnerve him, words did. His father looked gaunt, distinguished, eminently successful—and completely unlovable. Ernest knew what he himself must look like in contrast: a pale, scraggy and overgrown youth full of the usual inhibitions and frustrations, and yet at the same time an up-to-date edition of the very man he detested.

He failed, however, to achieve a bridgehead.

At any rate, he achieved one ambition that morning: he made his father speak! And it was amusing to remember now that his father told him scathingly—in answer to a remark about refusing to go to college or to any Ministry either: 'I should have thought you would have wanted the name of Bisham to be a household word! I know I did, when I was your age!' How queerly prophetic! It was a household word now all right: it went into every room, in cottage and castle; it even went into that very dining-room, likely as not, in that sinister house in Putney! Life, then, had the pleasing habit of righting itself, and apologizing for what it had done before. Did it stay right, and penitent? That was the next intriguing wonder. But in the days of the Putney house, life had seemed, as it often did to worried youth, most unlikely ever to right itself. In a burst of rage and daring he walked out of the house. Rather, he ran out of it. It was brave to think that he had walked out without any money at all, even though he had only gone along to Mrs Clarkson's peculiarly smelly house off Hammersmith Broadway. He wasn't the first person to have taken such a risk, and he wouldn't be the last; but at the time he thought he was, which was the important thing. Mrs Clarkson's house had green plastered walls, oddly like the walls of his study at school. And, so great was man's desire for a sense of safety and familiarity, that he pinned up one of his study pictures. It was called Dad's Girl, a rather out-of-date blonde sucking orangeade through a straw. The picture had often been used for target practice by the cads, and it had dart, boot, and kiss marks on it.

He hadn't taken to the idea of a public school, and rather regretted leaving the smaller pond of a preparatory school. He supposed he was rather feeble about it, and not a little ungrateful, yet somehow when the prospectus arrived from the Bursar that morning, he was far more aware of his silent father's antics with toast and butter and marmalade, than he was of the contents of the illustrated brochure. There were tough-looking boys swinging on ropes, and there was a large matron standing grinning threateningly in a brown doorway. A huge swimming bath looked singularly cold, and deep, and there was an immensely high diving board.

There was an unnerving picture of the Headmaster, with bull-like features and bulging eyes, with both ears torn to shreds through hearty games of rugger. He seemed to be riddled with learning. Staff: Headmaster (since 1908)—P. H. Quantam, MA, Late Scholar of Emmanuel College, Cambridge; VIth Form Master at Worcester College, Oxford; late Exhibitioner of Sidney Sussex College, Cambridge.

There followed an imposing list of Assistant Masters to the Senior School, only slightly less riddled with learning, and a list of the Assistant Masters to the Junior School, 'for boys under fourteen'. In small print at the top, The Visitors were mentioned, and they appeared to be Vice-Chancellors, Presidents and Wardens and Chairmen of Governors. Wardens? A mental picture of Dartmoor came, a little mistily. The pater's scrunching echoed sharply while he was thinking of Mr Quantam's birch rod, which he would be sure to have, because here it said: '. . . Any boy failing to take part in school games without special permission *in advance* from the Headmaster, thus spoiling the game for his fellows, is liable to corporal punishment.' And it said the playing field was the finest in the whole South of England!

He spent all that morning staring glassily at the prospectus, and accusing himself of being dreadfully ungrateful and feeble, and not like other boys. Yet he felt queerly pleased to be 'different'.

He felt he already knew the school inside out, and it was as chill inside as it was out.

It was also vast. There were five hundred boys.

There were four Houses, called North, South, East and West. He was to go to West House, under Mr and Mrs Deem. The pater had evidently already seen them, and he thought Mr Deem 'a fine man', and Mrs Deem 'extremely sensible'.

There was an OTC, and several vigorous sergeant-majors; there were various quite incomprehensible things printed here and there in Latin, and not only in Latin, but in Roman figures as well; there was a Chapel covered in ivy, lists of places which were out of bounds (penalty—a flogging), lists of Distinguished Old Boys, which appeared to be very broadminded, including abbots, airmen and actors. Nearly all seemed to have been shot in some war or other.

There was a picture of 'a lecture room', and 'the new laboratory', and 'a classroom', and 'the cloisters leading to Big School (fifteenth century)'.

He felt unsettled and uneasy.

But he liked things to be gentle and settled, he liked reading by the fire better than charging about with heavyweights in the bitter wind. He had never been flogged, and dreaded even meeting Mr Quantam, let alone being flogged by him. He was prepared to loathe everyone. It was a sentence, and he disapproved of prisons.

Also, the town was associated with his sentence of incarceration. He soon hated the trams and the wide congested Broad Street, and saw nothing picturesque about the Old Prison and the Old Castle, which represented to him nothing but a minimum distance for alternative Sunday walks. There was a smelly tannery on the route, and there was the empty shop where somebody had had his head battered in, though nobody had been hanged for it yet. The police knew who it was, but there wasn't enough proof. This was to be most attractive for a few terms, but soon it was a bore. It wasn't even fun any more, then, seeing strange men pass the shop, and thinking: 'Perhaps you're the murderer himself—walking about free!' The town was noted for museums and soap. Nearly every big building was either a museum, or else it was a soap factory. There were hundreds of lime trees and horse chestnut trees, and tram lines wandered everywhere, making cycling slightly dangerous. There were rows of big, dull houses, red and grey, with strong drain pipes, and they were one and all studded with brass plates: doctors, dentists, surgeons and psychologists, for there was a well-known hospital just out of the town of vast dimensions.

There was a college of dubious repute, several squalid schools one never played or mentioned, and a theatre which was now given over to the amateurs, when it was not a cinema.

The trams clanged continually through everything, and you could hear them in the distance at night. They made you feel that you were indeed in a cell. The world was very far away, and your sentence was years yet. You were only fourteen or fifteen, and you wouldn't leave until you were at least seventeen.

These were the years which were supposed to decide what a man was going to be and do in the world.

Queerly, hardly anybody asked Ernest what he was going to be or do.

There was too much routine, too much going on, for masters to ask that.

Each new arrival was the same.

He would reach the school gates and there, up the long lime

tree-bordered drive, with the cricket pavilion away over there on the left of School Field, was the school itself spread out in its familiar splendour. You couldn't see North House or East House, for they were right behind the quadrangle, near the laboratories and the sanatorium. But you could see South House away there on the left, and straight up the drive past 'porter's lodge' was West House. Taxis were going up the drive and down it, and up and down the other drive past the chapel, empty or laden with trunks.

Rooks sat about dismally on the tower of Big School.

Porter's white cat strolled out of the lodge, licking its chops. Porter and his fat old wife came out as if to sniff the smell of the new term. They were called Mr and Mrs Gray, but when you saw Mrs Gray, which was rarely, you said for some reason or other, 'Hallo, Mrs Porter,' and when you saw porter, you said, 'Hallo, Gray.' He was very popular and nice, and always on your side, even when he came into the classroom with a note from the Head to be read out. While the master was reading it threateningly out, old Gray always winked slyly, and at a certain point in the recitation rubbed what he liked to call 'yer bum', with circular motions of his free hand. 'Boys are reminded of two things: The new school fields in Elliot Road are out of bounds except for prearranged matches; two boys were severely flogged this morning for removing test tubes from the laboratory without permission.' The Grays' little cottage was practically hidden by its own drainage system, which was a sea of pipes, all of which dripped and gurgled behind patchy clusters of dirty-looking ivy. The atmosphere within looked pitch black, and smelt vaguely of tea.

He would say: 'Hallo, Gray—hallo, Mrs Porter,' and old Gray would twinkle and call out (he knew absolutely everyone's name): 'Ha'r, young Bisham, well, how are we, then, glad to be back? Watch out for yer bum this term, my lad; be sure to do that, sir! I've had to get in two dozen new birch rods, 'cos of the way you all went on last term!'

'Oh, get on, Gray,' one always called out. 'I know you're ragging!'

Mrs Porter would be bending over three square inches of flower border, and revealing parts the size of an elephant.

Ernest saw his younger self pulling his cap off and start throwing it up and catching it. Once, he had had a fight in the drive, well, a wrestling match, and his enemy had thrown his cap into the bushes, just there by the Head's garden. In getting his cap, the Head's face had appeared over the wall. His bulging eyes, thick lips and shredded ears. The moment had been extremely painful for all concerned, for not only were the bushes out of bounds, but it was also Sunday, 'the day of rest, have you forgotten, may I ask?' the Head had coldly wondered.

Both boys had been mesmerized in the drive, usually the scene of happier moments, when one rushed up and down at the school rugger match, shouting hoarsely: 'Play up, *school! Schoo . . . ool!*'

Old Rags had said through his nose (he always rasped things through his nose):

'Come and see me tomorrow morning at ten o'clock.'

It had been unusual. Boys who were boarders were rarely dealt with by the Head, they were usually handed over to their Housemaster. Anything was better than having Rags lamming into you. Which would it be, a flogging or a caning? Queerly, it was recognized that when the Head sent round a notice that a boy had been 'caned', it was far worse than being 'flogged'. The former meant six of the very best, and the latter meant only about three. It was freakish.

Appearing, however, at ten, after a light breakfast, it had appeared necessary to remind Old Rags what they were outside his ghastly study for. He really seemed to have forgotten.

'Er, in connection with an . . . incident in the bushes, sir, yesterday,' young Cobalt had got out. His eyes were like the eyes of a snared rabbit. Ernest had a new and odd sensation of being thrilled.

He had a silk handkerchief down his pants; they said that took off the sting, and wasn't noticed if he felt you. There had been an interesting pause. Lame Miss Nutley, wearing a green jumper and pince-nez, had come out of the study with a handful of papers. She was the Head's secretary. She went dot-and-carry-one and vanished, her right hip rather crooked. Mr Friday, short and white whiskered and Bursar, and wearing gold glasses flat on his forehead, and wearing a parson's collar, came out with his hands, as ever, tucked behind his gown, and walking with his little knees going outwards. The Head's mortar-board towered above his bull-like features, and he licked at his chops like he always did every morning in chapel, as if he was exploring avidly round his tremendous teeth, in search of juicy bacon rind. There was a glimpse inside the Head's study—which you could have and welcome. There was the famous cupboard.

Looking back, it seeemed to be a time full of quaint character studies, and other lessons.

An amazing time, now and then, but much more often tedious.

Growing up was a slow affair, and masters never grew up. They had no chance to.

No, he hadn't liked his public school as much as he suspected he ought to have liked it. Everyone else seemed to like it, and apart from surface grumbles, nobody else seemed to mind being birched, or made to go for long and stupid walks on Sunday afternoons to some curious woods where shop girls hung about behind bushes and went: 'Here they come, Doris! I'll take the tall one!' It was probably quite fun if you were ready for it, but Mr Bisham hadn't yet got hair down his front, and so the point was entirely lost. Another thing everyone but himself seemed to be fond of, was rushing about the rugger field in an icy north-east wind, with somebody else doing a hearty tackle and bringing you down with a thud onto the frozen turf. Ernest Bisham's idea of a thrill was rather different, and he found the only way to achieve it was to search for it in something by Conan Doyle. Another less known author also assisted his desire for drama, and there were moments when he donned a mask, made up out of a handkerchief soaked in school ink, and with a water-pistol tackled the more unmuscular from behind door or hedge. 'I say, it's that absolute swine Bisham,' thin, piping voices would declare, enraged to the Heavens. 'You scared me out of my wits, man!' It was humiliating to know that a water-pistol held no fears, and that he was recognized at once solely because nobody else wanted to play this particular game. It was considered childish. Once, holding up Mr Deem, in error for a prefect, Ernest Bisham got six of the best and the advice: 'If you want to dramatise yourself, Bisham, you'd better join the dramatic society.' But when he did so they made him play Ophelia, which was somehow or other unsatisfying. Later, he joined the debating society, and although he attacked the public school system with some apparent success, claiming that it deprived chaps of all individual attention at the most critical time of their lives, he was thereafter labelled as a pansy, and for some reason a socialist. His unpopularity was odd, considering his ready manner, and sometimes he would be asked why he deliberately made himself unpopular. He would always explode with a protesting laugh, but, unable to reply adequately, he would wander away to beat a tennis ball up against the wall by himself, and thinking: 'As soon as I leave here I shall be popular all right!' He attacked the system of imprisonment, instancing Dartmoor, rather well at another debate, but likened it to the public school system. For that, he had to run the gauntlet of wet towels dressed in his pyjama jacket.

Now, when he sometimes sat on a public platform, much more cautiously airing the same views, whatever he said seemed to be greeted with popular applause. He would wait confidently for his cue, knowing whatever he said would be successful. '. . . So I will now call upon Mr Ernest Bisham, the well-known announcer, who has very kindly come all the way to Manchester

to be with us today!' To a storm of applause, he would stand
before a sea of curious faces, and he would proceed to get in
as much of his views against prison life, and its silly inhumanity,
or his views against the repulsive habit of flogging, without
letting it be thought he was either a socialist or airing the views
of the BBC. At the end, there would be another storm of
applause, and silly faces would throng round him and voices
would say: 'We always listen when *you* read the news, Mr
Bisham! My mother-in-law thinks your voice is by far the best!'
Not one of them cared the slightest about his views on anything,
least of all sex life in prisons. But it amused him, as life amused
him with its odd antics. When magazines asked him if they
could print his photograph and an article about his life, he was
studiously vague about certain years. It was strange how lumps
of years could safely be dropped from an article. It was a technique. And it was often convenient. Impossible to say: 'Well,
as a matter of fact, during those years I was simply appallingly
broke. I had the dreariest of jobs—until my father died, you
know—mechanic, salesman, oh, and cat-burglar.' One item
would be very colourful. 'I must tell you about the afternoon I
walked into a jewel shop in the city. I asked to see some rings
and the bloke showed me about ten on a narrow tray. I said,
thanks, chum, and stuffed them in my pocket. I strolled out—
you mustn't run when you're a professional thief—each moment
expecting bells to ring and hands to seize my left shoulder. But
the shopkeeper must have had one or two, for in about two
seconds I was outside and lost in the crowds.' An asterisk and
italics at the bottom of the page could add, in a dignified way:
'By the way, I sent the rings back. When I got home that
desperate day I found I'd landed a job. And in any case it's too
risky trying to sell jewellery of that kind in London.' Yes, indeed,
and it was still a problem to know what to do with it. The
prisons were full of blokes who had tried to solve this unsatisfactory problem. He often thought old Mrs Clarkson might
have had some useful suggestion to make. Her house was full

of the most shadowy, stooping characters. They would creep furtively up her dark stairs at all hours, not a few going to bed during the day instead of during the night. But he had never risked it. He went on doing various little cat burglaries, just for the thrill, and to prove his beliefs about never getting caught, and in the hopes that one day he would think of what to do with the proceeds. Sometimes he chucked the proceeds into the Thames when he got bored with looking at them. Now and then he sent later proceeds to insurance houses he felt he might have cost too dearly. Mrs Clarkson would be curious about his little newspaper parcels and think they were fish and chips. She would accuse him of not liking her food.

He didn't know what he would have done without her help in the first days of his break with home. And he often wondered now if it was Mrs Clarkson who had first given him his interest in the word 'bulletin'. She certainly brought regular news bulletins to him for several years, scurrying back to the shabby little Hammersmith house to say: 'No, Master Ernest, I tried again—but he just won't speak. We shall have to wait.' When at last Mr Bisham Senior's obituary did appear in *The Times*, his will was reported to have mentioned a figure as large as thirty-three thousand pounds—five of which he was obliged to leave to his son through his mother's will. His son instantly got an advance, threw a lot of surplus jewellery into the Thames and drank gin with Mrs Clarkson until midnight, when they changed to draught Burton. By four o'clock in the morning they were both completely and contentedly under the weather. They lost no time declaring that the old man hadn't been such a bad sort after all, erroneous though the belief was in the cold light of day, Mrs Clarkson insisting that he had been a sort of Dick Whittington in his younger days, 'and very human about ladies, my dear, excepting his own family, that is.' Mrs Clarkson did not at once let drop certain pending surprises about the Bisham family, but proceeded to read the story of Dick Whittington to Ernest Bisham, who sat in her brown armchair with his feet on the table. It was Mrs Clarkson reading it.

He was never very partial to Dick Whittington's story, having no particular fancy for Lord Mayors or for cats, though Mayors were jovial fellows with plenty of food and cash, and Mrs Clarkson had a cat in her kitchen with a highly developed dramatic sense, being fond of springing from great heights across gaps of at least fifty feet, or hurtling itself from the very jaws of infuriated Hammersmith buses into the basement area.

Mrs Clarkson then slyly proceeded to make certain strange suggestions. She was going to have her house repainted, inside and out, and so Ernest was to take the opportunity, 'now that dear father has passed away', of going on a short visit to, 'a sort of family relation, a kind of distant cousin, in another part of London'. She said she had always wanted to see Master Ernest, and she might turn out to be useful to him over a career, or something in that line, you never knew. Startled, for Ernest had been unaware of any such watching interests in his background, he cross-examined Mrs Clarkson in some detail. But all he got was: 'Never mind about the whys and wherefores, dear. And don't ask her any questions, either. She is very reserved and a little prim, as the saying goes. But she likes young people and is keen on educational matters. Go and stop with her, it can't hurt, and I'll get on with the house.'

She was called Miss Wisdon, and her house was in Chepstow Walk, Notting Hill Gate. It was hard saying good-bye to Mrs Clarkson, and to thank her for all she had done.

'You'll be all right,' she said. 'And Miss Wisdon is quite decent. Don't rub her up the wrong way.'

'No,' Ernest said.

'And I expect her Mr Edwards will come and see you and see what he can do.'

'Oh?' he said, startled again.

'Don't rub him up the wrong way,' she strongly advised him. 'Then you'll be all right.'

'Yes. But who is he . . .?'

'You'll see in good time,' she said. 'Well, I'll see you again soon. Be sure to write, or it will rub me up the wrong way.'

'Yes, I will. Good-bye.'

'Good-bye, dear,' she said, and decided to kiss him, a little after the fashion of a mallet going conk up against a tub.

Conk!

Conk!

'Well, good-bye, Master Ernest!'

'Good-bye, Mrs Clarkson . . .!'

The parting seemed quite a sorrow, another rooting up. And although he did see her again soon, when the painting was finished, he had really said good-bye, for she died later that summer, and he was not again to live in the Hammersmith house.

He took a taxi to Miss Wisdon's. He had been told she was 'poorly', or she would have come to collect him herself. He reached Miss Wisdon's at six o'clock. He walked up the pathway of a tiny three-storied house. It was of the dimity variety, and in the garden were large stone toadstools. There was a note jutting out of the front door letter-box with his name on it explaining economically: 'Pull string.' He pulled and there was a long key on the other end, so he let himself in. In the little green glass hall was a second note propped up against a large brass pot with a fern in it. It was as economical as the first. 'Upstairs.' He felt Miss Wisdon was very rash with her trusting notes and he went upstairs feeling a little polite. On a door a third notice said: 'Knock.' He had reached the Robbers' Cave. A thin voice said to come in.

Miss Wisdon was a little old-fashioned lady who belonged to the Victorian era, and who had no wish to modernize herself. She turned out to be good-hearted and easily scandalized. She was one of the world's fussers, everything must be in its place before she could settle. The tea must be laid properly, with

things in the right position, and if one of her stone toadstools
fell over there was conversation to last the week. Tea must be
exactly at four and the silver must be polished on Tuesday
mornings between eleven and twelve. Maids who came in and
'did' for her rarely stopped long, they were 'rude', and they
went out into the night (and sometimes the day) never to return.
She liked being made a fuss of and was used to it, particularly
from the mysterious Mr Edwards, a gentleman she regarded
with considerable reverence and awe.

Scarcely anything was said about family matters, Miss Wisdon
explaining, with familiar reasoning, that Ernest's father had been
'difficult but least said soonest mended'. It seemed she was a
distant relation of Ernest's mother and had always wanted to take
an interest in him. She was shocked to discover he had no evident
plans for a career, but she had already spoken to her old friend,
Mr Edwards, who was an accountant, and so it seemed his future
was in his hands! There were introductions which he was going
to be so good as to give him, so that he could get started in a
job. Miss Wisdon said of him: 'He's such a very busy man, but
he has found time to dine with us on Tuesday.' Then she said
he was not able to come until Thursday. It seemed only fitting
that Miss Wisdon should keep a cat. She hated dogs. 'They water
my doorstep.' She said: 'And Iris is afraid of them.' Iris was her
cat, a dreary thing, Ernest thought, though he tried to like her.
She was a tabby. He never once saw her move from the kitchen
chair while he was in the house, even for most pressing reasons,
and could only assume she absorbed everything in some mysterious way. If he must have a cat, give him Mrs Clarkson's black
Tom, which fought like a virago, and feared neither man nor
machine. Iris just sat, and the expression in her pink eyes was of
an actress watching her understudy take over. When he gave her
any fish she just turned her head away. But when Miss Wisdon
did, she was good enough to allow herself to be fed piecemeal.
Miss Wisdon bent over her, looking like a Victorian music-hall
turn, turning to Ernest with pride in her eyes.

CHAPTER V

ERNEST was really rather dazed at this period of his life. He was 'resting'. He had a good think, but let life do the worrying for a change. And he met his first dangerous woman at Miss Wisdon's house, or to be precise, over Miss Wisdon's fence. She was a girl of sixteen called Violet. She was fond of chocolate, eating it with her mouth open the whole time, without spilling any of it, and without offering him any. She had raven black hair shaped like a worn-out mop, and a hefty-looking father who wandered about the narrow garden as if he was looking for something. Miss Wisdon didn't 'know' them; they were sanitary inspectors who had come into a bit of money, or they would have been still in Battersea by the gasworks. Violet was fond of standing on the manure heap at the bottom of her garden with her legs wide apart. She balanced herself there in order to stare at him and whatever was going on at any of Miss Wisdon's windows. The only thing which ever did go on at her windows was a dancing yellow duster, in the mornings. For the rest of the day there was just Ernest for Violet to look at. She thought he made a change. She asked him point blank to kiss her at their third meeting by the manure heap, chocolate and all. He thought it would be like kissing an éclair. 'You've never kissed a girl,' she challenged him, 'have you?'

'I may have done,' he told her, embarrassed.

'Where?'

'I can't remember.'

'When, then?'

'I can't remember now.'

'I knew you'd never! You went red as red!'

'No, I didn't! In any case, why should I tell you?' he said, stung, but curious about her and this odd phase of his unsatisfactory life.

'I didn't want to know,' she said, womanlike.

Then she said:

'All the boys are after me. I go to the pictures twice a week.'

'Oh?' he said.

'Joo go to the pictures?'

'Now and then.'

'I like Charlie Ruggles,' she said in a certain way. 'He's up the road this week.'

'I've seen it,' he said, deciding quickly.

'What's it about, then?'

'Well, if I tell you,' he said glibly, 'it'll spoil it for you.'

Her long red tongue travelled down a yard of chocolate.

'You haven't seen it. And you've never bin with a girl. And you're a dirty little liar.'

She ran up the garden and then ran back to say:

'You can call me Violet. But I shall call you Squit.'

Then she ran away again.

It was Squit Bisham, watching her!

On Thursday afternoon when Mr Edwards was expected to dinner, Violet came to her manure heap when Bisham was thoughtfully weeding Miss Wisdon's aster bed.

'Hullo, Squit,' she said.

'Hallo,' he said, generously.

'Dad and Mum have gone out to supper. Take me to the pictures and we'll be back by nine o'clock. We'll have a good time.'

She looked flushed and pretty in a rough way. She was still licking chocolate. He was rather interested in the feminine figure at this time. But was it wise to take up with her? He thought of women in terms of marriage, and there was something a little unromantic about marrying a Sanitary Inspector's daughter. He was very snobbish at this time. Violet was in a very chatty mood, called him Squit in quite a friendly way, and it obviously didn't occur to her that he could refuse. She told him all about her grandma, who had the dropsy, giving interesting details. Finally she said he was to slip out into the street in exactly an hour's time.

'See? Have you got any money?'

'Well, yes. But . . .'

'Enough for chocolates? I hate half doing things.'

'Look,' he faltered, 'I'm afraid I can't come tonight. Somebody's coming to dinner.'

Her brow darkened.

'Who? That Mr Edwards? . . . That's fine, leave them together, they're madly in love with each other, didn't you know that? Tell Miss Wisdon you want to go for a long walk.'

'It isn't so easy as that!'

'You dirty little squit!'

'I'd like to come some other night,' he protested.

'You're afraid,' she said.

'I'm not . . .!'

'Yes, you are! You're afraid of girls!' The contempt in her voice hurt badly. 'I shall never speak to you again!'

She turned and ran up the garden, long legs white in the sunshine.

The incident clouded an evening already a little overcast. Mr Edwards's arrival did nothing to cheer, nor did his after-dinner comments. During dinner he made no comments at all. Miss Wisdon had warned him in advance not to speak to him unless spoken to, Mr Edwards liking to eat in silence and to masticate his mouthfuls fifty-six times. He sat at table staring over his head at the bust of Robespierre on the bookcase. He was tall and stern and high-collared, and Miss Wisdon treated him like God. He treated her with great courtesy and respect too, speaking of her to him as 'a great lady, so good and kind'. There wasn't the feeling they were madly in love with each other, but he gathered at the finish he was a Trustee, and that she had done a great deal for the Chapel at which he was Sidesman. Dinner was prolonged and Ernest sat wondering what he would say to him afterwards, and whether Violet really thought he was afraid of girls, and whether he had better invite her to the pictures fairly soon. Miss Wisdon had said in scandalized tones before dinner: 'I hope I didn't see you talking to the girl next door, dear? She is not at all suitable and we do not know them.' At the close of dinner Mr Edwards gravely said a grace, and Miss Wisdon in hushed tones said she now thought Mr Edwards might like to speak to him alone, and she went gravely out. He opened the door for her and she went off to the drawing-room, giving him a little pat on the cheek as if to say: 'It's quite all right, your future is assured—thanks to Mr Edwards!'

'So kind and good,' Mr Edwards said as he returned to his place. He was getting out a little cigar not much bigger than a cigarette.

He thereupon grew very pompous and talkative, asking a lot of questions about his life, and about his schools, and about how he liked being with good, kind Miss Wisdon, and whether she ever spoke about him. He replied that she frequently did and he looked very pleased in a clouded sort of way. Suddenly he got up and went to the fireplace and clasped his hands behind his coat tails. He said he understood that Ernest was worried about his future, but that now it was settled, and that he was to start on Monday in the West End of London, in a Banking and Insurance House called Ponds Corporation Limited. There was a sinister silence.

It suddenly came to Ernest that it was time he emerged from his dazed condition and took a serious interest in things.

He tried very hard to convince Mr Edwards about certain musical ambitions, which he didn't really possess, but they sounded better than mentioning burglary.

Mr Edwards didn't look the type to understand cat-burglaries.

Unfortunately, he didn't understand music, either.

Ernest became aware that he had reached a time in life when certain decisions had to be made. He had some money now, but not so much as all that, and he supposed Mr Edwards was right in saying he ought to 'do' something. Why not learn banking, from the bottom rung of the ladder? It was so *safe*, Mr Edwards said he thought.

Mr Edwards said that music was 'very unsatisfactory', and, although Ernest knew he was pulling Mr Edwards's leg, he kept on about music, so as to keep off the difficult subject of banking.

He also said there was no need for Mr Edwards to bother about him. It was only Miss Wisdon's idea.

'Only?' frowned Mr Edwards.

'It's very kind of her, of course.'

'She is *very* good and kind . . .'

'I know. But there's no need for either of you to bother about me, Mr Edwards. Thank you very much. Things will sort themselves out, I've no doubt.' He added vaguely: 'I might write a symphony.'

Mr Edwards was horrified.

'Composing?' he said, standing. He seemed fascinated by him. 'But I thought you wanted to carve out a career for yourself. I know you have a little money now. What's better than to learn banking? Then you will be able to look after it.'

'I loathe money and banks,' Ernest said sadly.

This winded him completely. He looked quite at a loss until his brain cleared with:

'I must remember you are still very young.' He seemed much happier. 'How old are you?'

'Getting on for thirty.'

'Much older than you look. But nothing wrong with that age to enter a sound firm like Ponds Corporation. In fifty years—providing you work hard—you'll probably be earning between ten and twenty pounds a week. This music phase of yours—there's nothing wrong with it—will of course pass. Here is your letter of admission. I have already written to the bank on your behalf.'

Thus this ancient problem was no easier for Ernest than for a multitude of others. It had come to him later, that was all. Just before he was ready for it. Income versus Art, and all the arguments about playing for safety, or playing for your beliefs and your secret faith in yourself. He could never agree with those who thought an artist could not create what he wanted to create without that frightful preliminary toss-up. Perhaps one day it would be possible for the boy who wanted to paint or write or sing or play to get on with it at once without money worries, in the same way that the would-be businessman could get on with it from the word go, and paid for it into the bargain. Until the present, the would-be creators, who had problems enough to decide if they were even sufficiently gifted, had to set out into the darkness of probable hunger and squalor, at tenderer years than thirty. It was time that Dickens's garret was burned down and forgotten. Mr Edwards was no better and no worse than his predecessors. He put it down to Ernest's youth and said quite sharply: 'Take my advice and put music out of your head.' He would have said much worse about cat-burglary.

'Supposing Beethoven had done that,' Ernest explained, flushed. 'Or Schubert.'

He let out a guffaw. 'So you fancy you are Schubert?'

'No,' he said, getting bored. What ought he to do with his life? There was such a lot of it.

'We all have young ideas,' Mr Edwards said.

'Did you?' he asked.

Mr Edwards went into the drawing-room presently, shaking his head and looking very cross. Ernest heard him telling Miss Wisdon that he had been a little rude 'and ungrateful', and that he was afraid he was stupid into the bargain. He admitted Ernest looked intelligent enough to grow out of it 'in time'. When he had gone, Miss Wisdon asked him in scandalized tones if he had been 'polite to Mr Edwards? He's such a great man, and Chapel.'

'I tried to be,' he said. 'But I'm older than he thinks.'

'I hope you will make a better impression on Ponds Corporation, dear. You are not at all old. Thirty is nothing. For a man.'

'I want to learn about music. Not about banking, Miss Wisdon,' he decided to explain. 'When anyone wants to learn about banking, they're received with open arms! Everyone understands immediately. They don't get told, oh, you must go and write a symphony, here's a letter of introduction, you will start on Monday at two pounds a week. Then, after fifty years, if you have written enough symphonies, you may earn ten pounds a week.'

'Don't scream, dear,' prayed Miss Wisdon, scandalized afresh. 'You look quite flushed, I'm sure you've got a headache.'

And she asked him if he needed aspirin or Enos. He chose aspirin.

Next morning he saw Violet balanced as usual on her manure heap. He had been set to sweep in between Miss Wisdon's row of stone frogs, by the sun-dial. Violet was wiping her tongue along a stick of liquorice and eyeing him with that kind of disfavour which was also speculative. A high wind blew her mop in an easterly direction.

'Squit,' she said.

'Good morning,' he said, by now resolved to ease his ruffled vanity by some display of manhood. 'I wanted to speak to you.'

She turned her back, but he noticed she didn't run away.

'Would you like to come to the pictures?' he enquired nervously.

'Seen everything,' her back said.

'Well, we could go to a theatre.'

'What sort?'

'Something musical, if you like.'

'When?'

'Saturday. Tomorrow. I've decided to start a job on Monday and I'll be leaving here.'

She swung round.

'Leaving?'

'Yes. I didn't come here for always. Miss Wisdon only did it to oblige. My other house is being painted.'

She would not commit herself, but he felt certain she would turn up, if only because he secretly prayed she wouldn't. She ran in, and then ran back to say she had examined the papers and he could take her to the Shepherd's Bush Empire, a twopenny bus ride, and that *if* she turned up, she'd meet him there in time for the first house. 'I say if. I ought not to come out with you at all, after the way you treated me.'

'It's very kind of you.'

'I wouldn't do it for everyone.'

'Well, thank you.'

He retired to wait in dread for the following evening.

When it came, he told Miss Wisdon he thought he would go and make sure of how to reach Ponds Corporation, so as not to be late for Monday morning, and she was very pleased, though she told him not to linger long in the West End on a Saturday night. She looked very grave about this, and so did Iris. The future seemed a dizzy and bewildering affair, and his evening with Violet offered some light relief. Perhaps it was at the Shepherd's Bush Empire, once again within sound of music, or at any rate musical noises, that he decided Ponds Corporation could not be allowed to hold him for long, if at all. Violet turned up on the tick. She looked surprisingly nice, a trifle startling, wearing a little red hat with a huge white feather jutting out of the top of it. She was for a time surprisingly shy and subdued, blushing profusely when she said: 'Hullo, Squit!'

'Good evening, Violet,' he said, raising a felt hat bought that very morning. 'It is most kind of you to have come.'

'I bet you thought I wouldn't,' she said.

They went in. They were both very shy until a turn came on called 'The Orchestra Conductor', in which a man climbed up out of the orchestra pit with a fiddle and started to conduct the orchestra. A fat lady hurried on as if she was the outraged manageress about to send him off the stage. In two seconds they were fighting with such astonishing abandon, mainly involving the violin and the manageress's skirts, that the audience, led by Violet, was in an uproar of delight, Violet rocking to and fro and reaching crescendo with the cry: 'Ooh, my dear, she's got her behind in his face . . .!' It was a great success, and Violet kept up her enthusiasm with such verve that the gentleman in front kept turning round and asking her if she would mind keeping her hands to herself. What she said to him would not bear mentioning, but he got up and walked off to the bar with an expression of extreme horror on his face. Violet was very interested in the bar, but it was still a little improper for ladies to be seen in bars, so she had to be content with ice cream and chocolates. Out in the street again he had his first hint that something was wrong with the post-war world. Out-of-works were parading with banners round Shepherd's Bush Green. The banners cried: 'We want work. Where are your promises? We are the heroes!' He took Violet home on the 17 bus. When they got off it was dark and she said: 'We won't go in yet,' in sinister tones. She took him along a side street to some trees she seemed to know. He felt very nervous indeed. She said he had been 'sweet', and wasn't quite the squit she thought, and that the rest of the evening was on her.

'Oh?' he said, puzzled. He was very young about women.

'I love you. You're sweet.'

They were under the tree.

'It's very kind of you,' he began.

'No, don't you understand? I'll be your girl. I thought you were a sissy, but you're not.'

'A sissy?'

'Oh, stop kidding,' she giggled, 'you are a One,' and she dug him in the ribs. 'Shall I take off my hat? Or what?'

He supposed he owed quite a lot to Violet; for breaking the ice, as it were. She was quite nice about things, almost motherly. He supposed she was a naughty little girl. But he remembered her now as a cockney girl who got him the biggest black eye of his life. When they got to her door at last he thought the evening was over. But thrills were the spice of life to her. She whispered that pa and ma would be in bed, and that they would have five minutes in the parlour, 'so long as we are quiet'. Unfortunately, she omitted to inform him about the stairs leading off the hall to the basement. Tip-toeing in with beating heart, he missed his footing and fell with prolonged and resounding thuds down the twenty-four steps to Violet's dropsical grandma's kitchen. Dropsical grandma evidently slept there, for nightmarish screams broke out on the instant, being taken up by the sounds of creaking beds above, opening doors and a male voice bawling: 'Who's muckin' abart darn there?' Followed the massive vision of the Sanitary Inspector himself, replete with blunderbuss. Much of what he called him was now happily lost in the limbo where lurk all such unhappy misdemeanours, but he remembered a cuff which sent him reeling some four hundred yards backwards down the corridor. 'You whipper-snapper,' was one thing the Sanitary Inspector thought about him. 'You seducer of innicent gells! Get art—afore I chuck you art!'

CHAPTER VI

MISS WISDON was waiting on the doorstep in her nightie, swathed in a red flannel dressing-gown. Her eyes were round. Ernest supposed it was then that she decided he was 'no good'. She declared: 'Oh, poor Mr Edwards,' in a pitying voice, and she declared: 'Those poor Ponds Corporation!' If only the Sanitary Inspector hadn't slammed his door like thunder, Ernest might have reached his bed without losing Miss Wisdon's good opinion. Miss Wisdon put a piece of raw steak on his eye, saying what a good thing it was only a bit of skirt, a remark which baffled him at first.

She said: 'I realize, of course, I have had nothing to do with young men, but I had *no* idea things like this went on! And we don't even *know* them!' She always said 'we', presumably including Iris. 'Whatever will Ponds Corporation say to your eye on Monday? How did you come to get it?'

'I fell down some stairs.'

'On your eye?'

'I'm very sorry indeed, Miss Wisdon,' was all he could say. He was too exhausted for true penitence, and felt sick. In addition, there was that part of his conscience which smarted from the evening. He felt filled with shame.

He sat back balancing the steak on his right eye, and wondering if anything was happening to Violet. Wickedly, her giggle came back.

'You're sweet . . . Do you like me?'

'. . . Yes.'

'Say you love me?'

It had been most improper and undignified.

And he was as good as engaged. From his window next morning he spied Violet already on her manure heap. It was a

47

comfort to know she was still alive and able to suck liquorice and hadn't got an eye like his. Miss Wisdon was very prim indeed that Sunday, saying he was to stop in bed, and to keep the blinds down. He was to 'think quietly, dear. We should all contemplate, now and then. Especially on Sundays. And not only about the future—but the past.'

So he spent that Sunday in restful contemplation, his complexion a trifle red. He contemplated the creaky noises Miss Wisdon made downstairs as she moved about her little house, and the noise she made down there in the little drawing-room on her harmonium. She played hymns which were very fitting comments on his new and dastardly character, and he hoped they would encourage God to forgive him. She played 'There's a Friend for Little Children, Above the Bright Blue Sky', and she burst into song with 'O God, Our Help in Ages Past'. She had a trembling, sincere little voice with a catch in it; it brought out her gentleness. She was a dear old lady and he always hoped she never married Mr Edwards. She came upstairs and read to him out of the Apocrypha.

'Great travail is created for every man, and a heavy yoke is upon the sons of Adam, from the day of their coming forth from their mother's womb, unto the day for their burial in the mother of all things.'

She said it was out of Ecclesiastes, and he wondered why it should be so. It did sound as if this world was a kind of punishment meted out to people for sins committed elsewhere at some other time.

Thus he spent the day contemplating Life and Death, and wondering whether his sin of yesterday would debar him from passing St Peter at the Pearly Gates. Perhaps he would look gravely at him and say: 'There was Violet and the Shepherd's Bush Empire': and over there would be Violet with her black mop of hair and her white legs, ready to walk with him down that slippery incline into Dante's horrible Inferno. Miss Wisdon had a book of the most wonderful pictures of the Inferno, and all the various punishments for all the various sins. Dante had thought of everything. Opinion, however, informed him that Dante was definitely Freudian, and he thought he was repressed.

He didn't see Violet again. It happened to be two more weeks before he left Miss Wisdon's care, but Violet was sent away somewhere for a change of scene. A number of notes were exchanged between her family and Miss Wisdon, the latter reading them with a horrified expression and exclaiming to herself: 'Oh, how shameful, what dreadful people!' He kept very quiet.

On the Monday, at nine sharp, without knowing quite why, he presented himself at Ponds Corporation near Jermyn Street. He loved the West End, with its cinemas and theatres all being busily scrubbed and polished ready for the exciting night to follow. Restaurant mats were being shaken, names being put up in lights, and shop windows tidied and polished. Limousines were to him full of members of the public coming to buy tickets for the new symphony he had written, just then enthralling London. He asked for Mr Barclay without enthusiasm, handing in his letter of introduction. Ponds Corporation was a maze of wire and glass cages, you could make of it a bee-hive, its real workings hidden within sinister doors marked: 'Directors' and 'Board Room'. On the surface, marked with nothing, there was the hurry-scurry of the busy bees, darting at typewriters and comptometers and wire baskets full of papers. Several people glanced at his black eye, Mr Barclay himself starting back at it and exclaiming: 'I hope you don't fight! We don't want ruffians here!' He said he had heard from Mr Edwards and that he would have thirty-five shillings a week, and that he must wash a good deal and never have dirty collars or frayed cuffs. Mr Barclay had big, round features, making him think of a huge baby. He was podgy. He looked as if he lived with Mother and was made to have Ovaltine every night before he got into bed. 'You must keep your strength up,' Mother probably said. She probably lived in Beckenham.

'You won't, will you?' Mr Barclay said.

'What?' he said.

He stared. 'That wasn't very polite. You must call me Sir, young man. I say I hope you won't have frayed cuffs.'

'No, sir.'

'And don't ever be late. It's nine till six. You will usually have Saturday afternoons off.'

'Yes, sir.'

'Don't go into public-houses. Have you ever been in one?'

'No.'

'Well, don't. Just because others go into them, there is no occasion for you to. You must say, "No, thank you. I'm not thirsty." You can be quite polite.'

'Yes, sir.'

'Go into Lyons or Slaters. I'll tell Mr Grayson to keep his eye on you. You want to start as you mean to go on. You look a bit dreamy. I hope you aren't that; you want to keep your mind on your work.'

Ernest had the strongest possible feeling that his Destiny was not here. Why had he come here? Just because one could not write a symphony, but must 'do' something.

'You will be under Mr Grayson. If you take my advice you will learn typing and shorthand, it's the thing. You're keen, aren't you?'

'Keen?'

'To get on. Show keenness and you will get on. Mr Grayson will like it if you are keen. And so will I. And so will Mr Edwards, he's one of the directors. Well, go and sit over there and I will see if Mr Grayson is ready for you.'

'Yes, sir.'

He sat on a wooden bench with holes in it like a baby's chair. Mr Barclay picked up a telephone, holding the whole thing above himself, and shutting his eyes importantly. A worried little man came cringing up to him with very frayed cuffs indeed and looking about a hundred and fifty.

'What?' Mr Barclay opened his eyes and snapped at him. 'What? I am not aware that I said anything of the kind? . . . Go away.'

'Very good, Mr Barclay,' the little man said, and he hurried away to his lair in the shadows.

'Put me through to Mr Grayson,' Mr Barclay shut his eyes and said.

Miss Wisdon said: 'Well, how did you get on? I hope you were polite? And did they notice your eye?'

It was probably a claustrophobia which made people shrink intuitively from this environment or that, choosing by instinct the Army, the Navy, or the Air Force; the office or the open road.

Bank life was outside his range of things.

While, in banks and offices, there would be those to whom any other sort of life, with its risky freedom, would be intolerable.

Mr Grayson was a handsome, grey-headed man, very pleasant. Ernest felt able to confide in him his worry. He said he was not fitted for life in a bank and was interested in music, if anything, but preferably nothing.

'I wanted to paint once,' Mr Grayson confided in him. He shook his head ruefully.

He would say no more. There was no need. Ernest became the more convinced that if anything was to be done he had better do it now, in case it became too late. It was at these vague and dangerous moments that life was shaped.

So he had only two pay days at Ponds Corporation Limited. He could still recall Mr Barclay's astounded face when he told him he had decided, after due deliberation, to give him a week's notice. It had been insane even to start here, and, whatever the

future might have in store for him, it was neither music nor
banking. Mr Barclay, informed briskly of this, flopped back in
his leather chair as if he had been pole-axed. Everyone else
having told Ernest Bisham that he was very young, even for
nearly thirty, Mr Barclay now told him that he had better realize
that he was not young, and that he ought to have settled down
into a career long since. Mr Barclay would not have it that
careers often started at forty, or fifty, or even sixty, and ended
successfully. He thought they started the moment you left school
or college. Mr Barclay, not having heard anything much about
radio, and never having heard about television, had not the
imagination to visualize any possible career ahead for Ernest
Bisham. He leaned forward in exasperation and said to Ernest:

'If you will pardon my saying so, young man—you're an
idiot! I shall speak to Mr Grayson!'

'I've spoken to him already, sir,' Ernest said.

'When your money's spent, you'll soon wish you were back,'
he warned conventionally.

But he never did wish it.

He continued trying to puzzle out what he should do with his
life, and he went back to Mrs Clarkson, who wisely said, over
her teapot, and in a house smelling of new paint, which she
was not long to enjoy, why worry, why force things, let things
happen by themselves, you could sometimes safely do that. She
said he should take stock of his rosier position, financially, and
not be pushed feebly into unsuitable careers. So he took stock
of his rosier position. He first of all tried very hard to decide
why he had become a cat-burglar, and in such an exotic, superior way—he realized what the profession would think of his
attitude towards the gems he got away with, typical old school
tie, no doubt they would call it—and he decided that whatever
had caused such a lapse, the thieving days were over, whether
they were highbrow or not. It didn't occur to him that in the
same way that it was hard to give up drugs, or drink, or even

smoking Churchman Number One, it might be hard to give up any other exotic habits. And one night in Richmond he saw the top window of a large house slightly open. He shinned up a drain pipe and went systematically through the house while the owners were at dinner. He didn't take anything, because they hadn't anything worth while, and because he liked the sound of a girl's laughter. He went on home, via a second drain pipe, and resumed taking stock of his position. He pondered his case all night, feeling a little depressed, and continued taking stock all next day.

Most unfortunately, he took stock of it on top of a bus going to Kew Gardens. There was a girl sitting next to him with glossy fair hair. She was utterly unlike Violet, who had, however, taught him something, and before they entered the high gates of Kew Gardens he knew that her name was Celia. When they entered the Tropical House, she wanted to climb the green spiral stairs and she said all the boys she really liked called her Seal. Ernest forgot to take special note of her use of the plural in her reference to men, and could think of nothing but her glossy hair done up in a green net, and her long legs as they went up the spiral stairs. They were lovely legs. She was a long, lovely creature and only twenty-one, which was another thing he forgot to ponder upon. But he knew he was at the age which loved 'youth', even when it was sometimes ugly. He was getting on for thirty, and he now felt he knew all there was to know about what the pictures called 'dames'. At the top of the iron stairs she stood looking marvellous under a huge palm leaf, and he said he imagined himself with her in the jungle, protecting her from tigers, and coming back to their tent at dusk. They lit fags up there; she'd been brought up on Players, and she said she hoped he didn't think she was the kind who let boys take liberties with her, she'd been educated at great expense at Cheltenham. He knew already, in his subconscious, that she was what was called 'a little beneath him', despite her alleged visit to Cheltenham (which turned out to be untrue), but these were modern times and all that sort of thing belonged to the really dead past. He didn't even yet know he was a person who did things he only *thought* he wanted to do. As long as a girl didn't actually drop her aitches, it was all right; even if she did, it was still all right, because you could teach her the most attractive way to pronounce things. (One did not include Violet.) They blew smoke at an old spider that had come out to examine the day's prospects, and he noticed she had an attractive giggle. It was young. She said:

'I don't know why I talked to you on the bus. I don't know why I went for a ride on a bus. But they drive me balmy at home sometimes.'

He laughed.

She said it was a funny thing that hardly any families seemed to get on, and she said, rather cleverly, that family quarrels were so bitter because the parties knew so much about each other.

'Yes,' he said he supposed.

She seemed to know her subject.

He wondered about her, apart from her legs. His love adventures had not been very glamorous, so much as experimental, usually involving cash, which was sordid but gentlemanly. He had grown cynical about it.

She enquired even then about his ambitions, but he was dark about them, merely saying he wasn't a chap who was bursting to be a famous explorer or some other thing. 'Perhaps I ought to have been born with money!' he commented.

'What would you have done with it?'

'Nothing. Till I died. Then I'd have left it to somebody else.'

She stared at him curiously. He decided she was the homely sort, and he decided that her eyes were honest and her chin firm. He was hopelessly wrong in all three guesses. He would so like to have at least been good at judging character, if he wasn't good at anything else. (Well, except being a cat-burglar, which seemed terribly freakish in her presence, yet still darkly attractive.) They met a number of times, both declaring that their first meeting had been romantic. They hadn't 'got off' with each other. That was unthinkable. They frequently returned to Kew Gardens and the green stairs and their affair grew apace. Indeed, it grew at a tremendous pace. Without quite admitting it, he grew a little alarmed by it, and he was pledged to marry her almost without realizing it. She'd told her mother he had money. Somehow or other it seemed that the moment he slipped the engagement ring on her long finger her good points started to recede in an astonishing manner. Kew Gardens receded at once, they never went there at all. He had moved into a small flat she liked in Acton, of all peculiar places. In spite of her alleged taste for Cheltenham, and his for Hammersmith Broadway, she seemed to adore Acton, which was vaguely near Shepherd's Bush and was noted chiefly for its police-station and its road accidents. It was nothing, of a Saturday night, to hear blood-curdling screams in the main road, and to dash out and find bodies sprawling around with torn thighs, and the news, 'the beggars just drove on without stoppin', they ought to be 'orsewhipped!' Seal, however, thought it was 'life', and she loved rushing out with blankets, bringing them back soaked in blood. 'Take the plates out of the sink, Ernest. Fractured base of skull.' As for Acton police-station, she caustically thought it was 'a beautiful piece of work, and so does Mother'.

Mr Ernest Bisham's first mother-in-law had been an enchanting piece of work. She was early resolved to be every possible help to her daughter's marriage, if not her son-in-law's, and it could hardly be denied that she made every effort saying, when they got married, where the furniture ought to be put, and saying, when the crash arrived, where it emphatically ought not to be put. 'On no account let *him* have it,' she bawled at Seal from out in the road—she had a most positive voice, he remembered so well, none of the neighbours ever missing anything. 'What's he done to deserve our consideration, that's what I should like to know?'

Retiring, at that stage, to a pub called the 'Bull and Dragon', situated as far as possible from Acton, somewhere near Tower Bridge, Ernest had contemplated the situation at his leisure, wondering how on earth sensible human beings could get themselves into such a sorry mess with both eyes wide open from the start. But, looking back, he supposed both his eyes had been full of her legs on the green stairs at Kew. And then, at the same time, there was the crass stupidity of dear old Bess.

The unexpected appearance of Bess in his life was one more example of life's freakishness. He had never heard of her and it was a considerable shock to learn that he had a sister ten years older than himself. His father had never breathed so much as a word, and old Mrs Clarkson, who knew all about the family affairs, had never told him anything. She certainly knew because when the letter came for him, from Bess herself, announcing her existence, 'You weren't at Father's funeral, why not? Hatred I suppose—but write me a letter,' he shoved it under Mrs Clarkson's nose and cried: 'What on earth does this mean? She signs herself "Your Loving Sister, Bess"!'

Mrs Clarkson peeked guiltily under her spectacles and said, well, dear, as a matter of fact she'd sworn a sacred oath never to speak of Miss Bess.

'Why on earth not?'

'Because I'm a devout Catholic. And a sacred promise is a sacred promise. It isn't like C of E. Have I ever said a word about your dear, dead mother?'

'No. But you might have said a word about my dear, live sister. My father has been dead some little time, after all!'

But Mrs Clarkson said it was different if you were a Catholic. And she said it didn't matter now anyhow, because he could meet his sister that night in the Cromwell Road.

It was an unusual sensation telling Seal he couldn't meet her that night because he had to go and meet a sister he had never heard of. He went along to the Vanderbilt Hotel in the Cromwell Road. There, he was astonished to meet not only his sister but various members of his family who had been in hiding for years. They appeared to have taken refuge in or near The Wash, for most of the embarrassed conversation seemed to include The Wash. Bess was the only person who interested him in the little gathering, chiefly because she was so uncannily like his father, and it fascinated him. There was a pull between them, and, from the moment he admitted he was contemplating matrimony, she never let go. She took one look at Seal—over tea at Harrod's—and closed down like a clam. Two hours later she telephoned him feverishly and said: 'Ernest, don't be such a *fool!*' After that she said every day for a month that he ought to remember he was a Bisham. 'Surely breeding counts for something, Ernest, even in these days?' If there was one way, thought Ernest, to irritate a man into a silly marriage, Bess took it.

CHAPTER VII

NOT that it was any excuse. Ernest went into his first marriage with reasonable enthusiasm and optimism. Any doubts he may have had—and he did have several—he cast to the winds the moment they got clear of the registry office at Hammersmith. Wedding guests were a curious motley, with people like Mrs Clarkson mixed up with people like Bess, who had carefully brought the most appalling atmosphere with her, adding it to the equally careful one brought by the bride's mother. After the ceremony, the bride and bridegroom vanished with all speed, having earlier on declined any form of communal celebration, and drove at a great pace in Mr Bisham's new Citröen to Brighton. Seal had been as determined on Brighton as Acton; Brighton was the only possible place for a honeymoon, and you had to go to the Ship Hotel. And Ernest was so pleased to have money and a wife, even if his plan of life was vague, that he agreed gladly to anything she said. The first night went with a swing until midnight, when it was unromantically marred by the bridegroom having the most chronic toothache. The light was still on and he sat up and exclaimed: 'You've broken one of my teeth and it hurts like anything.' He started to pace up and down the bedroom holding his lower jaw. Almost at once, Seal showed her true colours. She said, well, of all things, to go and have toothache at such a time, what sort of a man was he, and blaming her, too, in that feeble way? She sat up in her very loose peach pyjamas and frowned unhelpfully. Ernest was beyond argument, due to the pain, and after a bit of a row he cried, 'All right, all right, but the point is we must at once find a dentist. Please ring the bell.'

She flounced out of the double bed and crossly rang the bell. 'Nobody will come at this time of night,' she said, cross.

Mr Bisham continued prancing up and down the room with his hands tightly about his jaw.

'We've got to do something,' he cried. 'I can't stick this—'

'I can't think why you didn't have your teeth seen to *before* our honeymoon,' she said, interrupting him. 'Instead of *during* it. You must have known they were faulty.'

Through the cloud of pain he managed to see her expression, and the expression of his marriage prospects. When he asked her if she had any iodine, she said he could hardly expect a bride to have thought of iodine, any more than expecting her to tour a dentist with them. He had the feeling she wasn't awfully kind in character, but he said in a muffled voice: 'Look, ring the bell again, will you? I shall go out of my mind!' She again crossed the room sharply and nearly pulled the bell out of its socket. As she did so, a waiter knocked and put his head in and said politely that he was afraid intoxicating liquor could not be served to customers after midnight.

So then Mr and Mrs Ernest Bisham started looking for aspirin. Two consequential-looking gentlemen in the next bedroom answered their knock by opening their door two inches and saying was it the police? 'No, aspirin,' said Mr and Mrs Bisham.

They were obliged with aspirin, but by morning the bridegroom was completely exhausted, physically and spiritually. Even after seeing a dentist, on whose doorstep the pain ceased instantly in the usual infuriating way, he was exhausted by the decision that Seal was the very last girl in the world he ought to have married, just as Bess had said. As Bess said, he needed the homely type, if possible with a spot of beauty thrown in, but it wouldn't have mattered much. Celia had just an artificial and sexual beauty of face and body, but even this faded the moment anything went wrong. For the rest, she smoked like a furnace, liked expensive clothes, adored neat gin and thought going to church was 'just balmy, *now*adays'. Every room she entered became immediately littered with things she had just bought, many of which she forgot to use at all or even undo. She just liked spending. She didn't like the necklace he gave her, despite its beauty, simply and solely because it only cost two-and-six. He tried repeatedly to discover why she so adored Acton, but never arrived at any conclusion. It was just one of those things. We all had some little weaknesses. Ernest Bisham had always recognized that; and he recognized it as he sat thinking about his latest escapade and how much he would like to present Marjorie with the pearl necklace in his drawer. He thought again, in self defence: 'And why should famous announcers be exempt from human frailty? The risk is their own and it is they who face the consequences—if there are any.' Even announcers were human beings and had lived before ever being announcers. Would the public really object if it knew the double life he led? Going downstairs, he gave a little knock on the door of the little room Marjorie liked to consider her own. He thought: 'Poor old Seal simply hated it if I knocked on her door! She thought it was indecent!' What cards would she have played, he wondered, if she'd ever guessed he would make a name for himself? What did she think now, when she listened in? It was quite amusing! Did she switch off—or switch on?

Well, she never had guessed. She had been much too busy in her own fashion to guess anything. They returned to Acton to live the kind of life which those peace years made so inevitable to rich and poor alike, with the difference that the rich were bored and the poor desperate for work. There was no work, and anybody who said there was, if only a man took the trouble to look for it, just wanted kicking. Ernest was fortunate in having some capital on which to subsist, and he fought Celia hard in order to keep the bulk of it intact. Her mother said he was mean and the whole affair drove him frantic, though he regaled himself from time to time with his secret hobby, sometimes going to the country for it, and more often in London districts. His greatest thrill was in thinking what his mother-in-law would say to him if he did get caught; the excitement was worth it, if only for that! He only took gems of rare beauty and he never robbed from the poor-rich or the nice-rich. He could always tell from the feel of a place what the people were like. When the papers tended to indicate that he had made an error of judgment, he returned the property through the post, taking meticulous care about such delicate points as finger-prints, paper clues and postmarks. He amused himself by a continual study of diamonds and stones, as well as safes and locks. He did this because it fascinated him. He also took lessons in revolver shooting, not because he would ever shoot anybody, but because it seemed a proper part of his hobby. You might as well do a thing properly if at all. Seal thought him just queer. 'You and that gun,' she would mutter. Or, 'You and those gems'; she meant illustrations of gems. 'Fat lot I ever see of any!' She thought him extraordinary over shoes, having so many different pairs, with what she called 'stupidly different rubber patterns'. Seal's hobby was to run up debts, which she did with greatest of ease, unless the shop owner was a woman. Men fell for her like flies; it wasn't even a hobby. Women gave her dirty looks automatically, but men's faces broke out like May blossoms the moment her quick footsteps were heard in the distance. The pink block of Acton flats, where they lived on the seventh floor, was being constantly rung up by the flats' porter to know if Mrs Bisham was in. The porter had long since fallen for Seal, so he liked to protect her from approaching tradesmen. But if Mr Bisham was in, he sent the tradesmen right up. The porter often came up to see if the piano was tinkling, and it meant Mr Bisham was in. Ernest never knew what he had done to offend, but he felt sure Seal had double-crossed him somewhere. The porter looked at him as if he was a pimp.

As sordid weeks grew into sordid months, he started to do

a bit of serious thinking. He did his thinking at the piano. He
had a natural aptitude for the piano and had learnt a good deal
at school. But he was not ambitious about it. He often wished:
'Why haven't I got a career like the piano?' Yet, surely, everybody
wasn't born with a terrific careerist-complex?

Then it suddenly dawned on him that Seal had been
unfaithful to him for ages.

A day or two later, in what he thought was a fit of pique, he
brought a blonde to the flat. She was apparently an amateur,
but he got talking to her in a local pub and she seemed mildly
amusing in the conversational way. When she suddenly
informed him who Celia was sleeping with during the daytime,
as a change from sleeping with her husband at night, he started
to prick up his ears. It seemed that this woman was a friend
of Celia's, and also of the man's, because, as a matter of fact,
the man was her own husband. Staggered, yet not really as
surprised as he thought he felt, Ernest ordered two more
double Haigs.

When they closed, that night, he allowed the blonde to come
back with him to the Bisham flat, quite careless of all possible
consequences. He had no interest whatever in her person, and
in any case was far too fastidious, and at the flat they just sat
and drank Bols gin so as to safeguard against a hangover. Then
they went vaguely to bed in different rooms.

Nevertheless, standing together at the flat window next
morning in their negligée, Ernest was astounded to see Seal in
the street below pointing them out to a man in a bowler hat.

When the front door bell rang, a few minutes later, he strode
to the door, expecting to confront Seal. But the man in the
bowler hat handed him a writ and a fountain-pen, while the
flats' porter stood back a bit, grinning.

The blonde explained she did hope he wasn't going to get
sore with her, but what was the point in going on in this way;
she'd always liked old Seal and always would. Looking a trifle

scared, she got her red hat with the daisies round it and
vanished.

Looking back, Ernest thought it by far the most undignified
moment in his life. He remembered, too, being manly enough
to decide upon dignity from then onwards at all cost.

He could still picture that younger edition of himself, taking
on new dignity in the very face of adversity, and closing the
door on that unscrupulous blonde, whose husband would now
have to divorce her in the way she wanted.

He went straight to his desk, signed the writ, although he
need not have done so, deciding to take his medicine. Seal
appeared at the front door, even as he sat drawing cheques to
settle her outstanding debts, bringing her mother with her. He
soon slammed the door in their faces, whereupon his mother-
in-law retired to open a flank attack from the main road—so he
slammed the window. Seal banged on the door for a bit, sobbing
out a portion of contrition, finally screaming out in a temper,
'those hateful Kew Gardens', and that was the last he heard of
her.

Well, he'd been a damned fool and he must take the consequences. He packed up all his personal belongings—they went
easily into two large suitcases, whereas Seal's things would
have needed eight pantechnicons—and, as a final act of puri-
fication, went and had a bath. A label of Seal's, stuck in the
soap, said 'Fresh Lobster'. It had been an endearing hobby of
hers to collect things from snackbar counters in Acton or
Piccadilly when she was tight. On an old bit of sponge there
was one saying 'Fresh Caviare'. This hobby, he decided, was
the only human thing about her, if you excepted her legs. He
left the flat for ever, passing the porter with a great show of
courtesy and dignity, and hailed a taxi. There were two things
he would never, never do again: he would never talk to strange
girls on buses, and he would never visit the Tropical House
in Kew Gardens!

He was divorced a few months later, 'for mental cruelty and misconduct with another woman, or women, and for habitual drunkenness'. It said so in the *News of the World* one cheerful Sunday morning, the report adding, fragrantly, that the trouble started on their very wedding night, when 'the petitioner's husband's conduct was so extraordinary as to make the petitioner terribly unhappy'.

'Was he cruel to you on *that* night?' wondered Seal's counsel, sympathetically.

The first Mrs Bisham burst into tears. She made a tragic figure in her black, but looked very brave.

'He was *callously* cruel.'

'Tell his lordship what happened—*if* it isn't too painful?'

'He wouldn't come to bed. And he went up and down corridors asking people for aspirin.'

'Was he . . . drunk, Mrs Bisham?'

'He was always drunk.'

His lordship seemed to think it an extremely sad case, and a grave one. Moreover, it was undefended, which indicated that the husband's gross depravities were admitted by him. Mrs Bisham was entitled to her divorce—with all costs against the husband. Very generously indeed, Mrs Bisham was not asking for damages. There were, mercifully, no children of the marriage.

Mr Ernest Bisham, in his new surroundings, kept calm and dignified, gently lowering the *News of the World* into the wastepaper basket.

CHAPTER VIII

DIGNITY had, of course, a danger of its own; it led towards pomposity if a man wasn't careful. It was important always to keep within bounds, and to be human and broadminded in proper proportions. There was nothing more awful than narrowness and smugness. In the new phase of life which greeted his return to the bachelor state, Ernest Bisham elected to study himself and to try and find some solution for the future. There was not so much of his five thousand pounds as he would have liked to have felt was still left, particularly by the time that odious blonde had brought her case to a successful conclusion, which conclusion provided for handsome damages against Mr Bisham for the injured husband. He paid up like a man and went for a walk in St James's Park. When he got back, there was a letter from his sister. Through Bess, he suddenly got an unusual job. He had appreciated the radio since the radio's crystal-set days at Savoy Hill, and had spent hours at home with headphones on; but it had never occurred to him that he might one day be, so to speak, at the other end of the line. Now, after a series of Boards, he suddenly found himself taking an even greater interest in music and the proper ways of pronouncing their composers' names. And he started to go on strange journeys. Sometimes he would only go to buildings in London, or to Broadcasting House itself; it would be painted white and the lights from the windows at night did all conspire to make it look rather like a lighthouse. But sometimes he would go to the Midlands, or to Scotland. He lived in a pleasant bachelor suite near the Westminster Theatre and had a somewhat erratic circle of men friends, droppers-in, not necessarily literary or musical, he might just have got talking to them somewhere. Ernest Bisham was now over forty and he had grown large and full like his father. Photographs of Ernest

Bisham sitting at the microphone always made his sister say: 'Yes, distinguished—but getting bloated,' which always made him wince slightly. He spoke a little ponderously, at the microphone or away from it, and was not the impulsive, casual person he had been as a young man. He dressed extremely well and spent a lot of money on his hairdresser. His hair was already slightly tinged with silver. He often felt there was something whimsical about going all the way to Manchester to announce: 'You are now going to hear a special performance of . . .', or to say: 'You have just been listening to a special performance of . . .' He felt glad that nobody knew who was announcing such things. He felt, frankly, rather feeble. But Bess said: 'You must earn something. And it will lead to something.' She also said that all jobs depended on what you brought to them. So, as well as considerable dignity, Ernest Bisham brought the art of being perfectly sincere at the microphone, whilst at the same time being amused at himself. Perhaps it was this that made his voice so real in the room. And then, with the declaration of yet another war, he discovered two things: he liked announcing, and he'd got a weak heart. He was announcing, from a building in London, for the Overseas Service soon afterwards, knowing that he was no good for the war. And suddenly, again due to Bess, he was to meet Marjorie.

Bess Bisham turned up at his Westminster flat and said: 'A friend of mine wants to meet you. She's fallen in love with your voice.'

He had heard of this sort of thing before, so he just smiled. Bess was already in the ATS and she flung her overcoat over his best armchair.

She said she and her friend were 'listening in'; she preferred this expression, where others liked 'tuned in' or 'switched on', 'and you announced something or other, and Marjorie said, "Oh, I wish I knew that man; he was the first person who spoke to me when I bought this old house, he's more than a friend."' Bess sank down on the sofa. 'I said, you *can* meet him, and he is more than a friend—if you know what I mean. He's my brother!' She rushed on with the news that it was most romantic, say what you liked, and that although Marjorie Bud was no longer exactly young, she wasn't as old as he was, and there was just time. 'Just time?' He was always amused at Bess. Bess blushed and said there was no point in a woman marrying unless she had a family, surely.

Ernest sat thinking. His manservant—an old fellow with one arm, but astonishingly dexterous with it—brought them some tea. He knew Bess wanted him to marry. And quite as much as she had once implored him not to marry. And she quite rightly suspected that he wanted to marry again. It was the only solution for him. Yet he was wondering if he had enough nerve for it. Also, it needed a good deal of energy, emotional and intellectual. There was a danger of his becoming lazy about it and absorbed by his work.

After tea she showed no signs of going so he gave her some sherry. She put on the electric fire with her toe and said she had first got to know Marjorie Bud at her club. She spoke diplomatically about Marjorie, 'j, not g', and took care not to put him off her by overdoing it. She said that as well as being neither young nor old, she wasn't beautiful and she wasn't ugly. She had breeding, and she said who her family were and where she lived, 'in that house, charming, but much too big for her on her own like that, and she's lonely'. Then she cleverly dropped the whole subject like a hot potato and wouldn't say another word about her. She chattered about the war.

He sipped sherry through her chatter. Marjorie. Not one of his favourite names. Not old, not young, not pretty, not ugly. It sounded ideal! How Bess loved men to get married—so long as they let her arrange it!

The flat was attractive in the firelight. There was something about this safe, masculine condition. It would be an effort, and it would be a wrench.

Yet—it was dull, wasn't it? Things could be as important

to us as people; but only for a time. They receded and
became the background they were meant to be. Then, you
wanted people; a person. And, for him, it still had to be a
woman.

He got up and wandered about with his glass. When he was
alone, it was a habit of his to wander restlessly from room to
room; there would be a glass in his hand, or a cup; a cigar,
perhaps. He would see the mute furniture sitting waiting there.
How furniture waited! Time ticked away, wars raged; sofas and
chairs just sat there, not dead, yet not alive. His furniture had
style, but it had grown very masculine. It was colourless and
'unwarm'. His flat suddenly seemed to be ash trays and bottles
and dusty records and dusty books. A row of his books, lit by
two bars of electric firelight, said *Evolution of Mind*, *Wild
Flowers*, *The Forsyte Saga*, *Chopin and Schubert*, *Edgar Wallace
(a biography)*, *The Dance of Life*.

There was a glass-topped cellarette full of glasses and bottles,
and in a glass cupboard along one green wall stood his collection of brandy glasses, a peculiar hobby he had started a year
before, a sort of sub-hobby. There they all stood, rather foolishly,
and very masculine, with the reddish firelight showing up in
shadow their differing sizes, all waiting to see if they were going
to be blasted in the blitz.

He didn't care for pictures very much, and the only thing
on the wall above the fireplace was a strangely illustrated verse
from 'The Hound of Heaven'. Interwoven with the contortions
of a young man were the familiar words: 'In the rash lustihead
of my young powers, I shook the pillaring hours, And pulled
my life upon me.' Then there were a few more strange drawings
and splashes of colour, and there was only room for:

> *grimed with smears,*
> *I stand amid the dust of the mounded years—*
> *My mangled youth lies dead beneath the heap.*

An old French clock was ticking. Outside, London tumbled past, and there was the thought of the black-out beginning.

This repetitive business of war was excessively trying.

Many people liked to say—and many more hoped in secret, without saying it—that one day we might achieve a condition whereby wars would be impossible and unthinkable. But, he thought, these people were not students of the Bible or the stock markets.

For most of us, the present time was always the urgency, with but an anxious eye to the future time. The future stretched out only as far as the life of our grandchildren, and it seemed difficult to guarantee them even a hope of any permanent peace.

We could but be cheerful and do our best. We would fight tooth and nail, if we could; and if we couldn't, we would be buried alive in Notting Hill Gate, or bored to distraction in the Ambulance Service in Fulham.

Failing that, we would sew and knit, or wrap up parcels for people, formerly most respectable, but now called—prisoners.

Mr Bisham viewed it all with an uneasy sense of guilt.

He wasn't satisfied.

It was coming to him increasingly that he wasn't satisfied with himself.

And that was the first impression Marjorie had of him.

She wasn't sure whether he felt he wasn't doing enough in the war; or whether he felt that reading aloud to millions of people, or announcing plays, features, talks and symphony concerts—or just plain gramophone records—wasn't a very satisfying thing to do with his life. She felt at once that he had character above the ordinary, and yet he was a problem still unsolved. He looked cut out for great things, and how great was 'announcing', when it was coldly analysed? Was it as great as being Noël Coward, or the Lord Chief Justice, or the Poet Laureate?

Whatever the answer, when she saw him in the curtained anteroom of that little French restaurant in Soho, she felt instantly stimulated—and ridiculously excited. And he had not been, then, Ernest Bisham, *the* announcer. He was just a voice that had filled her empty house. An attractive voice, to be sure, and the whole thing savoured strongly of the romantic, but she was allowing for that.

When she had learnt a bit about him later, she decided she would never have guessed that any such past could have been his. But we were so often deceived about people. It was because we formed an idea about them before we knew them. Naturally the two could rarely be identical. She would never have dreamed of him having been married before, least of all that it was such a marriage! He must have stooped to conquer, then? Perhaps he had changed since then. Did people really change at all? Except their skin? Had she changed, herself? Nobody ever answered these things. You were left for ever with the theory that you were always the child you had been, but were now merely tired and cautious; you'd make the identical mistakes a second time—if you dozed off for a couple of seconds.

It did make it rather intriguing. It was like a succession of duels. This time, you would *not* be caught off your guard.

Ernest, when they came to discuss it, called it 'sporting'.

When he came forward that day in the French restaurant and said: 'Bess is late. But I know who you are,' she knew at once that she liked him and that he thrilled her in an inexplicable manner. She dropped her guard even as she thought: 'Are you really just what you seem?' She remembered this, much later.

She could have killed Bess for her painfully obvious absence, and at the same time blessed her for it. She blushed stupidly, taking his hand.

Mr Bisham shook hands. 'I've booked a table for two,' he said. He dropped his guard and smiled. She decided he was as cool as a cucumber. Secretly, however, he was shaking like a leaf. He asked her if she liked Soho now there were no Italian restaurants and he took her in to lunch.

He was aware of an odd sense of panic. It wasn't because Bess had refused to come too. It was because the moment he saw Marjorie he knew that Destiny had some serious game to try on between the two of them. It was Destiny's idea of fun. He'd been left alone lately. Absorbed by his microphone, he hadn't even slithered down any drain pipes. Perhaps he never would again. At lunch, he looked at his new acquaintance, imagined them both married to each other, and silently considered the question of drain pipes. She had a perfectly beautiful throat. It was made for diamonds. Yet what was the good of that if the diamonds he could get her were too dangerous to wear? It was tiresome. He felt excited and ate his soup too quickly. She was miles behind. He had to pretend he hadn't finished after all.

They sat in the far corner.

They sat side by side. She said she hated sitting bang opposite people, it was formal.

The place was very elegant and everyone looked very highbrow. He noticed several delightful pearl necklaces about. He knew the restaurant well. All the waiters he had known had vanished. Most of the familiar food had vanished. There was still some good wine, at a price. And there was Algerian wine.

Conversation was a bit sticky at first. They both behaved rather as if they were conscious of being no longer young. They were somewhat formal, but with a sort of affectionate politeness caused by Bess having told each of them nice things about the other. This gave them something to start with.

She was larger than he had imagined and it was easy to imagine her as a singer. It was more than a popular notion that singers got fat. Singing did make you get fat. And you had to sing on a full stomach. But she was not actually *fat*. She had height and grace and she dressed elegantly. Her sense of colour seemed unusual, for she had light green eyes yet wore brown and carried about a large, mauve handbag. On both large wrists she had red bracelets. It was quaint. Her hair was light brown and he supposed she did something to it, for its shading seemed uncertain. He could imagine her dressing rather dreamily, perhaps while she looked out of the window at her pretty garden. Her garden would be sure to be pretty. He admired her petal-like skin and her mouth most. They were ideal. She had that schoolgirl complexion with which to set them off. Her tone of voice was unhurried and young, and the tune of it made her seem the motherly sort. She fused a shy youngness with this, a childish, polite gravity with a background expression of the eyes ready to smile at will. Here was no shrew, no cactus. Here was an elegant and very sensitive plant. It was tall, so if you let it get cold it would bend at the top and wilt into prideful tears. It flooded upon him that if marriage was meant for them he must never hurt her; she had been hurt already. The responsibility of this unnerved him afresh. He had no right to go any further with this. His guard was up again. When she elbowed her glass over, she looked worried to death by it and she blushed. How easily she blushed, didn't she? It was quaint too. 'Oh,' she said, 'I'm terribly sorry, Mr Bisham!'

He quickly laughed away her embarrassment. He said it was entirely his fault for putting it where he had, and he signalled the waiter.

When the waiter mopped it up she sat wondering whether to say it was lucky to spill wine, or whether it would sound too young for him.

He sat smiling politely at the proceedings and wondered the same thing, but thinking of the ritual which required dabbing some of the spilled wine under the other person's ears. She had fairly large ears, and she wore little green rings fitted to the lobes.

Later on, when they discussed that first lunch, it amused them a lot to think what a mutual ordeal it had been. Both thought it would never end, while hoping it would never end. 'I kept staring at your hands,' she told him. 'I do like good hands.'

At the lunch he had had to call her 'Mrs Bud', and it hadn't fitted her at all. It had never occurred to her to revert to her maiden name.

And when the ordeal of lunch came to an end both suddenly regretted that it was over. He said he had twenty minutes in which to get across a section of London and say into the microphone: 'You have been listening for the last half hour to Sandy Macpherson playing at the organ of the Granada, Sheffield.' For her part, she had to go and do some shopping. The afternoon suddenly stretched endlessly out for him. He would be in his little glass box, every now and again staring irritably at the clock to see if the programme was under-running or over-running, sliding to his feet and reaching over to the gramophone bank to play a fill in—which announcers did in those days—fading it out when the red hand reached the top. Then he would slide down into his seat again. 'And now, for the next twenty minutes, parents can listen to messages from their children in America.' The boy at his back would be coping with an armful of discs cut into bands. Each band would end: 'Good-bye, Mum and Dad. Love to Aunt Maude. Keep your chin up . . .!'

When she was putting on her gloves, he asked her if she would care to see him again.

'Of course I would.' She smiled positively.

'I'm glad Bess hasn't painted me in too sombre colours!' He smiled too. There was the awkward business of paying the bill without seeming to flourish pound notes about.

'Should she have?'

He couldn't think of an intelligent answer. He left it.

Feeling there was a mild pause, caused by her silly remark, she said:

'You wouldn't be with the BBC if you weren't eminently respectable!'

It seemed to make things worse. They were ending badly.

He assured her rather gravely that 'that is all changed. The BBC is no longer frightened of divorce. Times have broadened.'

'Let's hope so,' was all she could think of for that.

Her own troubles touched her forehead then. He noticed there were three little lines which could appear above the bridge of her large nose.

He thought: 'It's a nice nose . . .'

CHAPTER IX

IT was, however, Mrs Bud's beautiful white throat that enthralled him most. Nevertheless, remembering the fatal fascination of Celia's legs, he dismissed Mrs Bud's throat firmly from his mind, at any rate for the time being. A successful marriage needed other qualities. As Bess pointed out those qualities from day to day, 'I think she can cook, she *likes* cooking, anyway', and, 'she's sweet with children, I've seen her on walks', his cautious new defences started to crumble. As for throats, a beautiful throat like that needed the kind of jewel only very rich men could obtain. As well hang dynamite round her neck, as hang the jewels of his own collection there. Best to forget it. At any rate there were other things to think about for the moment. He would ask her to marry him, he had made up his mind.

Now, knocking on her door two years afterwards, he suddenly thought of her throat again. In the locked drawer in his room was something worthy of it, the papers said it was worth five thousand pounds. But instead he must put his hand in his pocket and give her the little thing he had seen in an old shop. It was only coral.

And just as when he had given her the puppy, now a long-legged animal called Lucas, her childish pleasure was a rich reward for him who had deserved no reward.

He was under the sad necessity of trying to save his marriage, while it still could be saved.

Her eyes were wide and looked a bit wet. She had been writing letters and she was turned round in her chair. She exclaimed: 'It's the second present you've given me of that kind, Ernest!' She stressed 'that' slightly.

He thought guiltily: 'Only two—in two years? Well, of *that* kind. She means other than it being a birthday present or something.'

'I'm trying to thank you for it,' she said, frowning quaintly.

He fidgeted a little and lit a cigarette.

'It's only a little thing.'

'But it's beautiful . . .'

'It's perfect in its way,' he said, rather briskly. He wished he could say something of what was in his mind. But it would be dull to say he'd rather give her a five thousand pound necklace than a five pound one.

She suddenly got up and kissed him and said, simply:

'Oh, Ernest . . .!'

She was thanking him. She wasn't much good at talking, either. She said now what she had more or less said two years before, about Lucas. 'You must have gone to such trouble to find it. That's what I appreciate so.' Bess had said, concerning Lucas: 'Don't go to a *shop*. Aren't men hopeless! Women like to feel a man has been to some trouble. Find one in a dogs' home.'

'They'll be dirty and . . .!'

'Of course they'll be dirty! *And* thin. Don't get a well fed one by telephone from Harrod's! Women like sentiment!'

He went obediently to various dogs' homes, finally coming across old Lucas. He was called that then. He'd been taken in from the streets and he was emphatically dirty and thin. Curiously enough, he still looked the same, only taller, though he ate like a wolf and never missed a meal, even early morning tea. His make was still distinctly uncertain and the best you could say about him was that his grandfather might have been a badly bred airedale.

When he left for London, he sat in the train and had new thoughts about his marriage. He again thought that, as when he had given her Lucas, the coral beads were a second clue to the success of his marriage. There had always been a flame burning dimly between them. It just wanted some little discovery to make it burn in the way it should and could. You couldn't rely on giving her things. What was it? He sat in the train and frowned.

Suddenly he thought it was because she was disappointed in him. He *was* what he seemed. (She had told him that she wondered if he was.) Well, he was. He was just a distinguished-looking man who read out loud. Where Bess was impressed beyond measure by it, Marjorie was not in the least impressed. He had as good as died on her almost at once. Chagrined by this decision, he thought again of his latest escapade, and Lady Stewker's necklace in the drawer at home. And it came to him that he was a cat-burglar because he was disappointed in himself too. Unless he had this risky double life—he wasn't a man of character at all. And he knew for certain he was going to take another serious risk of the same kind—again and perhaps again: so as to see what Destiny was trying to do with him.

The man facing him in the carriage recognized him.

He had large red ears and was one of those vacant, smiling men who liked to speak just loudly enough to be overheard by the rest of the carriage. Leaning forward, he pitched his voice embarrassingly:

'Excuse me, I know you won't mind my mentioning it discreetly? Aren't you Mr Ernest Bisham, the announcer chap? Thought so—recognized you at once, from the *Radio Times*, or was it *The Listener*? All you announcers' pictures were in it, a few weeks back.' He proffered fags and said: 'You'll be glad to know I'm not one of those that criticize the BBC. I reckon it does a wonderful job, all things considered. But this I would like to say—why on earth don't you give us more jazz, Mr Bisham? I'm fed up with all this classical stuff. It's all right for the few, but I like to keep my weekends bright. See what I mean? I wish you'd alter it.' He beamed, leaned back and said he did hope he wasn't speaking out of turn and hadn't butted in in any way. It still wasn't the era of the new General Forces Programme, which was something.

It was the cue for a pitched battle between classical 'stuff' and jazz. During it, other beaming faces discreetly wondered why Mr Bisham didn't have just two wave-lengths: one 'absolute low stuff', and one for 'the absolute high-brows'. It would solve everything: everything, that was, except why the 'Corp' had so many talks, too few plays, so many chamber concerts, too few symphonies. However, they said, they jolly well knew all this talk against the BBC was 'plain jealousy, Mr Bisham', and they said they were satisfied the BBC had no 'obstructionists' like other big bodies had, and everyone was keen, friendly and overworked. The BBC was something more than just a branch of the *Manchester Guardian*.

A little before Waterloo Station, the originator of the discussion, concluding a diatribe against the Brains Trust and for Monday Night at Eight, said he thought they would all agree, in any case, they all ought to hand it to the announcers. 'Because, it isn't only the reading, is it? Take these news bulletins, it's writing it all! I reckon you announcers do a really wonderful job, Mr Bisham!' In addition, they said, announcers were so good-looking.

Mr Bisham walked sedately towards the wartime look of Broadcasting House. It was a wartime black lighthouse instead of a peacetime white one. The Langham Hotel, its windows blinded with brickwork, was on the left, and the gutted Queen's Hall and All Souls, Langham, on the right. A couple of khaki-painted recording cars stood outside the entrance to the black lighthouse, which was dotted with Mr Commissionaire Eady, and his white gloves, and policemen. Young gentlemen with large moustaches and corduroy trousers went in and out; messengers went in and out holding armfuls of gramophone records, or armfuls of papers and manuscripts and memos. Mr Bisham thought about the conversation in the train, and generously supposed it was reasonable for most people to imagine announcers were entirely in charge of all radio broadcasts, and that there were no such elements as former newspaper editors, news writers, talks writers, play writers, feature writers, producers, actors, composers, orchestras, expert disc players, and an enormous army of eager technicians and aging administrators; and this didn't include liftmen, cleaners, waitresses, receptionists, departmental directors, typists, booking clerks, telediphonists, telephonists, charwomen and the Board of Governors. It was natural, perhaps, for the 'masses' to think only of announcers and the Director-General, for they were constantly in the news, whether it was press or radio, and whether it was pleasant or unpleasant. They would not have thought of a studio attendant, or of the person who caused horses' hooves or a door slam in the middle of a play; of Arthur, the handsome club steward, or of actors and actresses hurrying anxiously along at 10 a.m. to Studio 3A. Any bent, greying figure shuffling towards a temporary building belonging to the BBC in New Cavendish Street, might be a director going to yet another Board Meeting, or an author attached to the best-seller called *Front Line Family*, adored by the American public who were moved daily to sending parcels of tea and sugar to the Robinson Family (those emblems of wartime Britain). The public, happily, did not have to think of these urgent things, and thought only, 'what *is* wrong with the BBC?' pretending that something was much more wrong with it than with the MOI, or any other branch of the Civil Service. The public really knew they loved their radios, turning them on all day, the very moment they stepped into their flats or houses, and had nothing against the BBC whatever. They just allowed themselves to be influenced by professional writers who had quarrelled with somebody whilst in the BBC, and had then, for a couple of weeks or so, turned journalist. The public did not realize these things, and would drop dead if the Director-General announced: 'We are closing down! You think you can do better, so get on with it!' The public—which is pubs and drawing-rooms and club bars and soldiers and sailors and airmen and bored hostesses—did not think of red lights, or clocks with red second hands, or headphones, in 1944: the pictures could not portray such—or did not—and films always showed a stupid-looking man standing behind a glass panel, usually wearing a beard, and stabbing out a long forefinger whenever it was the cue for a player to speak his next line. The films seemed ashamed to depict things as they really were; and although it might be technically difficult to show a red light in a film story, surely there was nothing against showing the actors grouped round the mike, or mikes, holding their scripts without embarrassment or noise as they acted their parts: tiptoeing away afterwards to make room for the next. They were not like the children in Children's Hour—one of the BBC's charm-programmes—who were likely to suck sweets into the microphone, so that the noise they made sounded like the sea breaking on the rocks below.

Mr Bisham realized that a few years before he had been just as ignorant about it all as the film people and the public still were. He had not actually thought that announcers wrote the news, or that they decided how much jazz there would be today, and whether Mr Middleton would be asked to speak tomorrow. But he had been considerably in the dark and thought it all most romantic. The truth was, sadly, nothing was romantic once you had seen the other side. It became just an industry.

He often wondered about his job. What did people think of announcing now? There was the surprising feeling that it really was considered very glamorous indeed. Letters to *The Times* often criticized them, but the same letters spoke of announcers by name and hailed them as family friends. It was attractive to think your voice could enter the privacy of a strange room and win friends.

When he had first broadcast, Mr Bisham had not foreseen this possibility quite to this extent; for he had not then known, any more than anyone else, that his name would be announced one day as well. It had never occurred to him that millions of people might have the right to know something about you; they

knew your name and your voice—now they must know all there
was to know.

Well, all?

Bess just turned up one day and said: 'The radio. Just the
thing for you, Ernest. They need your sort, and as it happens
I can give you an introduction to somebody who knows the
ropes.'

Remarkable things usually came from quiet beginnings.

Entering Broadcasting House, he showed his pass briefly.
He went to Home Presentation, thinking distantly: 'Small beginnings?'

He was trying to remember the small beginnings that had
enabled him to get away with Lady Stewker's pearls.

There was a note for him, dated the morning before, and
marked Personal. It was from the dreadful woman herself and
it said:

Just to thank you terribly for being so absolutely *sweet*
over my broadcast. I was absolutely petrified and I could
never have done it without you. And I just know the result
of my charity appeal will be simply splendid—because
you announced it. I shall ring up, may I, and ask you to
dine?

One of the telephones rang and it was Home News Talks
wanting a second voice; they had a war story from Russia and
the quality of the recording was not clear enough on disc.

One of the other announcers sprawled on the day-bed and
said: 'Oh, Bisham, old Lady Stewker's 'phoned you four times.
She says she's getting masses of jewellery for her war effort—but
somebody broke in and pinched her most valuable necklace!
And it wasn't for the war effort!'

Mr Bisham was looking at the duty schedule.

'I suppose it was insured,' he commented.

'Yes . . .'

'Well, she won't really lose anything.'

Scarcely five minutes had passed before she 'phoned again. Mr Bisham felt amused, knowing how rich she was, and knowing how anxious she had been to collect other people's jewellery for the war effort. She was crusted in jewellery from top to toe, but she would part with none of that.

She said she was mortified by the robbery and had a splitting headache. She said she telephoned Mr Bisham because she had no husband to advise her.

'The police will surely advise you,' he said politely into the telephone. Really, the demands on announcers' sex appeal was limitless!

'Is she flapping?' somebody asked him.

'Yes,' he said. 'It seems it was worth five thousand pounds.'

Waiting, later on, for the red light and to start saying, 'This is the BBC Home and Forces Programme, here is the nine o'clock news, and this is Ernest Bisham reading it', he saw again the image of the necklace lying on the loose sheets of paper before him; and he tried to picture it on Marjorie's bosom. 'Russia,' he announced firmly to Marjorie and the other twenty million, 'has made a further advance in the vicinity of Kiev.' And he wished the young man standing at the gramophone bank behind him would stop fidgeting. It was a long time yet for his cue. Through the window, the girl at the control panel was calmly powdering her tiny nose. He became irritatingly aware of her actions out of the corner of his eyes. She had no soul! He had a very good mind to log it against her—but he knew he had a reputation of being rather kindly, if a little stuck up. 'Salerno,' he continued, his voice brighter through thinking of this, 'Salerno has again been the scene of fierce fighting . . .'

Marjorie was listening.

She always listened if she possibly could. If the three Misses de Freece, or the Wintles, were her guests, she always said, 'I'm sure you would like to hear the nine o'clock news,' meaning quite apart from the fact that Ernest was reading it. And if she went out to dinner she would ask her hostess, '*Could* I hear the news? Ernest has started a cold and I do want to hear if he sounds all right.' Everybody was always enchanting about it, not to say a little glassy-eyed, and she was often forced to feel that people envied her her tremendous marriage. What a lucky woman she was, their faces said. Her Ernest was not only charming, and well off presumably, but he was a famous announcer. His name was a byword (and it was her name) and he was a public figure (and so she was too). No wonder their attractive house was getting more and more popular. There were no cars any more, but people actually *walked* to have sherry or dinner with them. They sometimes came by train all the way from London. Titled people, too. Mr and Mrs Bisham were asked to open all the whist drives and bazaars, and huge handbills announced such items as: 'Ernest Bisham, the Announcer, has consented to open Lord Sudbury's sale of gems in aid of the Russian Red Cross on April 19th next at 21 Belgrave Square, London.' Placards frequently said, in italics: '*Mrs Ernest Bisham, wife of the announcer, will be in the chair.*' Secretly, Marjorie didn't like it very much. But she wanted it for Ernest, because she felt he wanted it. She told Bess she was really a background wife and had a dislike of public life. Platforms terrified her. But Bess said firmly it was her duty to help Ernest to become and remain a national figure. She owed it to the Bisham name. And when Ernest actually had to have a telephone conversation with Mrs Winston Churchill, though he could not say what about, it really did seem clear that Ernest had reached a public position which, at any rate in relation to society and the war effort, could not be taken lightly. And so far as life in 1944 was concerned there remained only one little cloud: neither she nor Ernest could truthfully say they were in love with each other. There was something wrong. There was some strange unseen wall built up between them which would not allow of anything deeper than a real affection and a mutual respect.

Twice he had seemed to try and break it down. But it was still there, and there was the feeling that both were trying in vain to make each other happy. What was wrong? To fall into marriage was an easy thing; to fall into love was a complicated thing.

Ernest, she knew, took the problem to Broadcasting House with him. She took it, with Lucas, to the pine woods and walked slowly along the canal staring at the barges. Things were better than they had been, admittedly. He was always kind, but, at first, life with him had been almost painful. He had often spoken of his father's silences, yet he seemed, at times, to have inherited them. He would read and she would sew. Sometimes he would play the piano to her, but her presence seemed to embarrass him and he would stop. When he was in London, she would turn on the radio, waiting to hear him, and wishing, hysterically, he would say, for a change:

'This is the six o'clock news, and this is Ernest Bisham reading it—but would you all excuse me a moment, I want to speak to my wife . . . Marjorie, are you there? Did I ever tell you I love you, my dear?'

He never did! Naturally!

A person in his position had to behave like a model machine. The slightest indiscretion and he was ruined. They would all be ruined. He knew that, and he would never hurt her. He was kindness itself. Wasn't it awful that kindness wasn't enough? Look how kind he could be to Bess, and she was very tiresome at times, though without meaning to be. Yet it would be nice if people went haywire sometimes; even Ernest.

Was his personality really such a model one? Of course it was. And what a good thing it was. You only had to think of the antics of some husbands.

Yes, she was very lucky. She was very lucky indeed and she was very wrong to complain.

But . . .

All the same, coming back from the pine woods one afternoon, in good time for the six o'clock news, she thought she felt happier. You had to be patient and give things a chance, didn't you? She had had an afternoon off from her many wartime activities and she had spent it counting her blessings. Ernest was off duty after the six, and he was coming home to a cosy dinner. She had been dreading it in case he telephoned to say he was going off on one of his journeys. He still had a good deal of routine announcing to do, and he was liable to go off anywhere at any time of the day or night. Two days previously, he'd rung her up and disappointed her by saying: 'I'm awfully sorry, my dear. I have to go on a little journey.' She was a tactful wife and didn't ask where, but she said: 'Oh, Ernest, but it's getting so late.' He'd been sweetly apologetic about it, saying in a schoolboyish way that he would 'try and make up for it'. Well, she supposed the coral beads were the making up.

There was no disappointing telephone message, so she went upstairs to dress. When a knock came on her door she was terrified in case it was a message.

But it was only Mrs Leeman with some worry about the dinner, and the difficulties of shopping, and to say the black-out had slipped in the master's room, and to say she couldn't very well be in two places at once. Mrs Leeman was not exactly the ideal servant, any more than Leeman was.

'I'll see to the black-out, Mrs Leeman,' she told her.

'Very well . . .'

'Dinner is the important thing,' she said pleasantly.

Ernest adored his food.

CHAPTER X

SEEING to the black-out in Ernest's room, she indulged in a few worried thoughts about the Leemans, who were their latest achievement. Though there was only his word for it, Leeman had been invalided out of the army since Dunkirk, where he had received what he called 'a bang on the nut'. It had certainly affected him, or something had, for he was thin and his face was always ashy white. Both his temper and his presence at meals were distinctly uncertain, and he sometimes flung the front door open to visitors in the most startling manner. Mrs Leeman was fat and looked old enough to be his mother. She was sour, but good with the silver. Strange relatives were rather inclined to appear at the back door on Saturdays, the Tredgarth back gate being swung on by sundry children of obscure appearance, like the Dead End Kids. When Ernest protested against this, on account of the din they all made, the Leemans had looked black as thunder for several days. But the Dead End Kids vanished. The Leemans had comfortable quarters and more or less free access to the spirit and beer ration, and of course they had 'the wireless'. They were not very flattering to Ernest, however, declaring a hatred of the news (sounding as if they meant announcers) and vastly preferring Enoch, yodelling, and Workers' Playtime. When Ernest politely agreed that Tommy Handley was very amusing, they both shrugged and said, 'Oh, yes, him.'

Mrs Bisham frowned slightly about them, but she and Ernest were terrified of losing them. One had to be grateful for small mercies. She sat in Ernest's room and looked idly round it.

He'd made it as nearly like his Westminster flat as the shape of the crooked room permitted. The differences were the beams and corners and the log fire.

86

He still had his books and his brandy glasses and his illus-trated poem by Francis Thompson.

There was a pile of letters and papers on his desk; it was in a mess as if he'd been having a turn-out at his leisure. Several things had fallen to the floor. There were some old brown snapshots of his public school, of himself as a boy in cricket clothes. There were a few up-to-date ones of him sitting, looking very distinguished—large and almost elderly—in a studio, before a hanging microphone.

There was a cricket cap and an old boxing glove and a cricket bat with signatures on it.

There were lots of little clues to him. He'd thrown two tennis rackets on his bed, and a dusty pile of music scores: 'Bird Songs at Eventide', 'All Alone', 'Love's Garden of Roses', 'When I Grow Too Old to Dream', 'When I Look at You'.

She turned them over and thought: 'But I still don't really know him from Adam.'

She was aware of the rather exotic sensation that she was looking for something: she was doing some detective work on him—she was searching for clues to him, *the true him*. She felt extraordinarily excited knowing afresh and for certain that she *didn't* know the true him. There was a queer sensation of mystery in the room. His room.

It was nonsense, of course. It was wishful thinking.

Wishful thinking? That was a funny thing to think. When everybody else thought him so ideal.

The three little lines appeared over the bridge of her nose. On the near chair was an illustrated advertisement of a safe. Was he going to buy a safe?

Suddenly she saw something else.

It was lying on an old brown volume of Shakespeare.

As a child, she had been quite used to the sight and also the feel of a revolver. Her father had had an imposing armoury; it had been quite a hobby of his. She knew how to load and unload a pistol when she was ten.

But to see a six-chambered, up-to-date little revolver in Ernest's room was a considerable surprise. What was even more surprising was that it was fully loaded. It was extraordinary of him to leave it lying about. And what on earth would he want with it? It was true that the Leemans had instructions never to enter his room, and she looked after it herself, but it was very unwise, wasn't it?

Frowning slightly, she put it in a drawer of his desk. The drawer was a bit small, but the others were all locked.

When she reached the hall, he was just coming in. He was smiling but looked a bit tired under the eyes.

Greeting him affectionately, she thought: 'Perhaps he's in the Secret Service.' A funny little current of pride and excitement touched her scalp. She knew that she wanted to think that.

She decided it would be intelligent not to say a word about the loaded revolver. He was intelligent, too, and he would see it had been put in the drawer. He would be pleased with her for it.

He kissed her and said at once: 'How are you, my dear? You're looking very nice. By the way, before I forget, tomorrow night I've got to go on a little journey. So don't be worried if I miss the eleven-five.'

She heard herself saying, 'Another symphony concert in Manchester, dear?' but she hardly heard his non-committal reply because by then she was thinking: 'He *is* in the Secret Service . . .!' She knew a little tremor of fear for him, mixed with the new pride in him.

When he was preoccupied during dinner, she was tactful and not at all talkative.

Almost the only thing she said was:

'When you have time, Ernest, would you do something for me? It will please Mrs Wintle, she's so worried about Jonas.'

She was sure he was in the Secret Service. He was not really

going to announce any concert in Manchester or anywhere else.
Tomorrow she would try and find out what the concert was
and if he did in fact announce it from up there. That would be
easy to find out. Then she would know.

She thought of this with rising excitement all the time she
talked about Jonas Wintle and asked Ernest if he could possibly
get him into the BBC. Poor Mrs Wintle was so worried about
him.

He was aware of what she was saying, and he answered her
attentively.

But his mind was elsewhere.

The spectre of Mrs Mansfield had arisen a little before he
was ready for her. However, one had to be opportunist, and if
he was as successful with her at her house in Mount Street, as
he had been at Lady Stewker's in Grosvenor Square, it was just
as well that he had ordered himself a safe. One of his rules had
always been to take sensible precautions, and locked drawers
were not sensible. You never knew. And he wasn't at all sure
that he hadn't now thought of an idea which would make these
night adventures a little more interesting. What good were gems
locked up in a safe, when he had gone to such pains to get
them?

Yes, the safe was an essential precaution meanwhile, while
he considered this.

He started to tell Marjorie about the safe. It was to go in his
room, he had many private papers and so on.

But she was on the telephone. She looked large and elegant,
leaning over the Bechstein and saying:

'I've spoken to Ernest, Mrs Wintle. He will be very glad to
do anything he can for Jonas. But of course he's only an
announcer, he's not . . .' A bit later, she said into the telephone:
'Ask Jonas to come round now for a few minutes, Mrs Wintle.
And since he has been invalided out of the RAF, I'm quite sure
the . . .'

When the front doorbell rang Ernest was reading the evening paper. An article regretted that there was no reason to expect an early arrest in the Stewker necklace case. The press said unflatteringly:

'The robbery presented the same curious features that have characterized a number of burglaries in recent years. The drawers in Lady Stewker's dressing-table had been ransacked in a very casual manner. The thief appears deliberately to have ignored five hundred pounds in notes, for he—or she?—left the wad of notes sitting on an alabaster ash tray.'

He thought: 'I don't like the word "thief" very much.' It savoured somewhat of the chap who picked pockets in the school locker room.

He sat frowning at it.

The paper said:

'Inspector Hood, of Scotland Yard, is in charge of the case. Beyond admitting that he had found no clues, he has no statement to make at present.'

Jonas Wintle stood in the hall unwinding a large scarf from his neck. He was inclined to wear a permanent frown as if to indicate the serious extent to which life had by now browned him off. He had frowned his way through Harrow, which had browned him off somewhat, towards the finish, and the war arrived just in time to get him into the RAF. As a night fighter pilot, he had had to frown legitimately, but his frown stayed for good when he crash-landed on returning safely from a very hazardous trip. The irony of this crash, which was due to sudden mist obscuring the landing ground, browned him off completely long before he left hospital and returned to the bosom of a doting family who had browned him off almost as soon as he left the cradle. Life he now regarded as 'complete hell', and the only prospect at all appeared to be this pompous Bisham chap who might get him into the BBC or at any rate advise him how to get in. Oh, well, he thought, might as well explore every avenue, as the saying went. Life had years and years to run yet. And perhaps old Bisham wasn't as bad as he looked (and sounded)—he couldn't possibly be, could he? He unwound his scarf and told Leeman his name was, 'Jonas Wintle, any objections?' and stared at the fellow as if he was a ghost. The house was full of eerie shadows and the fellow looked ghastly. And did he have to pull open the door in that violent manner?

Jonas strolled into the drawing-room fully prepared to be thoroughly browned off long before the interview was over.

The Bishams were sitting over the fire, and their dog was curled up near the fender. A huge cat sat staring down at the dog's tail from a high footstool. Fearfully family and drab, wasn't it! In about three minutes he would fly from the place, screaming! But what could you expect from the BBC? He'd probably be exactly the same himself in a few years' time. Bisham always looked just like his bally voice. He was superior and rather fat. Very well turned out, of course. Oh, he was probably all right if you could stand that sort of thing. Mrs Bisham looked sort of milkish and flowing. Her extraordinary clothes, no doubt. Well, she had the peach of a skin, so that was something.

Jonas shoved on a fag and accepted a large whisky. 'No soda and no water.' He knocked it back in one and there was his empty glass again. His brown hair fell over his face and his flannel suit appeared quite shapeless. Marjorie felt it was incredible to think he was barely twenty-one but had already faced death a score of times.

Ernest sat and listened to Jonas's raucous voice and prayed that he wasn't hoping to be an announcer.

'Well, what else is there?' said Jonas, startled.

'There's music, writing, or the technical side,' suggested Ernest patiently. He kept thinking of Mrs Mansfield's red hair. What an extraordinary woman she was, and *so* talkative. She really deserved it . . .

'All three would brown me off in no time,' Jonas announced. He frowned at his empty glass and suddenly helped himself.

'A producer?' suggested Marjorie.

'Announcer or nothing,' Jonas said, and had the thought of himself saying: 'And this is Jonas Wintle reading it.' He would certainly get some sort of kick out of it, if it wasn't exactly flying.

He got up, mid-conversation, and wandered about with his hands in his pockets, kicking the furniture. Finally he breezily accepted an invitation from Bisham to 'come up and have a look round'. And since it was pretty decent of the old bird, and since he wasn't giving himself the airs one had anticipated, Jonas was pleased to accept.

'All right. Where do I come to?'

'To the BBC,' said Mr Bisham pleasantly.

'Yes, I know, but what do I do, and all that sort of thing?'

'You pass a lot of policemen and ask for me!'

'But don't you have to sign something? The pater had to do a broadcast once, water weasels or some such bilge, and he said what with passes and slips and coppers and one thing and another he was utterly browned off long before he even reached the microphone.'

However, Jonas said the invitation was 'pretty wizard'. He strolled home with his hands in his pockets and kicked his front door open and went up to his bedroom. He lay flat on his bed with his hands still in his pockets and his long scarf still wound round his neck. To say that he was browned off now through sheer reaction would have been, of course, an under-statement, and when his little mother came into his room to tell him anxiously not to 'pose' he really did feel thoroughly angry. His father came in too, rather heartily, but nervously, asking him what luck he had had. 'Luck,' he said in despair and turned his face to the wall. His father and mother sat on the bed and stared at him. Why did he have to wear a scarf, and wouldn't it be better to get into bed properly, and had he been drinking, dear boy?

As his mother and father knew, and as he secretly knew himself, his attitude to life was really a pose. It just meant that he was temporarily unhappy. His two elder brothers had been killed in the air, and his sister, of whom he was very fond, had been killed in one of the London blitzes. There remained his little mother, and his tall, animal-loving father who divided his time between the Air Ministry and the nearest river where he hunted for water weasels. Very much on his own, Jonas endured the effects of a bullet that teased his liver and tried not to think about how much his parents loved him and worried about him. He knew he behaved very badly to both of them, refusing to believe in God any more, or to go to church. He often watched himself hurting his parents, and wondered why he did so. He knew quite well he had been rude to the Bishams, who were probably quite decent old sticks; obviously they'd been married for donkeys' years and lived a dull, placid life. All the same, there was no excuse for being rude to people who were trying to be kind; and how did one know what people were really like and how they really lived? Thinking of this and everything in general Jonas Wintle was human enough, but unmanly enough, to burst into tears. His mother and father were very tactful, and his father, who was old as well as tall, used a quavery voice to ask him if he would like to be taken to a theatre quite soon. His mother, hearing this rejected, timidly wished he would take Holy Communion again, 'just to *see*, dear, and to please mother, it may have the most wonderful results', but he blew his nose and tried not to hurt them when saying, no, thanks most awfully, he was going to the BBC to become an announcer. So mother was delighted and at once advised him to pray and not to spurn prayer. 'I will pray *for* you,' she said to him, like the song.

'That's right, Mother, you do that,' he said, sitting up to blow his nose and unwind his scarf. His father helped him and asked if he would care to come otter hunting one of these days soon. Mother closed in on this by asking what Mrs Bisham was wearing. She thought her blouses were usually rather low. 'But she has such a lovely throat, hasn't she?'

Jonas said they had smashing whisky, he'd say that for them.

'I take it the Bishams were helpful, then,' elderly Mr Wintle said indulgently. He had been racking his brains at the Air Ministry, trying to think of something to suit Jonas. But the only possibility available there just now was censorship, which really only appealed to hard-ups or semi-lunatics. Poor Jonas would be browned off at once, as he put it.

Mrs Wintle said she thought Mr Bisham was a charming man, as well as very famous, that was what was so queer. And she thought Mrs Bisham, except for her modern blouses, was a sweet person. She knew her solicitor, old Sir Tom, very well, but of course he was so old now he never went anywhere, and his wife was peculiar about whom she met. There was some vague talk about Marjorie Bisham having been married before, and divorced. But it was probably all nonsense.

'That's right, Mother,' Jonas said to everything. His father went on with rather a long speech, partly containing entertainment value, but partly motive, about the advantages and disadvantages of being a solicitor. There was the hint that perhaps Jonas would like to read for the law, yet at the same time explaining that the law very often meant coping with unseemly things like Savile Row tailors who, after doing their utmost to make you have credit, suddenly turned shirty and threatened to make you bankrupt. Being a solicitor, elderly Mr Wintle explained, certainly made you see the very dregs of life, but at the same time it depended how you looked at these things, it was sometimes quite good for the soul. Jonas, however, threw up his hands at the mere mention of Savile Row, and started using obscurely advanced terms such as 'Substituted Service', adding, with new anxiety in his tone, 'and I don't pay them by Thursday, I'm afraid I'm for it. Sorry, pater.' There was a tension. During it, the pater looked transfixed with surprise, and started automatically fishing for his cheque book. The mater started saying various things about it being a pity to lose the church habit, even if it *was* the fault of the church, and she looked very peaky and miserable and kind.

He had the quaint habit of kissing his father, as well as his mother, and when that was done they went off to bed saying to Jonas that in a few days they just knew he would be announcing the six o'clock news.

'There are other things at the BBC besides announcing,' he told them dully. 'There's music and there's writing and there's the technical side,' he said, adding inventively: 'And acting, I suppose, if you can get your nose in!'

Next morning, Jonas went up to London, and his mother went into Woking to the butcher's. Waiting in the queue, she met Mrs Bisham. They both laughed at the state of affairs shopping had come to and wondered if the butcher would have the nerve to look them in the face when peace came again. And they talked about Jonas.

'Ernest is going to give him a voice test,' Mrs Bisham was pleased to be able to say. 'But even if that fails, there might be something else.' She drowned Mrs Wintle's expressions of thanks by mentioning a certain fairly distant dinner party she hoped Mrs Wintle would come to.

She always felt sorry for the little Wintle family.

Accepting with pleasure, little Mrs Wintle beamed and said:

'What a pretty little necklace you're wearing, Mrs Bisham. I love coral.'

'My husband gave it to me,' Mrs Bisham said, and blushed like a schoolgirl. 'Some unknown admirer sent it him from Italy!'

She had already discovered, by using the telephone discreetly, that Ernest was not going to Manchester tonight, or anywhere else. She was quite satisfied that he was in the Secret Service.

And strangely, and suddenly, she had fallen in love with him.

CHAPTER XI

IT was extremely ridiculous, of course. She really was behaving like a schoolgirl.

But at least the secret was hers, and it was her own heart, to behave as it liked.

As to his being in the Secret Service, she had no proof of it whatever, and she didn't necessarily mean it *was* the Secret Service; she just meant that she was satisfied Ernest was not the mere vocal automaton he pretended to be. Why else would he keep a loaded revolver in his room? Moreover—it had gone from the drawer in which she had put it! This was the greatest discovery of all!

Whatever his double life was, it was clearly a dangerous one, and of course it was one which brought him great merit, even if it was never made public.

Perhaps one day she would confront him with her discovery— and tell him how proud she was of him. She would say: 'I quite understand that you couldn't tell me, Ernest. At any rate until the war was over. I'm not one of those silly sort of wives . . .' And about the day when she found his revolver, she would say: 'That was the day I fell in love with you.' He would probably point out how stupid women were. But women did like a man to have character. She might say: 'I wouldn't have minded what it was you did, as long as you did *some*thing! You *look* cut out for unusual things, Ernest!'

She had begun to see him in a new light.

It was an exciting light.

In another exciting light—that of artificial daylight—Jonas Wintle sat at the microphone convinced that he had the ideal broadcasting voice. He said so.

The first sense of doubt assailed him, however, when Mr Bisham said crisply:

'I'm afraid everyone says that here!'

When he began to sound a little hoarse, Jonas explained that it was merely nerves. His voice went dry whenever he was nervous. Indeed, everything about this visit had conspired to make him nervous and his throat went dry as a bone. The long, winding corridors, the hurry and scurry of people of both sexes and all nationalities and conditions, and the expensive-cum-alarming atmosphere of the studios, and this studio in particular, with its double doors, its glass windows, its peering faces and its peculiar chairs so reminiscent of Mayfair cocktail bars.

Jonas was also astonished to find that he and Mr Bisham were not alone. Somehow or other he had thought they would be. But Mr Bisham told him to sit down and wait for Mr Black, who was late, 'as usual, but I expect he's finishing another show in another studio.' Mr Bisham ignored a sign saying 'Positively No Smoking Please' and walked up and down the limited space examining a green copy of *Seven For A Secret*, by Mary Webb. Jonas stared about him nervously, at the electric fan, and at the large water-jug and two glasses on a round, brown tray. There was a lamentable absence of whisky. Mr Bisham told him to have a drink and ease his throat. His throat already felt as if he had just been dragged out of a salt mine. Mr Bisham, while the water gurgled, thought: 'I hope Mrs Mansfield is casual about windows.' He disliked Yale locks or hovering by front doors in the gloom, or even the fog. Mrs Mansfield was coming to Broadcasting House presently and he might sound her further, now that his mind was made up. He would say: 'How is the servant problem with you, Mrs Mansfield? My wife and I are fairly lucky at Woking, but they cannot remember to lock up last thing!' Another little point was that he was getting somewhat bulky for small top windows. He must go and have a look at the houses in Mount Street. They were pretty high, weren't they?

'What do I do now?' inquired Jonas hoarsely. He wiped his mouth and just then in came Mr Black. He was an extremely sinister figure to Jonas, with his corduroy trousers, brown, and his black, lowering eyebrows. But Mr Bisham treated him as if he was fairly human, if just a little beneath him. So far as Jonas was concerned, the sight of Mr Black browned him off utterly and his voice seemed to go for good.

Mr Black sat down and treated Jonas as if he was dirt. He put on headphones and started to speak into the microphone, ignoring Jonas completely. He was very polite indeed to Mr Bisham and apologized in refined accents for being late. 'But those ruddy Indians . . . Are you there, Disc Room? This is to be a voice test, for Mr Ernest Bisham. The speaker is called . . .' He gave Jonas a dirty look, and Jonas got out his name hoarsely. At the same moment two huge ladies came into the studio and said they had booked the studio, they thought, for half-past, which was in ten minutes' time, and would there be any objections to their sitting down and waiting, 'since you are not actually on the air?' They said they were concerned with a feature designed to put us all on better terms with Welsh coal-miners.

Mr Black, who was not at all Welsh, dealt coldly with the situation, using dirty looks and the word 'ruddy', and asked them how they would like it 'if a crowd of women came in and sat down in the middle of *your* programme?' They went out, looking daggers, but to Jonas's consternation remained just outside the door and peered in at him, still looking daggers, at two minute intervals. Mr Bisham read Mary Webb and seemed engrossed only by that. Adding to his discomfort, Jonas became aware that through the small window on his right several girls with their hair hanging in nets were giving him a frank once-over. They were distinctly observed to give each other the thumbs down sign, in connection with him, and they stood about grinning. There was, however, one kinder than the rest, and she decided to come up to the window and stand there looking sorry for him. This brought a flush to his face which stayed there. Mr Black seemed to call her Annabella. What she called him could not be heard, since only he had earphones on. Jonas just saw her lips moving. Annabella didn't seem to require headphones in her mysterious room. She just switched something on or off and now and again had a look at an extraordinary machine she was tending. After that she came back to the window and stared at Jonas and looked sorry.

'Now,' Mr Bisham said at last, and handed him *Seven For A Secret* opened at Page 111. 'Just take no notice of us, and when Mr Black signals you with his hand—start reading until I tell you to stop.' He said what was happening was that the girl through the window was looking after the cutting machine which was making a gramophone record of his voice, 'We call them discs here. That's absolutely all that is happening, but you can imagine you're on the air, you're speaking to your mother at home.' Mr Bisham said that afterwards Annabella would bring the disc in and Mr Black would play it on the gramophone-bank there. He leaned on the back of a chair and folded his arms.

Mr Black said:

'If you're ready, then, Annabella? We'll go ahead in . . . ten seconds from . . . NOW.'

To Jonas Wintle it was a horrible game, far worse than any of the games Alice had to play in Wonderland. His eyes became fixed on a dreadful red hand on the clock face, and at the same time, like a drowning man, he suddenly decided it was far worse than being shot-up in the sky, and he noticed a thousand distracting details. Mr Black had a huge wart on his raised hand, Annabella was yawning and powdering her nose, her lips distinctly saying to a colleague, 'Go down'; Mr Bisham was glancing idly at his gold wrist-watch, and the two ladies outside the double doors had started to outrival the chatter and thunder of muffled voices and music newly belching from Annabella's room; fusing with it came the strains of 'God Save the King' from another direction, and from a third the Chinese sound of a record being run backwards. A dozen hidden channels had sprung to life and open warfare. And, the moment Mr Black's hand descended, Jonas had the sudden and positive conviction he was actually on the air, and he all but said, 'Can you hear me, Mother?' He stared at the microphone, which was hanging from the ceiling instead of standing on the table, distracting in itself, and said in fright: 'Er, do I begin now . . .' Mr Black snapped: 'Shut up. Start. Sorry, I mean—begin now!'

His agony proceeded.

Hearing the record of his voice played over, some minutes later, Jonas was embarrassed to hear it begin:

'Er, do I begin now? Shut up. Start. Sorry, I mean—begin now. Trewern Coed was a typical border village, not quite sure of its nationality, mingled in speech, divided between . . . between, er, blue-roofed cottages of Wales and the red-thatched ones of Shropshire . . . oh, Lord, I'm going to sneeze, I'm thoroughly browned off by this . . .'

Mr Black stopped the record.

He looked uncannily pleased.

Never in his life had Jonas felt so humiliated by anything. Quite apart from the crash of his sneeze, which sounded like a last broadside from the *Scharnhorst*, his voice was ghastly. In fact, he was fully prepared to disown it.

Mr Bisham was very kind about it and said that everybody disowned their voice when they first heard it recorded, yet it was at once recognizable to others.

It sounded, none the less, like a death knell to his hopes of being an announcer.

When Mr Bisham had to hurry away—somebody named Mrs Mansfield had called to see him, wasn't she the wife of that chap who made so much money out of bricks?—Jonas started to trail despondently out of the studio with the little bit of paper Mr Bisham had signed in order to permit his exit. 'I'll let you know what they decide,' he said to Jonas. 'But there are other departments, as I said last night,' he said encouragingly but ominously. 'You noticed what Mr Black was doing—what about that? Fond of playing records?'

Mr Black gave him one look and left. Playing records? It was too browning off for words! Jonas Wintle's brown hair fell over his eyes and he looked sick. Suddenly Annabella was standing there. She was actually in the studio this time, and she was painting her nails with a little brush. 'Hello,' she said, rather as if they hadn't met—which they hadn't, really. She was wearing sandals and her long red toes stuck out at the top, though quite attractively.

Mr Bisham went along to the room known as the Drawing Room. It was the room in which distinguished people some-times came to discuss their pending broadcasts, or other business. Afterwards, they were often taken along to a smaller room in another part of the building, which room, although smaller, had more homely furnishings and the attraction of a large tray full of stimulants suitable for customers shattered by their recent ordeal of being 'on the air'. Here, the modest, the vain and the eccentric had the opportunity, if they wished, of flopping back into arm-chairs and gasping: 'Yes, please—and the merest splash!' then was the time for understanding that the poor old BBC ought not to be criticized quite so harshly; whether it was Variety or Intellectual, broadcasting was not the simple thing it had appeared, and when you thought of the organization involved in providing entertain-ments to please all minds for twenty-four hours every single day, including Sundays, well, let the critics come up and have a shot at it.

The Drawing Room itself had a slightly more forbidding aura. It was done in mahogany and leather, and although there was a cupboard full of mahogany coloured whisky, it was always kept locked. It was a kind of promise of things to come. To open it, you had to sign something. The *Radio Times* and *The Listener* sat on a round table, and Mrs Mansfield sat on the unusually long settee. She was very powdered. She had four rows of diamonds about her powdered neck, and on her fat arms were encrusted sapphires, rubies and emeralds in rich and tasteless abandon. Mr Bisham's smiling eyes were on her truly magnificent necklace and he was thinking, 'How wasted there; imagine Marjorie in it!' Mrs Mansfield was altogether exotic. There was her queerly red hair and her inaccurate daub of orange colouring along her large lips. She smiled broadly— grinned was the better word—at Ernest Bisham, the Announcer, and declared that for a long time she had been positively determined to meet him; (Lady Stewker had said the same thing). Several things occurred to Mr Bisham as he sat beside her and offered her a cigarette. She said: 'No, thanks—is it dreadful of me, I take snuff!' Snuff, thought Ernest Bisham, and felt like backing away! She sniffed up great gusts of it into huge nostrils which threatened to split. Her snuff-box was crusted with jewels and was most attractive. A pity Marjorie didn't care for snuff. Might she like to start a collection of snuff-boxes? He felt amused, but again wished Marjorie might benefit from his adventures. Mrs Mansfield started to talk about the 'little broadcast' which her husband had influenced her to do instead of him; he hated talking. How alike all these old dears were, thought Mr Bisham. They were determined to meet an announcer and assumed announcers would inevitably be in charge of their broadcast. He politely explained the routine, and that there were many departments here, and grad- ually led up to more personal matters. He wanted to make sure Mrs Mansfield would not suffer by his visit. For instance, she said her husband had given her the snuff-box. She was clearly sentimental about it, even though she sounded a bit bored by George Mansfield. So he would not dream of taking the snuff-box. But the necklace? Oh, she said, 'I just wanted it, and I made him draw a cheque. Someone else was after it, I was determined to have it.'

Mrs Mansfield thought Ernest Bisham was quite enchanting. He was just as she expected, he was just like his voice. And he was so attentive. Could he really be so interested in her jewellery and her chatter, and such kind remarks about her servant problems and whether they locked the back door at night? 'We don't have a back door in Mount Street, Mr Bisham! It's a basement kitchen and faces the front!' He was sweet. She told him, amused, that if he was really interested she always made her maids sleep with their windows open. Even that seemed to interest him. He said: 'But what about the black-out? The room must still be airless? Unless, of course, they have curtains.' She was delighted with him and said they had curtains. She also said how much they cost, and how many coupons for the material, saying the whole thing was a scandal. She explained that her broadcast talk was to be about reducing the costs of material—by economic use—and it was a strong subject of hers and her husband's. When she got on to the subject of jewellery, she was intensely enthusiastic. She *adored* it. Mr Bisham said how much he admired her diamond necklace and she said: 'So do I! In fact, I sleep in it!'

Mr Bisham looked rather thoughtful.

'She sleeps in it,' he thought to himself. 'This is going to be unusually exciting . . .'

'Well, now about the broadcast,' said Mrs Mansfield.

And, much as he had done with Lady Stewker, Mr Bisham explained that he did not know if he would announce her on the air or not. He said there was a rota, and it depended who was on duty.

'I shall hope, of course, to be on duty at the time of your broadcast,' he said courteously, and wondered where her maids slept. She said she had two.

He tried not to sound too courteous, in case she was one of those embarrassing women who wouldn't leave announcers alone. She had asked if he was married. Women sometimes sent presents to the 'voice' they admired. If the presents were wine, cigarettes or cigars, it was pleasant. But sometimes they were rather more unusual. He had once received a live cobra, for example, from overseas. On another occasion, he received an iced cake bearing the words 'Baby Mine'. Mrs Mansfield seemed capable of sending a cake of this kind. There was something arch and puffy about her.

He explained, a little briskly, which department would handle her broadcast, and said that she would be telephoned by another department, and he was tactfully brief about what would probably happen to her script if she had written it herself. If she hadn't written it herself, but wanted them to, there was nothing to worry about, except possibly her reputation as a writer.

She told him he had been most delightfully helpful.

'I can't thank you enough, Mr Bisham. And I had simply no idea I ought not to have approached you. I quite thought announcers arranged everything.'

'Many people do . . .!'

'You must come to dinner. My house in Mount Street is charming, though I say it myself. How soon can you come?'

Mr Bisham smiled and said he would come very soon indeed.

'A bit sooner than you expect, madam,' he thought rather brightly.

He was there in a matter of hours.

CHAPTER XII

A GOOD thing, he thought, that he had warned Marjorie he might miss the last train. Thanks to those two policemen, there was now no hope of getting the last train.

The policemen seemed to have taken up a permanent position at the corner of Mount Street.

He walked along just inside the Green Park parallel with Piccadilly. He liked this idea of having parks without railings.

Now and again a policeman flashed a torch at him, for the night was excessively dark. On one occasion, a policeman flashed his torch and said:

'I beg your pardon, Mr Bisham.'

It made him even more thoughtful.

American officers were strolling about saying to each other that this little old town of London wasn't such a bad place after all; it was full of bright guys. They said to Mr Bisham: 'Say, buddie, have you got the right time?'

He passed the time wondering what sort of a job it was going to be. With Lady Stewker it had been almost too easy, for she had talked so much. She even told him what time she was going to have a bath, which was nice. In the end, all he had done was to take a taxi to Grosvenor Square. He'd strolled along to her front door, which she'd said was always on the latch, and he'd walked in and up the delightful staircase. He had his mask on, for he was often recognized now in the streets, though at times he substituted a raincoat with an unusually high collar; this, with a hat well down, was quite effective. There was something, though, about a mask which appealed to his sense of drama. The Stewkers had been at dinner, as he had known they would be—she'd asked him to the dinner, had she not?—and there was nothing to do but wander upstairs and find the old girl's room and the wall safe behind the picture of Napoleon. She'd told him the combination—which was 'Bisham'! Simple—yet quite exciting, in a Christmas charade sort of way. There had been one or two tense moments, to be sure, such as when a maid came in as he opened the safe, and when the butler came to put a green log on the fire. But they had passed.

He thought of those moments as he gave a stealthy heave and climbed into the top room of the house in Mount Street. He fell noiselessly into the room on his face. The window had been easy and there was no black-out there; the room appeared to be empty. Now and again a distant searchlight tended to become a bit dangerous, but it was useful too. He kept away from the window. Footsteps were walking slowly down Mount Street towards the park. A copper, he thought.

Mr Bisham had on a light overcoat, slouch hat and blue scarf. Marjorie had given it him for his birthday. He wore shoes with plain rubber soles and he wore tight fitting rubber gloves. His torch had two ends, one for light and the other, well, for people who were tiresome enough to sleep with their valuables on.

He swept his torch briefly round the room as he got to his feet. It had a blue, quiet light. It seemed to be a dusty, disused bedroom which was now used as a boxroom.

He moved silently to the door and softly opened it.

Then he softly shut it again. Two female voices were chattering confidentially out there in the passage.

Keyed up, Mr Bisham sat on a trunk and cautiously lit a cigarette. He was careful about the light from his lighter, and about the smoke, which he aimed out of the window, and about the stub, which he presently snuffed out and put in his pocket.

He sat there for a long time and smoked two cigarettes. So there were two stubs. He thought of Marjorie and wondered if she was the sort who could understand. Not that he wanted her ever to know, but it was nice to wonder. Somehow he felt sure she was. She wasn't 'ordinary'; well, she was and she wasn't, she had brains, intellect; he wasn't thinking of her high-brow reading, as neighbours called it, or her relieving grasp of affairs which came from her spontaneously sometimes. He was thinking of her personality. At that first Soho lunch, at their simple church wedding in Brompton, on the unspectacular honeymoon. She was 'quiet'. Her personality was quiet and unobtrusive. She was unassuming and she actually thought she was plain and dull. She was neither. Take Bess, now. She didn't think she was either plain or dull; yet she was really both if you looked into it. And poor old Bess would have a heart attack if she even dreamed where he was now. It would be outside her range. Would it be outside Marjorie's?

A light in the passage clicked out and suddenly the chattering ceased. He heard a door close and in the distance Big Ben was striking twelve. His colleague would be reading the midnight news.

He moved to the door, as he did so thinking of the new idea which was now formed so as to give his robberies some point. It was quite simple. All these efforts to aid Russia! Why should he not aid her too? Simply, when he had collected a handsome amount of jewels and gems—and he already had quite a collection locked up at home—he would seek means to send them anonymously to Russia. He would not rob from the rich who seemed not to merit such treatment, and he would not rob from the poor, that went without saying, for in any case the poor didn't have gems and jewels. He would take from the Stewkers and Mansfields—and Sudburys, perhaps—from whoever his sense of fair play and humour judged best; and his risk, such a very grave one, would be his contribution to the war effort. It wouldn't be much of a contribution to Marjorie, which was sad; yet, indirectly it would, for one day the papers would blaze the news that an anonymous cat-burglar had sent the proceeds of his crimes to aid the prosecution of the war; and without knowing it Marjorie would be married to the attractive, mystic figure. Perhaps he would tell her on his deathbed. Thinking rapidly about the snags and pitfalls of all this, 'if I'm caught before the stuff gets to Russia, of course, nobody will believe my intentions, not even Marjorie,' and, 'now, more than ever, I must never be caught,' he softly opened the boxroom door.

He moved quietly into the passage and cautiously shone his torch. In the blue light he saw the curve of the top stairs.

Mrs Mansfield kept her portable radio beside her bed; it was convenient for the midnight news and the seven o'clock news in the morning. Since she had become fascinated by Ernest Bisham's voice, and particularly since she had contrived to meet him in the flesh, she never missed a news bulletin. But when Ernest Bisham was not 'reading it', she usually turned it off after hearing the headlines. Tonight she had done so, and after listening to a little dance music she turned that off too. She was more than usually cross with George. What a worm the man was. How had she ever fallen in love with him? All he ever thought about was bricks. She was cross with her daughter Alice, for the way she gadded about London and set her cap at all the men; she'd never get a man that way. They'd almost had words, before Alice slammed off to bed. Life was utterly unglamorous and dull. And she was cross with both her maids; they had had the cheek to ask for another rise, and it was maddening when one realized that they simply ate her out of house and home and made off with the sugar ration. She told them so, and now no doubt they'd both leave. Through the wall she heard George pottering about in his bedroom. After a bit she heard him put out his light and get into bed. What a din the man made, but he was as fat as an elephant, wasn't he? She put out her own light and made her own bed creak; it was an arrangement with George so that he would know what was going on. She heard him give a great yawn, and she answered with a yawn, and there was silence in the dark house. She shut her eyes. To soothe herself, she started to think about Ernest

Bisham. It would be thrilling seeing him again when she broadcast in a few days, if *only* he was on duty! It would be too disappointing otherwise! How she had chattered to him. Had she talked too much and bored him? But he'd been so distinguished and attractive, not fat and greasy like George; he was a gentleman. His hair was greying at the sides in a most attractive manner. He hadn't said much about his wife; what was she like? She was probably too dowdy and suburban for words! Why on earth did they live in Woking? How on earth anyone could live anywhere but in London . . .

Mrs Mansfield dozed off. She started to dream that her script about economics had been altered into a talk about Polish war relief, and that at the last moment it had been confiscated by the Pope. She had to face the microphone for George without any script at all, and Ernest Bisham started saying: 'You are now going to listen to Mrs George Mansfield, wife of the eminent industrialist who has done so much for . . .' As she started to protest in alarm, she became aware of a strong smell of ether, and somebody's hands seemed to be at her arms and her neck. She started to cry: '*No, no, no,*' and through a haze saw a man in a mask bending over her; she was in bed in the Middlesex Hospital. No, she wasn't, she was in her own bed, but she couldn't scream or move, she lay flat. Somebody seemed to be moving about and opening or shutting drawers and cupboards. The smell of ether started to recede and her eyes opened. She distinctly saw a man in a mask cross her room silently and go out, closing the door. She put her hands swiftly to her throat and found that her most precious necklace was gone. She sat up in bed at once and let out a scream that could have been heard in Tooting.

George Mansfield came tumbling in in his purple striped pyjamas. He looked rather like a polar bear that had dressed up for a zoo tea-party. Almost immediately Alice Mansfield came in in her white nightdress with a chinchilla cape thrown round her thin shoulders. Mrs Mansfield had time to notice that she looked too awful without her make-up on and had great rings round her eyes. Alice said, 'Hell and green gin, what on earth's the matter?' By the time both maids had dashed in, Mrs Mansfield was in the throes of hysterics. Everyone was talking at once and the master was asking if the sirens had gone. But no, it was much worse than that, madam's necklace and bangles had gone. And so had the more valuable jewels from the case in her dressing-table. Suddenly the burglar alarm started to go too.

Mr Ernest Bisham allowed himself a small swear word. He was on the roof, which he had reached via the maids' bedroom. He hadn't time to decide where he had touched off the burglar alarm. Probably in madam's bedroom somewhere, or on the stairs, perhaps. No matter where, it was going off like a fire engine. He jumped nimbly over a couple of roof-tops and found some iron stairs. Unfortunately, somebody was coming up them at a great pace, perhaps a firewatcher, perhaps a copper. He retreated again in the direction of Mount Street, away from Hamilton Place, and was relieved to find a drainpipe, though it was square. There were convenient balconies to each of the five floors, and he got down pretty quickly. Footsteps were running in his direction as he touched the pavement, and there was the sound of a car. He whipped off his mask and walked boldly into Mount Street. He was stopped at once by two policemen, who flashed torches in his face.

'Good evening, officer,' he said to the nearest.

CHAPTER XIII

THE advantage of wearing a light-coloured coat instead of a dark one he had proved on a much earlier escapade, when a police sergeant had eyed smears of paint from a window-sill which had got on his lapels. It had been ticklish and only pure luck had got him out of it. Since then, he wore light colours, in case of paint or dirt from drainpipes and roofs.

Reaching Broadcasting House as it struck one, he reflected on the several advantages of being such a well-known figure. These would, of course, be suitably weighed against him if he ever faced a judge and jury; but in the meantime they had their inestimable advantages. The police officers had recognized him immediately, for they too worked now and then in the black lighthouse. Moreover, they very kindly let Mr Bisham stay around and watch the burglar hunt. The Flying Squad flew up, and a cordon was thrown round the building, in fact round the whole Mount Street block. It seemed that these burglaries were getting beyond a joke and were causing Inspector Hood a severe headache. Mr Bisham expressed a hope that he might meet Mr Hood, but it seemed Mr Hood was too busy inspecting drain-pipes and window catches. Quite a lot of people opened windows or came into the road in dressing-gowns, including Mr George Mansfield, the industrialist. But nothing much happened except that the sirens went and so everybody had to disappear to various posts as wardens, firemen and ambulance drivers. Not caring to have lumps of shrapnel falling on his head, Mr Bisham walked away to the black lighthouse. It had been fairly exciting, but not very. However, his haul for Russia was exceedingly satisfactory. The most ticklish moment had been when he was undoing the necklace from Mrs Mansfield's fat neck. Not an easy matter in rubber gloves. A pity he had

had to stoop to ether, but it would have been too risky without. It was to be hoped Mrs Mansfield wasn't feeling sick; ether was filthy stuff.

The all-clear sounded as he got back.

Broadcasting House was its familiar night-time self. Strange bursts of Indian music came from hidden channels. Weird figures moved sleepily about in dressing-gowns. Others wandered about with brown suitcases looking for a vacant studio bed.

He went to the Green Room.

There were rows of sleeping figures in bunks in the dim light. He would have liked to have examined his haul, but it would be unwise. Somebody might wake up, or come in. He left it where it was in his overcoat pocket, beside the revolver there. A pity he had been obliged to miss the train. He was rather in a mood for Marjorie's warm presence. The beds here were rather narrow and short.

He got into his sheet and carefully pulled his coat over him. Pleased, he fell asleep and didn't wake up until seven. Then he had a light breakfast in the canteen and took a taxi to Waterloo.

It was a lovely late-April day and Marjorie was in the garden cutting flowers.

Seeing her there, in all her reality, her basket of daffodils and tulips, and her funny little brown hat, and with the sun shining down between the two weeping willow trees in such an every day sort of way, the image of himself standing in Mrs Mansfield's bedroom holding a torch stuffed with cotton wool and ether, seemed quite incongruous.

Yet, at one time, the idea of himself addressing millions on the air would have seemed equally incongruous.

Why did we never get used to the fact that simply anything could happen? We never did. But the strangest things happened all the time, every day. Illustrations of it were scarcely necessary. It should be quite ordinary that he had stood in dire peril in a strange house, for his own reasons, and risked ugly, unhappy years in gaol, a fate he regarded as worse than death. He had flashed the blue light of a torch on a figure in a fourposter bed. It was snuff-taking Mrs Mansfield. Her snuff-box had been sitting on the radio there, but he hadn't taken it because it had sentimental value for her, or she said it had.

The present calm moment was now his to enjoy by contrast, and contrast was everything.

She was saying:

'Lord Sudbury telephoned, Ernest.' She said it was just about the sale of gems in Belgrave Square in a few days, and he wanted to make sure Ernest would open it; it was for Russia.

He thought: 'It looks like being an all-in day for Russia!' He had heard a good deal about Sudbury and his interest in gems.

She said: 'And your safe has come, dear.'

The cuckoo was trying out an old tune. He watched it fly from a clump of pine trees. The sky was a crystal blue with only one very white cloud in the entire expanse of it. He was sitting on the wooden seat by the rose path. A tall yew hedge was behind him, cut into peacocks. In front of him was the rambling house which always made him think of Hans Andersen. Marjorie called it their ginger-bread house. Wisteria, purple and white, would colour it a bit later on, and meanwhile the green foliage clung from window to window as high as the Leemans' bedroom. A large rook sat on the chimney stack. He could see it blinking.

In the next garden a motor lawn-mower was at work. At intervals it stopped at their fence and there was the drone of voices. Shorter liked to chat, and he stood by the fence with bits of bass sticking out of his pockets. Marjorie had discovered Shorter somewhere in the village. He walked about all day with bits of bass sticking out of his pockets, and on Saturdays with bits of boys pushing loaded wheelbarrows. He was resolved that most of the garden should be given up to vegetables, but he allowed Marjorie some flowers because of the local soldiers' hospital.

Ernest Bisham was wondering how he would get his collection to Russia, and how soon. And he was wondering what would happen if and when Russia discovered who the original owners had been. It was a delicate point and a point that would have to wait. There was no particular reason to assume the point would arise, for the gems would probably be broken down for many uses. Diamonds were used for many things in wartime. How would he get them there? By air, probably. It was surely not an insuperable problem? It could wait too, but not for too long. While they were in his possession there was constant danger.

There was the pleasant sound of Marjorie's scissors. She was clipping red and yellow roses with very long stems. He got the scent of them. Bombers droned across the sky towards France. He watched them for a time and then dropped his eyes from the glare. On the seat was Marjorie's newspaper. There was a colourful account of the latest cat-burglary in London, and she had evidently been reading it. He had read several versions in the train coming down. He asked her if she had read about it and she said she had. She seemed amused at the idea of a burglar having the nerve to take your jewels from you while you slept. Her eyes laughed and she seemed rather to admire it. The necklace was worth about ten thousand pounds. As he sat smiling at her, his fingers touched it. What would she say if he pulled the necklace from his pocket and said quietly: 'For you, my dear!' He sighed. He dropped his eyes to the paper again. Mrs Mansfield defended herself with an article called 'Why I Always Sleep In My Jewellery'. She said: 'I have never believed in safes. Almost anybody who studies the subject can get to work on a safe, either with, well, brains or dynamite. But I never thought a cat-burglar would dare to take jewellery from a sleeping woman. He must be a very unusual man, and it *was* a man, it was a man in a mask.' Mr Bisham was amused to see that he was now called in all the papers the Man In The Mask. They had dug up other exploits in which victims recalled getting a glimpse of the mysterious man in the mask. But he always got away. It sounded romantic. 'My necklace,' Mrs Mansfield explained, 'was insured for ten thousand pounds. My husband bought it for me from the late Duchess of Manse. The clasp alone is worth fifteen hundred pounds.'

Marjorie was calling Lucas, who was chasing the cat in and out of the greenhouse. 'Lucas, Lucas . . .!'

He suddenly thought she looked so much happier.

As she turned to him, she made a noticeable picture, holding the basket of roses. She still had a confused notion of colour, with her brown hat, and her large red blouse, and an oddly cut green skirt. She had no stockings and had made rather a hash of browning her legs, and she had on grey sandals with her long, square toes sticking through the tops.

She was getting taller, wasn't she, and just a bit larger in the body?

He suddenly asked her if she was happy.

She exploded, just like a schoolgirl: 'Oh *yes*, Ernest! *Very* happy . . .!'

He felt a little embarrassed by her reply and dropped his eyes. Three little lines at once appeared above the bridge of her large nose. He knew she was thinking: 'But . . . are *you* happy?'

He went indoors.

He would have a bath and change into something comfortable.

The safe was in his room and he crossed to it excitedly, as to a new toy. He locked the door of his room and spent fully an hour transferring his collection from the locked drawers. They were imposing on strips of black velvet and sometimes in their cases; cases were often too bulky for the pocket. There were emeralds and sapphires and diamonds and rubies and jade, and they glistened from bangles, necklaces, earrings, tiaras and rings. He crouched before them, a pleased, bulky figure, and decided to lose no time in finding means to get them sent on their mission of goodwill. Perhaps he would send some to Poland. The sooner, the better—on the floor a piece of torn newspaper said: 'Five years for cat-burglar.' He locked the safe. The combination he chose was 'Marjorie Russia.'

He went whistling into the bathroom. He had a new craze for whistling a modern tune, 'When I Look at You, I Think of an Angel!' It was attractive. Marjorie hummed it too; it had become 'their song'. He recalled that when he and Seal had been married 'their song' had been 'Stormy Weather'. It had been fitting. Amused, now that it was all far away in the dim and shady past, he smiled to himself and recalled too that Marjorie said the tune she and Captain Bud had considered their song, for about a week, anyway, was 'I Am Chu Chin Chow from China'. They had been to a revival.

Mr Bisham was very fond of bathrooms. He liked marble or alabaster bathrooms, with plenty of crystal glass. He liked large bath towels too, and not those little thin things that tore in shreds the moment you tried to do your back. Marjorie had arranged all these and other points soon after their honeymoon. They had spent their honeymoon here at Tredgarth, but had gone to London for shopping and to see all the musical shows. Marjorie liked dancing too, and when they were dancing he felt they made a very sedate couple. Everyone else seemed wildly abandoned by comparison, though Marjorie said he was the best partner she had ever had. Marjorie went off into dreams when she danced, gazing at the gold ceiling, and being a bit heavy on the feet. She smelt nice and was always pleased with everything. When he remarked that he thought they must seem sedate, she teased him by saying it was his self-consciousness. Lying in the green bath he reflected that she teased him a good deal in a quiet way. She did it with her large eyes. She had a trick of saying things with her eyes and a half-smile, and she had quite a trick, especially at dinner parties at home, of conveying all sorts of amusing thoughts. She was a marvellous woman, wasn't she! You did want a sense of humour in a woman. Seal had never seen the funny side of anything, least of all of herself. Marjorie had all sorts of little jokes and often he felt she was secretly laughing when he didn't know what the joke was. It had been her idea to have toy yachts to sail in the bath. She had made him admit, during the honeymoon, that his childhood had been a lonely one, and he admitted that one of his chief disappointments had been in not having boats for his bath. Well—now he had four! They had little red sails and they shot across the green, soapy water just above his stomach in the most thrilling manner. He pretended that the loofah was a large rock, and the nail brush was a Nazi submarine. Then he pretended that each yacht carried a cargo of stolen gems to allied countries, to aid the war effort. They had been stolen only from people who could really afford this little extra donation from their safes and chests of drawers. The little ships got through all right, and finally sailed back with the news of the gems' true origin. It raised such a laugh in the press that the owners had to put a brave face on it and present their gems to Russia as a gift. Of course, thought Mr Bisham, it was all very childish, this yacht business. The mirrors around him reflected the picture of himself which he imagined everyone else would get if they were snooping in at the window there—of a thoroughly eccentric and middle-aged gentleman with greying hair. Nobody would dream of thinking it could be Ernest Bisham, the announcer. Playing with boats in his bath at Woking—it just didn't come over in his voice! He lay flat and stared, pleased, at his yachts. Marjorie had got them with great difficulty at Hamley's in Regent Street. She'd been amusing about it, waiting until the Leemans were out of earshot and then producing the parcel. 'I had to tell Hamley's it was for my four-year-old son,' she told him. And when the Leemans had gone up to bed, she and Ernest had hurried to the bathroom and filled the bath. It had been fun. He wondered if Marjorie had played with them much when she had a bath. She was rather prim about her baths and locked the door—'Well,

I'm getting rather plump, Ernest.' Her bathroom craze seemed to be bath salts. There were rows of large square bottles full of purple crystals. He reached out and took a handful from the nearest bottle. He thought: 'I shall miss all this if I ever find myself in prison. You don't get boats or bath salts there! Or large bath towels!' He thought silently of some of the things you did get. A little warning shudder touched his spine. He stood up, humming, 'When I look at you I hear lovely music'. Then he started to think about the speech he would have to make at Lord Sudbury's affair. A tedious affair it would have been in the ordinary way, but his little hobby threw a new light on it. He had heard plenty about Sudbury's little habits, and about how he treated Lady Sudbury. It was quite certain Sudbury had plenty of gems to spare for Russia, apart from the ones he was putting up for sale. Lord Sudbury was a retired pawnbroker, though he called it something else. It would probably be a tougher nut to crack than any of the others. Though, you never knew.

The day of the sale happened to be the day of Mrs Mansfield's broadcast, and he bumped into her in front of Broadcasting House. She was exceedingly distrait. She said the police were still hunting high and low for the Man In The Mask, and they never ceased riddling her with endless and most ridiculous questions. Where had she been, and exactly whom had she met the few days before? As if *that* mattered. 'Why, I even had to mention *you*, Mr Bisham!' She declared that the mere idea of being asked such a stupid thing made her feel quite ill. 'I said, but he's at the *BBC*, Mr Hood!' She said Scotland Yard was absolutely hopeless, particularly Mr Hood, who was supposed to be in charge of the case. 'I *ask* you! He's been after the Man In The Mask for years, he says so himself. Why on earth don't they put somebody younger on the case?' She looked puffier than ever, but she was still coy. She was *mortified* when Mr Bisham said he could not announce her broadcast because he was opening Lord Sudbury's sale of gems to raise cash for Russia. 'Lord Sudbury!' she exclaimed disparagingly. 'Don't talk to me about *that* man. I hate mean, grasping men, and his wife is the nicest person, plain but *quite* sweet!' She said Lady Sudbury was supposed to have gems and jewels by the dozen. 'He gave her I can't tell you how many, a collection it was, for a wedding present. Wedding present!' She rolled her eyes heavenwards. 'My dear Mr Bisham, she's never been allowed to lay a finger on one of them! They've never been out of their cases; she told me so herself!'

Mr Bisham felt oddly pleased.

'Indeed . . .?'

'Now, if the Man In The Mask paid a visit to him,' said Mrs Mansfield venomously.

'Perhaps he will,' said Mr Bisham thoughtfully.

He was very thoughtful when he entered the house in Belgrave Square.

And on the platform, waiting to make his speech, he stared thoughtfully and carefully about him. Deep in his overcoat pocket, his fingers rested on something hard.

The use and mis-use of a loaded revolver was, to Mr Bisham, a matter of psychological interest and consideration. A man might sit and feel unusually secure because his right hand touched a revolver in his pocket; but it didn't follow that he would use it should the occasion arise. Indeed, there had been interesting moments in the past when he had had occasion to study the reaction of man to a revolver thrust in his face. He had not yet come across the man who would challenge it. The man who was thus threatened had but a little time to make up his mind on two things: was the pistol, staring at him, loaded? If it was, would the man really be likely to fire it? In all cases, prudence was the safest guide. Besides, if the man wore a mask, you could not judge him by his expression.

Mr Bisham passed the time thinking about it. Lord and Lady

Sudbury made quite a fuss of him. Before mounting the platform with them, he had been introduced to endless rows of people, all of whom thought his radio voice 'too marvellous, Mr Bisham! We *always* listen in when *you* are on the air.' Once on the platform, Lord Sudbury made a long and rambling speech in praise of the BBC and its announcers. His lordship looked an artful customer. He looked rather like a restless farmer and wore loose-fitting clothes. He had a ruddy face and leaned forward as if he had been at the plough all day long. The gems were arranged in attractive tiers at the foot of the platform and were roped off. A beautiful chandelier lit the proceedings, a little unnecessarily, for it was not yet dark, but the effect on the gems was delightful. It was like liquid fire shot with silver and gold. There was a wide staircase forming a background to the proceedings, at the foot of it an auctioneer's dais. There were rather a lot of packing cases about, for there were statues for sale as well as gems. The place was extremely crowded, unusually so, when you thought of income tax. Who could afford jewellery nowadays? A bracelet for three hundred and fifty pounds ten?

Inspector Hood was wondering.

Mr Hood, as he preferred to be called, was leaning against a stone pillar a little way up the staircase. He felt rather like a journalist who has covered this sort of thing a thousand times before, but doesn't want to miss anything just through being bored and cynical. His mack was undone and he had his hands in his trousers' pockets. His hat was on the banisters beside him.

Now and again he smoothed his silver hair with a restless hand, and his eyes roamed restlessly from the auctioneer to the figures on the platform—and back to the table full of such valuable gems. He had seen the same scene a thousand times before, and no doubt he would see it many times yet. But still, you never knew, there might be some little point to fasten onto. There might even be a robbery here, it was what he was supposed to watch for, but he felt it was unlikely. It wouldn't be exactly easy. It was a well-dressed gathering, wasn't it? Very smart. A couple of the War Cabinet here too. Not to mention others . . . All the same, he would have much preferred being at home in his little house in Shepherd's Bush. Yet there was *some*thing about this particular gathering which was out of the ordinary, at any rate so far as he was concerned! Ernest Bisham was here! It wasn't that announcers impressed *him*—but they impressed Mrs Hood! She was absolutely balmy about them, and when, at their daughter's wedding celebrations, a game had been played in which you had to choose whom, out of all past and present history, you would like to go out to dinner with, Mrs Hood had chosen Ernest Bisham! Well, it made you think, and there must be something to it or they wouldn't have caught the public fancy like they had! For his part, he would sooner have gone out to dinner with Crippen so as to have got the real low-down about Belle Elmore. But Mrs Hood had chosen Ernest Bisham, the announcer! And there he was over there!

Mr Hood gave him a bit of a once-over. The reason he really did so was because he knew quite well Mrs Hood would fairly riddle him with questions about what he looked like 'close to'. Was he like his voice? Was he like his photographs?

Well, he wasn't really like either. Or was he? He looked pretty decent. Genial, anyway. Photographs were misleading. Usually people only published photographs of themselves when they were younger. He looked kind of distinguished, didn't he? But so had Patrick Mahon! Smart, anyhow. If Mrs Hood thought Mr Bisham was young, though, she was sadly mistaken, never mind what his voice might sound like. If she thought he was young and flighty. He was very stolid, wasn't he?

Mr Hood felt rather glad. He had been getting rather jealous of Ernest Bisham in recent months.

He turned away.

'Shall we begin, ladies and gentlemen?' hammered the auctioneer. He thumped with his hammer and said more loudly: 'My lords, ladies and gentlemen; before we do begin, I am asked to stress that Lord Sudbury is of course only offering for sale part of his wonderful collection of valuable gems. But he and Lady Sudbury have very kindly consented, as a surprise, to permit, on the first floor, in the Jewel Room there, a private view of Lady Sudbury's own collection, given her by Lord Sudbury as a wedding present. There will be a special money-box collection, outside the Jewel Room, in aid of Russia.

'My lords, ladies and gentlemen, Lot Number One: a diamond tiara, once in possession of the Italian Royal Family.'

CHAPTER XIV

LADY SUDBURY was charming to Mr Bisham. She was a gentle creature, and a small bit frightened in manner. She wore a veil and behind it she could be seen taking a nervous interest in the proceedings. When she lifted her veil and pinned it up, her blue eyes showed a lost look, and her mouth said that life had long since died on her. The whole thing was now too pitiful to be true. She said to Mr Bisham in the saddest way: 'My life has been spent amongst gems!' And she said: 'I'm afraid we don't have the radio.' She smiled apologetically about it. She went on to say that her father, who had been fond of her husband, had also been an enthusiastic collector of jewels. But she looked bored to death with jewels as she took him up to the Jewel Room to show him 'one or two pendants; there is one in particular of almost priceless value.' She seemed amused at his interest in how she and Lord Sudbury safeguarded themselves against thieves. So many people were curious about that, weren't they? It was natural. But, she explained, Lord Sudbury had his own ideas. He didn't disbelieve in safes, but he regarded them as 'a temporary convenience—whilst you go into the next room, so to speak!' She took him into the Jewel Room, where a long table was roped off and laden with gems, and she said: 'We just keep everything here exactly as you see them. We close the cases, of course, because of the dust.' Then she smiled and said: 'There is our real safe, over there!' Mr Bisham had been looking at a pendant on the table. It was a magnificent piece of work. It outrivalled anything at present in his possession. So did several other pieces he could see there. When she said, 'There is our real safe, over there,' he followed her glance. A lot of people were standing excitedly and admiringly about the long table. At the entrance door, a girl in spectacles was standing with a collection box. Lady Sudbury's private secretary, no doubt. Following the direction of her glance, he could see no safe. There was no safe to be seen in any part of the rectangular, high-ceilinged room. Except for the table of gems, there was no furniture in the room of any kind. Where there had once been windows, there were now nailed boards which had been painted green. He heard himself saying perplexedly: 'I don't see any safe, Lady Sudbury.' But she smiled and said: 'He has been with us for some years now,' and Mr Bisham found himself looking at a thick-set man of singularly unprepossessing appearance. He was like a gorilla, with long, swinging arms, and a sloping forehead with sticky black hair shooting upwards from it. Lady Sudbury said: 'His name's Bardner. He's talking to Inspector Hood, from Scotland Yard. Mr Hood always comes on these occasions.' Mr Bisham gave Hood a quick look. He had often wished to meet him. So that was Hood! He didn't dislike him. He looked a sentimentalist—though doubtless he would deny such an accusation to the last ditch, if you said it of him. He became aware that every now and again Hood glanced at him with some slight interest. A little later on, Lady Sudbury rejoined him and said: 'Mr Bisham, Inspector Hood very much wants to meet you. He says Mrs Hood is a great admirer of your voice on the radio!'

'Delighted to meet you,' said Mr Bisham cordially. He became aware that the gorilla which Lady Sudbury described as being the family safe was standing a little behind Hood, watching him. Bardner's expression was somewhat ferocious. Was it his natural one? He looked a nasty bit of work, but perhaps he was kind to children and animals. Mr Bisham wished Lady Sudbury had been a little more explicit about her safe. How exactly did he function?

Hood was thinking: 'Well, I've met him! So Mrs Hood can't say I didn't!'

They started some small talk and the room filled more quickly. Mr Bisham started to wonder what had better be his line of attack. Obviously the place was full of plain-clothes men, not counting Hood and Bardner. Hood said something about Mrs Hood being most interested when he got home to Shepherd's Bush and told her he'd met him, and he said something modest in reply, and laughed. The gorilla had stopped staring at him and had moved away. Lord Sudbury was charging round the huge table, and round the crowd of guests, wearing the fiery expression of a farmer who is afraid the rooks may have been secretly walking off with some of his crops. 'What do you think of Bardner?' Hood was saying pleasantly. 'He's a beauty, isn't he?'

'Yes . . .'

'He used to be a warder.'

Mr Bisham was thinking: 'Well, I've got all the time in the world—so long as I'm back in time to read the seven o'clock news tomorrow morning. I must on no account miss that, for, as it happens, there's nobody to take my place.'

He had started to think quickly. A rather tensely defiant mood had settled on him. He felt like a warrior at whose feet had fallen another gauntlet, rather a large one this time, but it only made him more defiant. He took his leave of the Inspector, who said, a little disconcertingly: 'I hope we meet again, Mr Bisham. And I dare say we will, all right.' When he moved away, Hood was leaning back against the wall of the Jewel Room with his hands in his pockets. It seemed to be a characteristic pose.

When he had said his good-byes to Lord and Lady Sudbury and a few others, he noticed Bardner watching him again. Bardner had the eyes of a farmyard pig.

Turning away from them, in the din of conversation, he found himself facing the Sudburys' secretary and her collection box. She grinned expectantly.

'We think your broadcasts are absolutely marvellous,' she said unexpectedly, and stared at him through thick lenses, looking like a hungry thrush.

He dropped something into her collection box.

'I'm very glad . . .'

'Ooh, thanks most awfully! Look, do tell me, are those cooking hints after the eight o'clock news recorded, or real? I've got a bet. *I* say they're—'

She was interrupted by other departing visitors.

He muttered something and slipped down the wide staircase. At the foot of it he saw a maid and asked her if he might use the telephone.

She took him to a cloakroom on the ground floor and left him there. He telephoned Marjorie. Leeman answered the 'phone and it was possible to hear Lucas barking. Marjorie was out, so he left a message to the effect that he had to go on a little journey and might miss the last train.

'Very good, sir,' came Leeman's voice.

'In which case I shall not be back until dinner time tomorrow.'

'Very well, sir . . .'

'I'm reading the seven and eight and the one and the six.' He disliked telling Leeman this, but Marjorie liked to know so she could listen.

'Yes, sir,' Leeman said, bored.

'Good night, then.' He rang off.

He crossed the small cloakroom and stood staring at the window. Softly opening it, he saw that it opened onto a side street. Surprised at the simple convenience of this, he examined the catch and looked for alarm wires. But there didn't appear to be any.

In a similar state of tension, Jonas Wintle paced about in a similarly small room; but it was a room high up in Broadcasting House, and he was not searching for alarm wires. There were alarms enough in his new department, without wires. Except for himself, the room for the moment was empty. He sat on a leather sofa, or he got up and paced to the narrow window, there to stare down at Portland Place. He several times thought

of suicide, but it seemed such an unpleasant end. The clock
on the buff wall was ticking, its repulsive red hand jerking
round to the moment of his next crisis. In this the most
harrowing and responsible department in the entire
Corporation—called Recorded Programmes Department—his
short life in it had produced crisis after crisis, and at any
moment it would produce yet another. The public called it
'playing gramophone records'—if only it was as simple as that!
Mr Wintle, as he was now called, had not yet got over his last
job, which had been the six o'clock news, and over which Mr
Black, his Shift Leader, had told him he had made 'a complete
hash, Mr Wintle. What was the trouble, if I may ask?' He
loathed Mr Black as no man loathed a member of his species
ever before, and in vain did he protest that the 'trouble should
be accredited to that Mrs Mansfield woman, who had had a
coughing attack in the middle of her broadcast, and again just
before the end cue of it, thereby confusing the cue altogether.
I was in consequence eight seconds late in playing the trumpet
voluntary, Mr Black.' Mr Black, cold, said that the whole point
of the trumpet voluntary had been to round off the talk, which
goodness only knew needed something. He hitched his brown
corduroy trousers and said, cold, that eight seconds late on a
cue was worse, far, than murder 'here', and he was still waiting
for an adequate explanation. He said that coughing attack or
no coughing attack, Mrs Mansfield was entitled to her
concluding fanfare of tin trumpets; they had been recorded
with great trouble in Stalingrad itself, and if Mr Wintle had an
atom of intelligence—which he clearly had not—he would have
drowned Mrs Mansfield's disgusting coughing with trumpets
from Stalingrad. 'You should have faded it up and drowned
it, Mr Wintle,' Mr Black said, cold.

Even colder, and looking daggers, and sweeping his hair out
of his angry eyes, Mr Wintle pointed out that he could not
possibly know if red-haired Mrs Mansfield was going to stop
her disgusting coughing and say her concluding sentences. She

might then have spoken right *into* the trumpets from Stalingrad. He trembled.

Mr Black, trembling too, said he was supposed to use his judgment 'here'. He pointed out that in the short time Mr Wintle had honoured them with his presence, he had (*a*) left some discs in a taxi, and with only forty minutes to go before the programme was due on the air, and (*b*) said 'oh, dear' in a studio without looking to see that the red light was on—'we were deluged with letters, one even came from Aberdeen, Mr Wintle, postage paid'—and (*c*) been exceedingly rude to Mr Mundy about Brahms. Mr Black said did he not like Brahms? And he said he must in any case bury his feelings 'here' and think only of the public, no matter what the public might think of him. As for the hash he had made of the six, he should realize that the public got home feeling exceedingly tired and irritable for the six, because it had not had its dinner, and now, in consequence, the Corporation would be deluged with letters, 'phone calls, telegrams and cables all asking what happened at six; there was some very curious coughing at the end of Mrs George Mansfield's speech, followed by a long pause and then a roaring burst of trumpets from Stalingrad; had Russia concluded the war, or what? There was also a grave risk of having offended Marshal Stalin, not to mention Mrs Mansfield, when she heard about it. In short, Mr Wintle would undoubtedly go on the carpet first thing in the morning, and probably out on his ear sometime during the late afternoon. And serve him right. At this rate, he had better be an announcer, and just speak. He couldn't say anything more scathing than that, unless it was to put him solely on 'dubbing'. Dubbing, as Mr Wintle knew already, was an appalling invention whereby you were obliged to stand with a large stop watch in one hand and a telephone receiver in the other, while you watched a disc rotating at frightening speed on a black turntable. Somewhere else in England, the noise it was making, whether it was a trumpet fanfare or an extract from one of Mr Churchill's speeches, was being re-recorded on a cutting machine tended by somebody far less friendly than Annabella. Annabella was the one saving grace in the entire building.

Jonas Wintle paced about, thinking of Annabella, and of Mr Black, who was at the moment in the bowels of the building attending a recording of 'What I Think of Sergeant Majors, by A Little Wren.' It was to be played by Mr Wintle after the seven o'clock news next morning, as a punishment, the punitive quality being in the necessity for rising at six for fear of being late. He thought wistfully of Annabella, wondering what his mother and father would behave like if he brought her down for a weekend. Could he trust them not to be too old-fashioned? If so, it would be quite wizard.

Forgetting everything, he glanced again at the Schedule lying on the yellow table. He wanted to make quite sure which studio his next job was in, for it was a job for Mr Mundy. Mr Mundy wanted one of his Brahms programmes dubbed, because somebody had expressed a curious dislike for his last programme and had gently lowered all his discs into the gentlemen's lavatory basin. They had become scratched and he felt the public was entitled to as good a reproduction as he could give. On the Schedule it said: 'Dubbing Brahms for Mr Mundy, Studio Five, nineteen hundred hours to twenty hundred hours', and in pencil it put, 'Mr Wintle, and *please* don't be late, it's that swine Mundy.' Mr Mundy was a bewhiskered producer and Mr Wintle shared the general regret that his interest in Brahms caused him so constantly to rush up and down the studio with his arms in the air. Just as you were trying to negotiate a tricky change-over from the end of the first disc to the beginning of the second, or from the end of the fifth to the beginning of the sixth, Mr Mundy seemed to anticipate the erratic cut of a bar that you were probably going to make, and he liked to let out a roar like a gored bull. The result, so far as Mr Wintle was concerned, was that he jumped at least eight bars and wished he was dead.

Thinking of this, Mr Wintle felt extremely browned off and went down in a lift to the studio.

Mr Mundy was already bending over a long row of rotating discs on the vast gramophone bank. He was making marks on the discs with a long yellow pencil and above his tousled head artificial daylight lent an artificial gaiety to the scene, suggestive of torture in a beautiful Chinese garden. He ignored Mr Wintle and plied his yellow pencil. Mr Wintle started to click on various switches and stared in a glazed fashion at the control panel. A needle was protesting in frantic terms against Mr Mundy's view of Brahms. Mr Mundy kept lowering the needle over the disc, and then shoving up the pot'meter so that there was a shattering roar of Brahms, to which he made hearty vocal chorus and swung his arms heavenwards. Through the window, Annabella was eating an orange. It was too much for Mr Wintle. An orange? On a sudden impulse, utterly unnerved by Brahms and oranges, he rushed out and along to Home Presentation.

Haggard, he put his head in and said:

'Could I speak to Mr Bisham, please?'

He was quite resolved now. The sight of Mundy had done it, not to mention the fiasco at six. And the sight of those Brahms discs, and those yellow lines, and those waving arms . . . He would be an announcer or die in the attempt; it was a nice, quiet life, you just read out loud . . .

He was told that Mr Bisham was off duty.

'Well, when will he be back?' he cried frantically, drawing curious eyes towards him.

'He's reading the seven in the morning.'

'The seven . . .?'

The seven. He too was concerned with the seven. That little Wren, he would have to play the disc. Well, he would implore

Mr Bisham to get him out of this dreadful department. Meanwhile ... Brahms!

With leaden steps he went back to the studio.

Mr Mundy was standing motionless and for some curious reason was tugging his beard and singing 'Lead, Kindly Light'.

At the Bolivar, an hour and three minutes later, Mr Black, cold, approached a flannel-suited heap slumped over the cocktail bar. He said:

'So there you are! *What* happened?'

He then said (getting no reply) that Mr Mundy thought he had 'no love of Brahms, or indeed, of music', and that he had 'no musical sense'. He 'didn't know where a bar of music ended, or where it began', moreover he 'had played the opening announcement last, and the closing announcement first, and, in consequence, the whole thing would have to be dubbed again if Mr Mundy was not to disappoint Scottish listeners.' And who would have to do it? 'Why, *I* shall, Mr Wintle! Instead of going to the Feathers. After this, perhaps you'd just better do plain recordings, or give ten-second cues.' He said that Mr Wintle had let down the whole department and that it was probable he would have to go before the Board of Governors. He then had a gin, neat, and went out. Mr Wintle decided to go along to the Dover Castle; it had a nice country kind of atmosphere, even if it was polluted by BBC officials. He stayed there until it was time for dinner with Annabella, thinking.

He thought about his other experiences in his new, exotic life. He divided his thoughts into two, alternating between profound gloom and attempted optimism. He always felt optimistic when he had occasion to contact the Lady Announcers, whose beatific glamour, even when they knitted and waited to speak to the boys over there, inspired him to all that was soulful; under such an influence, he had once even achieved a successful transmission of a cut version of the Brains Trust, for short wave, notwithstanding rows of discs chopped riotously into sections by a yellow pencil, and notwithstanding having to 'set up' four change-overs with the headphones on, whilst running, and only a split second or two to do it in. Indeed, so smoothly had it gone that the Duty Engineer entered the studio, wearing an uncanny expression, and asked him if he was sure he had got the right discs—there must surely be something wrong somewhere? Duty Engineers were pale and not like other people.

Relapsing, however, once again into gloom, he remembered sadder moments, such as when he was down for Radio News Reel, and disagreed with the producer as to the exact sound of a Spitfire at ten thousand feet, and was sent as a punishment to the simpler task of recording Cardinal Prugg in Studio One. Cardinal Prugg arrived in full regalia, escorted by two choristers. He had stubbly hair and a ruddy, jovial countenance, and was exceedingly muscular. His closing cue was '. . . behind the chapel', but the Cardinal kept thinking of new things to add, about chapels, and so Jonas had to start the whole thing all over again, saying heavily: 'No, sir, *please* don't start until I've given the ten-second cue . . . We'll be going ahead in ten seconds . . . from . . . NOW.' Ordinary recordings were very simple and humiliating.

CHAPTER XV

ANNABELLA stood powdering her nose and talking to a friend called Mavis in the Control Room. Mavis had long black hair and bare legs with gold plated ankle bangles. They had been given her by the director of one of the departments she had been in before being promoted to this department. The Control Room was electric with voices and lights, both artificial. The artificial daylight was uncanny. Mavis put plugs in switches and answered telephones.

Whenever she had a second, she continued an animated theory for Annabella's benefit about how either writing or producing Talks was the best job in the BBC. The secret of radio writing, she said, was to do it as if you were talking: you put 'it's', instead of 'it is', and if ever you got stuck you just put, 'fade up sound of tanks clattering through country village', or, more simply still, 'up sinister music link—and hold'. About being a Talks Producer, Mavis said you really didn't have to do anything, except steer fiery colonels into studios for their war comments, and stand staring at them with a large stop watch in your left hand. Mavis started to think of several other interesting jobs, if only you could get a transfer from one department to another without having to resign first, but was distracted by her telephones and switches. When a programme started to end in Studio Two, she listened to the closing music and watched for her cue to buzz in Studio Eight A, which, to the theme song of 'An Old Violin' was to start an eerie hour of a new series called 'The Violin Murders', with a famous actress in the cast; she wasn't there in the flesh, of course, it had been recorded on tape, because soon she would be in a new West End play and they were rehearsing. Mavis told Annabella she would rather have liked to have gone on the stage, her people

thought she was quite like Fay Compton in *Blithe Spirit*.
Annabella said: 'I don't know how you stand Control Room,
with all these plugs, and all those pale engineers.' Mavis said
she used to be in the disc library. All those archives, simply
anything was better than that, except possibly the telediphone
crowd, who had to wear headphones and rattle down foreign
dispatches from war correspondents onto typewriters. The
really best job in the place, she said now, was announcing, of
course, if you were born with a golden voice. But if you really
wanted a cushy time, you should be a producer, most of them
couldn't produce kittens. Dabbing a pink puff on her high
cheekbones, Mavis invited Annabella to gin in the canteen.
They went along, chattering, and there was Mr Wintle, half
seas over. He was sitting on a black glass table, talking to a
friend about the New Recorded Programmes Manager, a Mr
Lark, who complained that he had fallen in love for the fifth
time in five weeks. It was difficult for managers, Mr Lark had
explained to the shift, with so much music and beauty around.

Mr Ernest Bisham was sitting on the window-sill of the little
cloakroom. The catch had given no trouble. He was dressed
as he had been for the little night visit to Mount Street. It was
dark and he carefully flashed his torch with the blue light. It
was a little after nine. Lady Sudbury had been good enough to
inform him of a dinner engagement to which she and her
husband were committed elsewhere, and so far as he had been
able to discover she only employed the maid who had taken
him to the cloakroom telephone. There was, of course, Bardner.
Thinking very considerably of him, he opened the cloakroom
door. The hall was in pitch darkness. It was eerie and dramatic.
He moved forward, thinking how often in life he had enjoyed,
or wanted to enjoy, emulating the dramatic and sinister figures
in fiction, moving silently up behind someone and saying softly:
'That thing sticking into your ribs ain't my finger, buddy!' Was
it a weakness in most of us? He thought it was, though he also
thought it was left to the few to carry things out. Those who

did, ran the risk of being accused mad. Starting to creep up
the wide staircase in the darkness, he considered this fine point
too. Was he mad? It was easy to say such and such a person
was mad—but were they really mad? To be mad, or insane,
meant that you had 'a disordered mind'. To be sane therefore
meant that you had an ordered mind. Your mind was disordered, or abnormal, they said, if you killed somebody—providing
it was peacetime. But the moment it was wartime nobody said
killing was mad. You could press buttons with your thumb and
release bullets and bombs. You could have a tommy gun, or a
Bren gun, and you could excitedly mow down retreating
Germans and Japanese just below the knees in a sort of sawing
motion so that they all sloped forward without legs, the more
slowly to endure the punishment they had brought on themselves by greater cruelties to women and children in Europe
and China and Russia. It wasn't 'mad' of you. Your mind wasn't
disordered. The only risk you ran was the risk of getting a
medal. You could finally return to your family in England and
nobody would ever remember that you were a murderer fifty
times over, least of all yourself. Yet, if you crept up some stairs
in the darkness and chanced to shoot somebody you would be
hanged, sent to prison, or sent to an asylum. Mr Bisham, feeling
extraordinarily sane, was just groping his way round the bend
he remembered in the stairs, when the door of the Jewel Room
opened and Bardner came out. In a yellow light, Bardner was
seen to go along the corridor there and come back carrying a
light divan bed. There was then the shadow of him moving
about the Jewel Room and making up his bed. Mr Bisham
thought: 'I mustn't be long over this. The Sudburys will probably be back from their dinner fairly soon.' He adjusted his
mask carefully and put his hand in his pocket for his revolver.
Then he moved quickly up the remaining stairs.

Bardner put down his divan bed in the corner and proceeded
to prepare it in the usual way. He thought once again about the

unusual life he led, and once again fell to reflecting that it was better than being a prison warder, which he had once been, and having to cope with all that red tape, and all that constant risk of a sex-starved prisoner suddenly going crackers and creeping up behind your back to dot you one. There was that unnerving incident when a prisoner with a secreted razor blade had leapt on the back of the Chief Warder and slit his throat from ear to ear. That sort of thing made an imaginative person very touchy and nervy, and you never really got over it. You were no good for the Army. For a long time he had not got over his nerves even here, where there was never a burglary of any kind. And why should there be one? It was selling the stuff that gave them such a headache. Otherwise there would no doubt have been a few attempts. And it would be easy enough, really, providing it was properly planned, and providing they'd learned the one or two little snags an amateur wouldn't think of. He made up his bed and yawned. Things were a bit tame, though, month after month, flattering though it was to your reputation as a 'safe'. A human safe! And Lord Sudbury was a mean old beggar and not easily pleased. Bardner had now and then wondered what Lord Sudbury would say if he went off with some of the valuables himself. But perhaps he knew he couldn't face the risk of being sent back as a prisoner to the place where he'd been a warder. It would be just terrible! The bathrooms down there, and having to bathe together! And those cell doors banging to, and the keys turning in the locks; hour after hour in those cells with the walls green and sweating in winter. And never seeing Gracie. Gracie was the Sudbury maid, the only one left, but to Bardner she was becoming more than just a maid. She had weakened a lot lately, in her sharp way. She was a tasty bit of work and he felt sorry she was out tonight. Where had she gone? She never said. When would she be back?

Having made up his bed to his liking, and put his fags and matches ready on the floor beside it, he gave the jewel table a once-over and decided he would turn in. The most likely burglary hours were after midnight, in his opinion, and he always got up then and put all the lights on. He clicked off two lights now, leaving a light over the jewels, which were just as they had been with their cases still open. He would have to dust them and close the cases in the morning. It would be a job, but Gracie would help.

He bent down by his bed to pick up his matches, resolved to shut the door after that and settle down.

Suddenly, as he stood up, he felt a peculiarly sharp sensation in the pit of his back. It was as if something was sticking into it.

Needless to say, he was imagining it. Gracie had slipped back and was in one of her witty moods. He started to exclaim: 'Now, Gracie—' when a very quiet, masculine voice told him to stop talking and to walk pretty quickly over to the opposite wall.

Bardner felt himself turning green.

This hadn't happened really, not *really*, had it?

The next thing that happened was that he did walk pretty quickly over to the opposite wall.

'Now,' Mr Bisham whispered sharply, 'put your hands up and touch the wall with both palms.' He jabbed the revolver into Bardner's muscular back.

Bardner felt the cold wall with two sticky palms. The blood which had rushed from his face now flooded back. He turned his face slightly to the left and managed to get a glimpse of a man in a mask. As he did so, the man in the mask pulled the handkerchief from Bardner's breast pocket and proceeded to tie it round his eyes. 'Doesn't want to be seen,' thought Bardner agitatedly. 'Doesn't seem to mind if I holler, then?' But he didn't make a sound at all; for the moment, his throat was too dry.

Bardner tried desperately to do a bit of useful thinking. While the knot was being tied, he had a desperate wish to take a chance and swing round. But he had no wish to be shot, it was all very well. And this chap seemed on the big side.

Then suddenly the man in the mask said something marvellous. He said:

'Keep your hands on the wall and don't move, or it will be the worse for you. I'll just shut the door.' '*I'll just shut the door!*' Bardner thought. 'If he does shut the door he'll regret it the rest of his life! And I shan't get the sack after all!' Tense, he waited.

Surely enough, he heard the man's footsteps move quietly to the door . . . And it shut. '*Got you,*' thought Bardner, exultant. That was a self-locking door and wouldn't open, now, until six a.m. Trembling with excitement, he waited.

The man's footsteps went towards the jewel table. There were the expected sounds there and they lasted quite a bit. The man was pretty cool, whistling 'When I Think of You, I Think of An Angel', or was it nerves? He'd get angels!

Suddenly there was the sound of Gracie.

And immediately there was the sound of the man's footsteps darting to him, and the feel of the gun in his ribs. Now, that wasn't a pleasant feeling, was it? After all, to be shot in the back for a chap like Lord Sudbury, who treated everyone, even his wife, like—

'Count ten before you make any reply,' warned Mr Bisham in a sweet whisper.

There was a pause.

Gracie's voice called through:

'Mr *Bard*ner? You're never in bed already? Mr *Bard*ner?' She rattled the door and said the master and mistress would be a full hour yet.

Mr Bisham jabbed with the pistol.

'It's loaded,' he whispered.

'. . . I'm in bed,' Bardner got out throatily. After all, the man couldn't get out till six. And his lordship was always up at five. He never missed coming down here very soon after five of a morning. Then he'd know something was wrong—if he didn't discover it tonight. Ten to one he'd come along to the Jewel Room before going to bed.

Gracie called something disparaging.

'Go to bed,' called Bardner in a sleepy voice.

To his relief, Mr Bisham heard her moving away. After a little while he heard a distant door slam. But even as he sighed his relief and prepared to make his getaway, he heard distant voices. The Sudburys were already back and the door slam had been the front door as they let themselves in.

The wall under Bardner's palms was now quite hot and sticky. 'Here they come,' he thought.

But there was a long, long interval. He stood there with his arms aching and the gun sticking into his back. To his consternation he finally heard the usual sounds indicating that the Sudburys had retired for the night. He could hear them overhead.

Hearing them overhead, Mr Bisham judged that his luck was in. He backed quickly to the door and without taking his eyes off Bardner he warned him, 'Don't move, and don't make any noise,' and groped for the door-handle. He guessed Bardner would raise plenty of noise the moment he got through the door. He would have to lose no time getting down the stairs and opening the front door. He had already examined the front door catch and there was no difficulty there. But there seemed to be some difficulty here. The door-handle didn't budge.

Bardner stood waiting. A grin spread across his face and, beneath the handkerchief round his eyes, his eyes were laughing. 'Now,' he thought sardonically. He'd say to Lord Sudbury: 'That was my brains, don't you see, my lord? I let him bandage me up with my own handkerchief—knowing he'd never be able to open the door!' His lordship would be very pleased indeed with him and might even give him a bonus. After all, there was some money here. And Scotland Yard—that fellow Hood— would give him another for catching the Man In The Mask. He suddenly said quietly: 'The next move's yours, chum,' and he sniggered. Then he stopped sniggering, because of the ensuing silence, and because of new anxieties. What if this chap lost his temper and plugged him? His face straightened.

'Combination lock?' suggested Mr Bisham thoughtfully.

'Yes . . .!'

'What time does it open?'

'If you care to believe me,' Bardner said, grinning at the wall, 'it don't open till six!' There was a pause and he added: 'His lordship always gets up at five. There's quite a routine.' He just couldn't help grinning.

CHAPTER XVI

Mr Jonas Wintle sat up in bed and looked at his watch in the dim light.

It was a quarter past six.

He fell out of his bunk and pulled on his trousers. Loud snores around him were mocking reminder that a day of new crises was already upon him. Somebody was being called by a white-coated attendant. 'It is now six-seventeen, sir. Sir? I believe you said you were on the air at seven, sir!'

Mr Wintle threaded his way through the dark rows of bunks and fumbled in his pockets for his comb. He would have a quick wash, a quick cup of tea in the canteen and go and collect the disc. It should either be in his departmental office, or in the news room under the care of the Duty Editor. He hoped that it was in the office, for he was scared stiff of Duty Editors; they were rarely very friendly, all being tinged with touches of genius and many of them suffering from pulmonary disease of the heart—entirely due to the exacting nature of their work. Work in a newspaper office, they said, was a rest cure by comparison, for at least newspapers only went to press once in a day, or at the most twice, and on Sundays newspaper men went home and lay in bed criticizing the Sunday papers. But here the news room went to press at seven, at eight, at one, at six, at nine—and at midnight; and Sundays also. Duty Editors were, therefore, entitled to seem preoccupied, what with their staff, and their multitudinous telephones, and their maps and their cables and recorded dispatches constantly being delivered on that thin paper so difficult to hold, let alone read. Mr Wintle had once been permitted in the news room for a short time, for instructive purposes. When he came out, he felt very much older and hurried to a mirror to see if his hair had turned grey. His brain swam with shouting voices screaming about news items from Cairo, Algiers, Sicily and Corsica, and with other shouting voices telephoning the Ministries of Food, Health, and Air, not forgetting the War Office and the Admiralty. Mr Wintle therefore entered the news room rather timidly and he was relieved in a perverted sort of way to be told by the Duty Editor, 'Of course it's not here. Do you suppose Home News Talks would remember a little thing like that?' Mr Wintle was too scared to reply. It was one thing to risk your life over enemy territory, anybody could do that, but to answer back a Duty Editor—that was what VCs were made of. He dashed along the passage to Home News Talks. Nobody was there and the black-out was up. There was no sign of the little Wren's disc, and the only thing shaped at all like it was a large tin of stomach powder. Mr Wintle dashed up a few floors to his own office. The disc wasn't there either, and the only thing there was a note in black chalk saying: 'Mr Wintle, I hope you are going to pull your socks up today? And don't forget the Wren disc goes out at eight as well as seven. Don't go to breakfast by mistake; better have breakfast afterwards. Signed—D. Black, Shift Leader.' It was six forty-two. Crisis Number One reared its ugly head, and so far from hoping to play the Wren's talk at seven, it looked as if it wouldn't be played at eight either. What on earth would Mr Bisham say when he arrived? And just when he wanted to have a friendly talk with Mr Bisham about becoming an announcer after all. What would Mr D. Black say, above all?

He dashed down many floors to Annabella's cutting room.

There was no sign of Annabella, but there was Mr Peat in his horn-rimmed glasses. Mr Peat looked like the Aga Khan. The only difference between Mr Peat and the Aga Khan was that nobody bothered to preserve Mr Peat's bathwater, for he had an objection to baths. His Harem girls, as he called his wartime staff, spent most of their time going to the showers instead of attending to their machines. Mr Peat spent his days, in white gym shoes, going from the showers to the cutting rooms, trying to find out where his girls were. Voices came through channels from studios saying, 'Are you there yet? I want to give you a ten-second cue.' And in anticipation of yet another day having to shout down a telephone, 'Don't give a cue yet, Miss Stead is having another bath,' Mr Peat was already a little off colour. However, he found the disc for Mr Wintle, who started to dash off with it. 'Here,' shouted Mr Peat, very unlike the Aga Khan in speech, 'you can't go dashing off like that; you haven't signed the forms.' He gave Mr Wintle the five green forms to fill in. Mr Wintle signed them with one eye on his wrist-watch. The label on the disc said, amongst other things: 'What I Think of Sergeant Majors, by A Little Wren.' Mr Wintle seized it and rushed headlong to the news studio. He would just have time to try over his disc and set it up before Mr Bisham came in. He pinned up his pink cue sheet which said 'Announcer—"And now to end the news here's a talk by a little Wren who thinks that sergeant majors are different in this war".' Then it said: 'End cue—"And so that is what I think of *our* sergeant anyway, she's tip-top, and we all say the same".'

Mr Wintle put on headphones and tried the disc on the turntable. The little Wren sounded like an adenoidal thrush. He set his machine with room for an artistic pause after Mr Bisham's cue, and he offered up a prayer of thanks that the talk didn't run onto two or more discs, involving a change-over mid-sentence. He offered up a second in that the turntable now ran at the right speed; it had been broken yesterday, or wanted oiling.

Then he looked at the clock. It was four minutes to seven. But there was nothing to panic about now; Mr Bisham never entered the studio until fifty seconds to the hour. Then he sat down and waited for the red light and began.

The news room had been looking at the clock too, but from force of habit. Crisis hour was always the hour before each news bulletin. Mr Bisham, being regular and very reliable in his technique, was always expected in the news room at a quarter past the hour, when he would sit quietly down beside the Duty Editor and work systematically through each loose page of news, checking questionable pronunciations and querying punctuations, and being entirely unmoved by the din all round him, or by the Duty Editor rearranging the order of news items up to and often beyond the last minute. The Duty Editor was surprised, however, this morning to see that it was nearly twenty-five to and there was no sign of Ernest Bisham. He reached frowningly for a telephone.

The news room, even at half past six in the morning, was a hive of industry. The walls were lined with huge maps, and at desks and tables writers and typists worked with an eye on the clock. Being so early it was all rather sour. The clatter of tape machines coming from a door at the far end was permanent background music, and at intervals cables and tape were brought in and handed to the editor. He scanned each succeeding piece of news as it reached him, and if it concerned the situation in Russia, he threw it to whoever was covering Russia; if it concerned Italy, submarines, Fortresses or the price of potatoes, he threw the items in the appropriate directions. A waitress came in with a large tray of teas and coffees.

There was no news of Ernest Bisham at twenty to seven. He could not be found in his customary bunk, or in any other bunk. He could not be found anywhere.

The Duty Editor put through a call to Mr Bisham's home in Woking, just in case by an unusual oversight he had returned home last evening. He had never gone home under such circumstances because of the difficulty of getting back in time for the seven, and moreover, he knew that on this particular occasion there was nobody here to take his place. Mr Bisham had promised most faithfully to read the seven and knew his colleagues would not be available. The Duty Editor, who suffered from duodenal ulcers caused by years of emotional strain, started to look unusually haggard even for him as he heard Mrs Bisham say:

'He isn't here. He hasn't been home at all . . .'

It was a quarter to seven. Ought he to telephone the police? Perhaps something had happened to Mr Bisham . . .

When he had rung off, Marjorie sat up in bed and stared at the little blue clock on her bed-table. She switched on her radio. Somebody was singing something out of Gilbert & Sullivan, 'Patience', wasn't it? But she was thinking, not of 'Patience', but of the British Secret Service. Suddenly, in a feminine way, and though ashamed of the thought, she wondered if Ernest was, well, having an affair with another woman. It was a dreadful thing to think, but the idea just slipped into her head. She *knew* he wasn't that sort—yet . . .! Her heart beat a little more quickly. She didn't really think such a thing at all but, well, was it really *likely* he would be in the Secret Service, tied up as he was with his announcing? He would surely have let her have some little hint of any such activity? Of course he would. Wasn't it just a childish idea of hers? She had *wanted* to think it.

She knew a mild panic.

Ernest to miss a broadcast? He prided himself that he never had missed one, and she just couldn't imagine such a thing. Had anything happened to him? Had he been run over and been taken to hospital? Ought the police to be telephoned?

Her thoughts travelled this way and that; forwards and backwards. She thought of the Ernest she now knew (or thought she knew), and the Ernest she had known before; they were slightly different, weren't they? There *was* a touch of mystery, wasn't there? That loaded revolver. Not being in Manchester that night. Being somewhere last night. Where had he been all last night, if he hadn't been run over?

She leaned back on the pillows and felt afraid. She tried to think of nice reasons for these little mysteries; nice answers. She thought of the nice memories, their memories, for they would be clues to him, as the clock hand crept round towards seven.

It was getting nearer. To the sound of the Leemans moving about upstairs, she thought of the nice memories of the wedding, and the quiet honeymoon at Tredgarth. The nicest moments at their wedding had been when she entered the church on Sir Tom's arm, and the old man had taken the wrong turning and led her down the side aisle by mistake, away from the direction of the altar. Ernest said he had craned anxiously and nervously round only to see the future Mrs Bisham heading away downstream, so to speak. The vicar started up a bit of whispering, and the verger went scurrying after their retreating figures, and they presently arrived looking rather flushed from their little expedition. She had chosen brown, for her costume, and she wore the orchids he had sent her, and she wore a blue and white hat. She felt very large and tall, kneeling beside him on the cream footstool, and she heard herself saying the responses in an extraordinarily loud voice. It was nerves and he did the same. They must both have seemed rather defiant, as if they were both saying: 'We made a hash of it before, but there are no flies on either of us this time!' Another nice moment was getting the ring onto her finger; he'd had to shove and shove, and finally the vicar whispered to leave it. Ernest had finished the job in the vestry. On the honeymoon, the nicest time was when they arrived home. They wandered all over the house, and talked about the new bathroom and having some sailing boats and crystals for the bath, and they'd wandered arm-in-arm all round the large garden which was full of winding little paths and weeping willow trees. There was the rusty sun-dial which said all the world was a stage, but appeared to end with some other ending than Shakespeare's. The evening had been loverlike in an elderly sort of way, both of them being a little reserved, deciding to have a 'den' each of their own, with a bed in it, but speaking in praise of her double bed too, which he said he admired; he had a quaint hatred for beds with brass knobs. When she put on her rather large lace nightdress, he said he admired her little mauve shoulder jacket with red and green ribbon, and he'd sat on the blue eiderdown and made her feel a little self-conscious until he started discussing men's clubs. He said he wasn't much of a club person, and she said she hated women's clubs; yet, if she hadn't belonged to one she would never have met Bess, and therefore she would never have met him. Life was amusing like that. Then he asked her about her toes. They were very long and square, he didn't think he had ever seen such square toes. They compared toes and wondered if toes were as interesting a study as hands. They were very polite.

'I wonder if there are toeprints,' she had remarked self-consciously. Would he get into her bed, or would he go off to his own? She was far from sure, for they weren't exactly young.

When they compared hands, she said:

'Mine aren't very feminine, I'm afraid! But people say that the woman who has really beautiful hands is usually rather stupid. And I should hate to be thought stupid!'

Memories!

And then he had said he was relieved to see she powdered her face before she went to sleep. He said, 'My other wife always plastered herself with grease, last thing—and then expected me to kiss her!' He said she had had beautiful hands, now he came to think of it. But he said these things in a kindly way—it was conversation. He hadn't asked her anything about Captain Bud, because he had already said he 'couldn't bear to think about it'. Men were odd like that. Women didn't seem to mind very much what a man had been up to, providing it was a genuine error. But men went green when they thought about the reverse process, whether it was genuine or not!

Her mind overflowed with memories of him. She'd woken up next morning to find him asleep beside her with his mouth wide open. And she'd laughed, imagining what the public would have thought, had they seen him.

Had she really loved him then, without quite knowing it? He was so kind. If anything had happened to him, she would die.

She looked at the clock again.

It was a minute to seven.

Mr Ernest Bisham was running. He had never before been quite so acutely conscious of the time, and he was a time-conscious man. It was saying something. His wrist-watch was difficult to see in the early morning light. But he thought he heard a clock striking six. He supposed it was six. It certainly wasn't seven; he knew the feel of seven without having to look at his watch or hear a clock strike in the distance. One thing, he thought—running would help his figure.

He raced heavily up a side street.

But there was another policeman at the other end.

He doubled back and went boldly through a courtyard and found himself in a mews. There was the unpleasant sound of the men chasing him, like in a nightmare, so on an impulse he plunged through an open door. He found himself in a mews flat and he shot up some stairs looking for a window on the other side. He saw a door.

It was locked, so he dashed up another flight of narrow twisting stairs. A large lady was coming down with a towel over her arm. Mr Bisham hesitated only for a fraction of a second, then he said: 'Good morning', and brushed past her. She was a florid blonde and she was singing 'Welcome, Stranger, to Samoa'. She stopped singing and started to say: 'Good . . .' then she broke off and screamed. A door opened somewhere and a man's voice shouted: 'What's up, Ethel?' She cried: 'There's a strange man in the house . . .!'

'Man . . .?'

'He's gone up the stairs! A man!'

Mr Bisham discovered another door and he opened it. It seemed to be madam's bedroom. It was empty, which was a relief, but on the other hand madam was still letting out catcalls and heavier footsteps than hers were even now thundering up the stairs. Mr Bisham hurried to the window. He couldn't open it, so he dashed back and locked the bedroom door. Then he dashed back to the window and tried to get the catch undone again. A fearful kicking started on the bedroom door. The window catch seemed rusted; didn't they have any air here? The bed was thrown back and a lot of shoes lay about the floor. Sordid clothes hung from a chair, making a splash of colour: red, yellow, black. Mr Bisham picked up a small stool and shoved it through the window pane. There was a shattering of glass, like in the blitzes, but he got the catch undone from outside and slid the window up. He got quickly out of the window and hung by his fingers from the sill. Then he dropped. It wasn't too bad a drop. He landed in another mews and ran for it. There was the sound of the milkman and his horse and bottles, and there was the sound of madam yelling from the window, '*Police, police*—George, why didn't you stop him, silly idiot . . .!'

He ran the length of the mews at a steady pace, and slowed into a walk at the top. To his relief, there wasn't a soul in sight in the main road.

He moved quickly, hoping to find an early taxi. He had been chased a long way and in the wrong direction from Broadcasting House.

CHAPTER XVII

HE was fortunate enough to find a taxi and he sat back in it feeling relieved but rather exhausted. It had been an unusually strenuous ordeal. Those hours with the man Bardner, and then the simple and dull solution. But then, he had known the only solution was to shoot out the lock; it was obviously the only thing to do. But—the flattened bullets just might provide a clue for the hunters. It was why he had hesitated for so long, hoping to think of a better solution, or, rather, hoping Bardner was lying about the door not opening until six, and about Sudbury getting up at five. And a little before five he had made up his mind to shoot his way out. Bardner, with his hands tied behind his back with a bit of string, and with his eyes still bandaged, had been asleep on his side on the divan bed. The three revolver shots had been deafening. The door swung open easily and he hadn't stopped to search for the flattened bullets, there was no time for dawdling. Indeed, it was touch and go as it was, for there was some hidden complication with the front door too, and he'd had to dash back across the hall and down the basement stairs there. There was the sound of old Sudbury yelling upstairs, and Bardner shouting, and then a scream from Gracie, who evidently slept in the kitchen. Why did people scream so? It was unnerving. At the back door he took off his mask and turned up his coat collar. He slipped out into the grey misty light—straight into a covey of police approaching at the double. Sudbury must have had a private line to a police-box or -station. He doubled back and ran for his life, heavy feet thudding after him and twice a tearing at his shoulder. But he outstripped them and felt grateful for something learned at his public school—cross country running. He got over a blitzed wall, raced through a gutted church and found a lane. Unfortunately, police whistles were sounding from the far end of it. He chose another direction and carried the chase towards the world of Belgravia mewses and mews flats. It had been touch and go.

And it was still touch and go.

He entered Broadcasting House at a minute to seven. Dashing to the new news studio, he wondered who they had chosen to read the news in his place, and what the papers would have to say about the new name. He also wondered what explanation he would give, and whether, if he was now in time to read the seven, there would be any stinkers to pronounce like Dnepropetrovsk. The Duty Editor, Mr Wintle and an understudy were standing looking green as he walked briskly into the studio with his hat and coat on. They stood staring as he sat down and almost at once the red light came on, and he said brightly to Marjorie: 'Good morning, everybody! This is the seven o'clock news for Wednesday, April 26th—and this is Ernest Bisham reading it!' After all, he thought, even announcers were entitled to their occasional little lapses. Pressing engagements were apt to make anyone late—and it was for the war effort. His pockets were heavy with the night's highly successful haul.

Hearing him, Marjorie felt an inexpressible relief. Her anxiety had been for nothing. He sounded so bright, there couldn't be anything wrong. She would have to say about the telephone call from the Duty Editor, and no doubt Ernest would offer an explanation. It would be something perfectly simple. The explanation of the loaded revolver was probably simplicity itself too. Why, of course, the Home Guard! How absolutely ridiculous of her not to have thought of it before. He hadn't bothered to tell her, and he kept his uniform, if he had a uniform yet, up in London. More than half satisfied with this new idea, she felt much happier as Mrs Leeman came in with the early tea. Ernest was talking about sugar beet, he had told her the farming news was always in the seven, and the eight, before the farmers went off into the fields.

As Mrs Leeman came in with the tea she thought once again what vast haunches madam had got. She made quite a mound in the bed. She'd be like an elephant when she was fifty. There wasn't any news about children, you noticed. Didn't they want any, or what was it? An odd pair, weren't they? Still, as people went, they weren't so bad, not really. They weren't mean, anyhow. And so long as that sister of his kept her face out of sight, things weren't too bad, and so long as Leeman kept reasonably off the drink. 'Good morning, madam,' she said in her sharp way, and thumped down the tray with a clatter. 'Sh, please!' exclaimed madam. 'I'm listening to the master's voice.' Her Master's Voice, thought Mrs Leeman! It was quite a case, wasn't it! She was nuts about him. The master knocked off while she drew the curtains and said something or other about a little Wren talking about sergeants or something or other. The first two words of the little Wren's remarks could not be heard at all. Atmospherics, no doubt? Madam apologized for being sharp. 'Oh, that's all right,' Mrs Leeman said. She drew back the pink curtains and looked down into the garden. There was dew on the grass and a huge blackbird was having swigs out of the rockery pond, and two pigeons were having larks on the garden seat. Madam put on her bed jacket and started tidying her hair. She said it was a marvellous morning. Mrs Leeman said yes it was, and she was about to go when madam started talking about the master's approaching birthday. 'It's next week,' she said to Mrs Leeman. She looked just like a girl, didn't she, when she spoke about him?

'Next week,' said Mrs Leeman.

'May the third. I was wondering if we could get hold of a pheasant. It would be a luxury, but the master does so like a nice dinner, and I will cook it myself.' She turned rather red.

Mrs Leeman stood with her hands on her hips hoping she was looking expressionless. Cook it herself! Well, if the pheasant turned out anything like the last effort, which had been a duck, Heaven help the master's digestion!

'It's whatever you say, madam,' she said, cold.

'And I will make a sherry trifle.'

'Oh!'

'Then we will have the Australian cheese Mr Bisham's Admiralty friend brought—Mr Leveson, d'you remember—who is soon going to Russia.'

Mrs Leeman thought: 'Well, that will be something, to get rid of that. It's been stinking the larder out for nearly a fortnight.'

'That will be all, then,' madam told her, and poured herself out a cup of tea.

'May the third,' thought Mrs Leeman as she went out. And it was to be supposed that life at Tredgarth would now revolve round that date. She was certainly in love with him; she was carrying on like a schoolgirl; it was a case.

She went to the back door to give Shorter his tea and she warned him:

'You'd better start growing plenty of vegetables for May the third! Cupid's coming to town!'

She went cackling back to Leeman. Leeman was sitting looking yellow and rolling a fag for himself. He'd been having a bit of a think. This kind of life was all very well for a bit, it was all right for a woman; but after a bit it made you think. He put a drop of rum in his tea to cheer things up.

She moved about the kitchen, chattering about May the third. 'I suppose Miss Bisham will come up for it, and I suppose the Miss de Freeces will be asked, and the Wintles,' she said, and he sat looking thin and sipping at his rum and tea. He stared out of the window at the laurel bushes and the back gate.

'I've been having a bit of a think,' he said thoughtfully. He sucked his teeth and gave a drag at his fag. 'I'm getting kind of tired of this place.'

She swung round at him, as he knew she would.

'Now, then,' she began in alarm.

'Shut up!' he told her flatly. 'Oh, shut your face!' he said more loudly as she started a crescendo.

She stood with her arms akimbo and her face flushed, staring down at him. He sat with his sleeves rolled up, and his thin face all yellow, and his weak chin wanting a good shave, and his thick lips pushed down into his teacup.

He finished his tea, eyed her significantly, and went out of the kitchen. He went thoughtfully up the back staircase and shut himself in his room.

When the eight o'clock news was filling the house, and filling the houses and cottages and flats and rooms of millions of people, not to mention the myriad moving vehicles such as ships, cars and 'planes, he was having a quiet poke round Mr Bisham's 'den'. There was plenty of money here at Tredgarth, wasn't there? Yet there was nothing very handy, so to speak. Mrs Bisham didn't seem to go in for tiaras, or anything of that kind. She didn't seem to go in for rings, and her necklaces weren't worth the taking. In Mr Bisham's room there was nothing but fags and cigars. You didn't exactly see bundles of notes lying around. But it was comfortable. You could say that.

He took a fag and sat down in Mr Bisham's armchair. The best part of having a boss like Mr Bisham was that you knew where he was at a given time. It might be convenient—if there was anything for it to be convenient about. But there wasn't. Or, if there was, it would no doubt be in that safe. Come to think of it, what did he keep a safe for? He'd said something about papers, but what sort of papers would he want a safe like that for?

He sat staring at it.

When he grew tired of staring at it, he lit another fag and stared sourly round the room. Mr Bisham had a nice taste in brandy, as well as old brandy glasses, and he reached out an arm to help himself. Mrs Leeman started calling him to come and see to the breakfast, but he was having a glance through the morning paper. Hullo, another cat-burglary again last night? The Man In The Mask too! He was a bit of a lad! Got away again, too? Well, it wasn't everybody's luck, and his wouldn't last for ever either. They'd catch him one of these days. Shot his way out, chased in the morning light all over Belgravia, thought to be a man in a light coat and felt hat, very well dressed and rather on the hefty side. Might pass for Mr Bisham himself! Or Mr Hood himself, or Lord Sudbury himself! There were photos of all three of them, at the sale of gems, and there was a photo of the man Bardner. Bardner said: 'He was armed. I couldn't do anything. There was a gun in my ribs the whole time and he was desperate. He bandaged my eyes with my own handkerchief so as I couldn't see him, and he tied up my wrists with a bit of string. He had a voice like velvet and spoke just like an announcer. In fact, when we were listening to the eight o'clock I said to his lordship, "He sounded just like that, my lord."' Lord Sudbury's statement said: 'Amongst the stolen gems is a pendant belonging to Lady Sudbury which is almost priceless. Other priceless jewels were taken. The thief must have hidden in the house after the sale yesterday, or something of that kind. I am offering a thousand pounds reward for apprehension of the Man In The Mask, or whatever the thief is called, and for recovery of the jewels. Lady Stewker and Mrs George Mansfield, two recent victims of what may easily be the same robber, are offering five hundred pounds each for recovery of their property.'

Inspector Hood's statement said:

'I've got a clue this time—three flattened bullets. We had to cut them out of the wall. There has never been a clue of any kind before, not a fingerprint or a footmark. But that's just luck. A man of this kind starts slipping sooner or later, and when he starts he goes right down to the bottom. An arrest may be early expected.' In a later interview Inspector Hood commented on the curious fact that no attempt to sell any of the stolen jewellery had ever been tried in the usual underworld channels, 'a curiously consistent aspect of these cat-burglaries which also tends to indicate the work of one man, perhaps an eccentric.' He didn't think it might be the work of a woman, but didn't deny the possibility. 'Some women have deep voices,' he admitted. 'But Bardner is sure it is a man. And the police officers were sure it was a man they chased through the streets. So is the woman who passed him on the stairs in her mews flat. At any rate, he had a very mannish appearance and sound.'

'Curious aspects,' thought Mr Hood, reading the newspaper account of his statement. 'Yes, yes! Curious is perhaps the word!' He stuffed the newspaper in his pocket and went into a shop he knew well in Pall Mall. He took out the three flattened bullets and wandered unhurriedly into the inner room and shut the door. It was an unhurried action he had many times done before. Yet never, perhaps, before had he come out of that little room feeling quite so surprised about anything. Of all surprising things, the bullets—and the gun that fitted them—had been bought not so very long ago by Mr Ernest Bisham, the announcer. But then, he thought, there was nothing to be surprised about in that. Quite obviously somebody had pinched his gun from him, and the bullets. There would be some answer like that. Still, it was a bit of a surprise. Perhaps the feeling of surprise was due to a little coincidence; two, in fact: Mr Ernest Bisham's name had been mentioned in this Man In The Mask case twice already—by Lady Stewker, and by Mrs Mansfield! They had both chanced to see him over a broadcast a few days prior to each robbery. Most odd! And then, of course, he was at the Sudbury affair yesterday! Well, at any rate Mr Bisham looked a nice kind of fellow and he would be sure to be most helpful. And Mrs Hood would be tickled to death to hear he had had to meet him again. Well, things certainly seemed to be getting warmer.

Mr Hood walked up crowded Regent Street, thinking hard. He paused at the window of Hamley's, a shop that had always fascinated him. As a matter of fact, though it was very silly, of course, he had several times bought Mrs Hood dolls there. It was regrettable they couldn't have any children, and although at the Yard they would laugh themselves sick if he was ever daft enough to tell them, Mrs Hood had a little weakness for dolls. Well, she had two little weaknesses: dolls—and announcers! We all had some little weaknesses, no doubt. Other people might laugh, or even frown. The motive was the thing. He always felt a bit embarrassed when Mrs Hood's relations turned up and saw the dolls lined up in their bed, if it was daytime, and in a large cot if it was night time. They seemed to think it affected, or even indecent, but for his part he always studied the reason in things before criticizing.

But this was no time to be distracted by Hamley's, was it? There was work to be done.

He suddenly took a taxi and went along to Lord Sudbury's place. There was nobody there except Bardner, which was all he wanted. He had another frown round by the cloakroom window, where the man must have got in, and then he wandered across the hall to Bardner.

'I've been having a bit of a think,' said Mr Hood thoughtfully. A most extraordinary train of thought had stuck in his mind. He said: 'What made you say this chap sounded like an announcer?'

Bardner stood rolling a fag and looking very much on the defensive. What had Hood come back for? Did he think *he* had a hand in it?

'Announcer?' he mouthed vacantly.

'It was a queer thing to have said.' Or—was it? Wasn't it the same way in which we used to say, 'Oh, so and so spoke like a public school man'?

Bardner looked like a scared baboon.

He started to say he hardly knew what he'd said. He said Lord Sudbury was in a very funny mood, and he didn't know whether he was going to have the sack, or what.

'I can't make out how you could let a man tie up your eyes like that. The man had a steel nerve, I should say.'

'He had a steel rod, I can say that, and . . .!'

'I know that,' said Hood, mildly disparaging, 'but he's got to drop his gun so's to tie the knot, I suppose? That would have been your chance, I should have thought?'

Bardner's eyes were wide.

'What? Good gracious, and a shot in the back . . .!'

'He'd never have shot me in the back! I can tell you that! And as for the string round your wrists—!'

'What?' Bardner exploded. It was too much altogether. 'Look here, if you think *I* had a hand in this affair—'

'Calm down,' interrupted Hood. 'I never said anything of that kind. No. But didn't you get the slightest glimpse of him, out of the corner of your eyes?'

'Not a glimpse! I *tried* . . .!'

'And he sounded like a . . . well, a gentleman?'

'Yes.'

'You couldn't even see what colour coat he'd got on?'

'No. I tried, but . . .'

'But he sounded like an announcer. In fact, like the announcer who was reading this morning's news, eh?'

'Yes . . .'

'Mr Ernest Bisham was reading it,' said Mr Hood, as if to himself. And presently he wandered out. He thought: 'Just before we go on a little jaunt to Broadcasting House, we'll take the trouble to pay one other little visit.' He got into a taxi and went to the mews flat where the Man In The Mask was said to have passed a woman on the stairs. The woman was called Mrs Mantlestone.

Both Mr and Mrs Mantlestone were delighted to see Mr Hood. They had seen dozens of people the whole morning, and told them their story. Mrs Mantlestone now told it again, explaining that she had got up early to go to her war work, which was making screws, but as the police had delayed her she was having the day off. She had yellow hair done up into a sort of huge sponge. Mr Mantlestone had black hair done in a sort of fringe over his forehead, and he smelt of horses. In the

midst of their excited chatter, Mr Hood said all he was trying
to get at was what did this man *look* like.

'It was too dark on the stairs to see that,' Mrs Mantlestone
said shrilly. 'Except he had a soft felt hat well down over his
eyes.'

'What colour felt hat? Could you see that?'

'Brown, I should say.'

'No, it was grey,' said Mr Mantlestone. 'The glimpse I got
of him when he dashed up the mews.'

'Well, what colour coat had he, then?' said Mr Hood rather
wearily. It was always the same, nobody ever noticed the smallest
thing about anybody else, or if they did they got it wrong.

'Light brown,' said Mr Mantlestone, to that.

'Light grey,' said Mrs Mantlestone. Then they started arguing
the toss. Mr Mantlestone made whistling noises through his
lips as if he was grooming his horses, and he started saying
how he'd had to kick their bedroom door in, and he didn't
know where he ought to send the bill in. Mr Hood examined
the window-sill for a bit of thread or cloth, but of course there
was nothing. There never was anything. Who would be a detective? People thought it was exciting and romantic! If only they
knew! About the only thing the Mantlestones were sure of was
that they couldn't see his face, 'becorse his coat collar was up';
they couldn't be sure how tall he was, he was anything between
four foot and seven, and they couldn't be sure what his voice
sounded like when he said good morning to Mrs Mantlestone.

'Well, was it a gentleman's voice?' said Mr Hood, cold.

'Well, yes and no,' Mrs Mantlestone said, frowning, and
bolstering up her sponge hair with a knuckly hand. 'He sounded
rather like your uncle,' she turned and said to Mr Mantlestone.
'But then, he's a butcher, isn't he? But still, he went to the
council school, didn't he?' She told Mr Hood the Man In The
Mask sounded very quiet and kind.

'Well, why did you scream, then?' enquired Mr Hood
unkindly. 'I hear you nearly brought the house down!'

'Jack the Ripper,' exclaimed Mrs Mantlestone, flushed and hurt, 'was quiet and kind—at first! And so was Neil Cream!' She said she had made a study of these things. 'But there was plenty of screaming afterwards,' she pointed out indignantly.

Mr Hood broke into a small laugh and apologized. He hadn't meant to be rude, or even cynical, but this Man In a Mask affair was getting him down. And his latest train of thought was so fantastic that he knew in advance there could be nothing to it.

But there you were, if you felt you were getting warmer, you had to follow it up. Sometimes, in the past, he had had the most fantastic ideas, and even when they proved to be indeed fantastic, they did none the less very often lead him on to the right goal. It was funny, but he'd noticed it many times. He thought of it when he reached Broadcasting House. At the Reception Desk he asked the charming and beautiful receptionist for Mr Ernest Bisham. 'If it's possible to see him for a minute? Some other time, if not, you know.' The lady enquired who he was, and when he told her she reacted in no way whatever, as if to prove, which it did, that she had so many clients in every walk of life that, to her, a visitor was yet another important broadcaster. When she had telephoned, she informed Mr Hood that Mr Bisham had been on the air doing routine announcing most of the morning, and he had also had rather a tiring night.

'Oh?' said Mr Hood, interested and sympathetic.

'He's now resting before reading the one o'clock news. But I spoke to him and he asked if the visit was urgent. Are you about to broadcast, or . . .?'

Mr Hood blushed. Imagine if Mrs Hood heard that!

'No fear,' he apologized. 'I once had to make a little speech at a police concert and it turned me hot all over! Mrs Hood was quite disgusted!' He said it wasn't at all urgent, and please to say so to Mr Bisham, with apologies. 'I'll make an appointment. He may remember we met at Lord Sudbury's, and—'

'Just a minute,' the girl said kindly. She was motherly.

She spoke to Mr Bisham again.

'Not urgent,' said Mr Bisham into the telephone thoughtfully. He felt a mild relief. All the same, it was a bit odd, the pace was speeding up a bit. They'd obviously traced the bullets already. That was quick work. What else could bring the inspector here? Curiosity got the better of him and he said: 'I'll come along. Ask him to wait a minute.' He rang off and got up from the settee.

It was a little disturbing and he couldn't resist finding out just what, if anything, Hood had up his sleeve.

As he walked slowly along to the lifts, he thought carefully. His statements must be carefully thought out. And they must coincide in every way with the statements he had made to Marjorie—would she forgive him these white lies if she knew? His conversation with her this morning on the telephone had been a long one. The Duty Editor had 'phoned her and she'd been worried to death. Ernest told her at once that she must never worry about him at all, he would *never* miss a broadcast. His explanation had been simplicity itself, to the point of dullness. He hadn't been able to sleep, 'those bunks, so narrow and short', and after about three o'clock he'd got up and dressed. He went for a very long walk, so far, in fact, that he suddenly became aware that he had gone too far, he was going to be late. 'And do you think I could find a taxi, Marjorie? Nowhere! Until at last . . .' She had laughed at her fears. Even the Duty Editor had laughed—in a strained sort of way. Duty Editors were not expected to laugh. And then poor old Marjorie, in her relief, burst out with the most disconcerting remark, over the telephone too. 'Ernest, don't think me silly, but . . . why do you keep a loaded revolver?' It had made him a bit breathless, not to say self-accusing. Was he getting careless? It seems he had left it in his den one day, and she'd seen it and put it in the drawer of his desk. He remembered wondering how it had got in his desk. And then, it seems, she had been so disconcerted that she'd gone again to the drawer only to find it had vanished.

She assumed he had taken it with him. 'And then, another thing, Ernest—that night I thought you were announcing in Manchester. *Where were you?*' It was ticklish.

It was an eye-opener to discover how she watched over him! He didn't know much about women, did he! 'Why, my dear child,' he cried down the telephone, inventing regretfully as he went on, 'as a matter of fact I was walking again. I didn't want to worry you, but as a matter of fact I can't sleep up here; it's the over-warm atmosphere.'

'Oh, Ernest, not to tell me . . .!'

'As for this talk about a revolver, my dear. Don't alarm yourself! I never keep revolvers.' There was a slight pause.

Her voice came:

'But, Ernest, there was a loaded one in your room. I put it in the drawer. Next day, it was gone and I presumed . . .'

His laugh came.

'Yes, well, we must look into it, Marjorie. It's very curious. Perhaps one of our guests left it there. Many people come to my den for a chat, don't they? We must look into it . . .'

If you must lie, he always thought, be simple and vague.

He would follow the same line with Mr Hood, if necessary. These detectives were pretty sharp. He'd be nosing round Tredgarth before one knew it. Perhaps chatting cunningly to Marjorie.

He advanced on Hood with a broad smile and at once took the line that he had invited Hood to see Broadcasting House, and that he had been interested enough to come along so soon.

'How do you do, Mr Bisham,' Hood said, slightly taken aback by this welcome. He felt rather like a stage-door fan who had arrived at an awkward moment with his autograph book. Mr Hood again thought what a distinguished man Mr Bisham looked, and he couldn't help thinking how thrilled Mrs Hood always was whenever he was on the air, and in consequence couldn't help feeling ridiculously overawed by his personality and his suave manners. But he succeeded in shaking this off as

Mr Bisham led him along to the famous Drawing Room. Two very famous men came out of the Drawing Room as they went in, and when they stopped and spoke to Mr Hood as well as to Mr Bisham, Hood was tickled to death, as he said afterwards. 'I was their bodyguard, so to speak,' he explained modestly, 'for a time, when I was a younger man, Mr Bisham.' They sat down together on the long green leather settee and exchanged politenesses about this altogether pleasant meeting.

'Well, now,' smiled Mr Bisham politely, and, having lit their cigarettes, sat waiting.

Mr Hood sat waiting for his brain to work. He smiled politely across at Mr Bisham. He found himself looking at two rather humorous but tired eyes around which were the lines and creases of a man past his youth. His cheeks were a little full, not unduly so, and not uncolourful, and his hair was thinning and rather grey. He wore a very well cut blue suit with starched white collars and cuffs. A Savile Row and Bond Street man. A man well past forty, judged Mr Hood accurately. And a nice man. No doubt the women all fell for him like flies. An honest man? Well, that question depended on how you judged the word 'honest'. But if this was the Man In The Mask, he'd eat a policeman's helmet! That fanciful notion surely went by the board straightaway. One made mistakes, of course, and it was only human to do so. Moreover, it happened to people like himself, who often had to pretend to themselves that they suspected this one, or that, because it was their duty to do so. Told you so, said Mr Hood to himself! No such easy, if fantastic solution as that, my lad! (Imagine what Mrs Hood would have said, had she known his passing doubts about her idol!)

Mr Bisham sat looking at a pleasant and witty-eyed man with an over-red face. He was probably nearly sixty. He was a bit short and a bit thickset. A human sort of man in an untidy brown suit. Brown socks, brown shoes, bowler hat on his knees. It was a childish face, but a shrewd face too, the whole covered by a small smile. Mr Bisham had the absurd notion that this

shrewd old man was shy of him! He certainly didn't feel the
detective had come here with any sinister intent. Unless this
quaint approach was . . . guile?

Mr Hood started to make various remarks to Mr Bisham
about being sorry to intrude when he was resting, but saying
how very interested Mrs Hood would be when he got home to
Shepherd's Bush for lunch, and they listened to him reading
the one o'clock news. 'Oh, she'll be quite tickled, Mr Bisham!'
Mr Bisham smiled politely, used to this sort of thing, but a trifle
anxious, inwardly, that such remarks should come from him.
Was he being genuine? 'Though,' Mr Hood went on, smiling,
'to you it must be just a job.'

'Quite right,' smiled Mr Bisham economically.

'I know the public likes to weave its own romances out of
things, eh? The life of a detective is supposed to be the most
exciting life!' He laughed. 'And so is the life of an announcer,
Mrs Hood assures me of that,' he laughed again. 'And so is the
life of a cat-burglar. Or so I suppose! I suppose the public will
be very upset when the Man In The Mask is sent to prison!
There's something very unromantic about years of penal servi-
tude!'

Sitting rather still, Mr Bisham found himself staring politely
at three little flattened bullets. They looked like florins that had
been put on the railway line.

CHAPTER XVIII

MR HOOD, still looking rather shy, said you could have knocked him down with a feather when the gunsmith traced the bullets to Mr Ernest Bisham, the announcer. 'I mean, only having seen you yesterday at the sale, Mr Bisham. And I said then, didn't I, I felt sure we should meet again? And now I have the same feeling, I reckon we shall meet a third time—if you believe in threes?' He smiled broadly.

Mr Bisham's smile was broad too, and carefully arranged.

But he was just a shade hot under his collar for, as a matter of fact, he did believe in threes.

Instantaneously, he made up his mind that the time was coming, if it had not already arrived, when he ought to call Finis to his little career as a cat-burglar. If his hand was showing signs of losing its touch—and there had been several little signs, these bullets, and these increasingly near squeaks—it might be wise not to tempt Fate's mood once too often. The wise man was the man who knew when to stop. There remained, however, one intriguing adventure, concerning a diamond which would get into a match-box, and concerning a semi-eccentric and vain millionaire. He was called Commander Legge and he was down to broadcast shortly.

And thinking of Commander Legge, even as Mr Hood discussed the habit of carrying revolvers, Mr Bisham then and there resolved that if this one further little adventure was successful, it would be his last. Then he need lie no longer to Marjorie. He had felt oddly unhappy about that, even though they were what he called white lies, and were designed to give her peace of mind. The affair of Commander Legge's diamond, which was emphatically priceless, would, from the early sound of it, require exceptional nerve and skill. To start with, the

Commander was a VC and probably went in for revolvers himself.

'But *I've* never really had the revolver habit,' he told Hood breezily. He told him quite frankly about his wife's surprising conversation about revolvers. 'She thought it was mine, of course. But it wasn't.'

'When *was* that?' wondered Hood.

'Oh, some little time ago . . .'

'Ah.'

'Do you think someone has been impersonating me at the gunsmith's?'

'It's possible, Mr Bisham, I suppose,' frowned Hood. 'You're a public figure.' He pulled a piece of flimsy from his pocket. 'But is this your signature, or not? It's your name . . .'

Mr Bisham felt rather pleased. He recognized the false signature which he had scrawled when purchasing the gun. It had been a useful piece of foresight, as it turned out.

He presented Mr Hood with his pass. 'There's my signature,' he said calmly. 'And it hardly compares with this . . .!'

'Who would be a detective?' remarked Mr Hood.

Mr Bisham was sympathetic. He said it was time for him to go to the news room, he always went there at a quarter past the hour. He took care not to mention his one lapse, this morning. Although, if the Inspector did find it out, it was nothing to go by, was it? . . .

All the same, he'd sailed close enough to the wind this time.

'I shall have to be a bit of trouble to you yet,' Hood regretted. 'I shall have to have a list of everyone who's been to your house, Mr Bisham. After all, your wife saw a strange pistol, and it wasn't yours. That's not to say it fits these bullets, but it's something to work on, if you see what I mean?'

'Quite so . . .'

'And a list of your friends and acquaintances here at the BBC.' He laughed ruefully. 'That'll keep me busy, no doubt. But it's got to be looked into.' He got up and put the bullets back into his pocket. 'I'm sorry to drag your friends into this, so to speak. But you can rely on me to be careful in my investigations.'

'I'm sure I can.'

'You haven't any enemies? Nobody with a spite? I mean, impersonations; it seems queer . . .' He broke off, frowning again, and suddenly said: 'What about the staff? At home, I mean? Perhaps you wouldn't mind if I came down to your place one day . . .?'

Standing watching him go, Mr Bisham had the picture of a frowning man scratching the back of his head below his hat. What was Hood really thinking? Had he really fallen for that line about the revolver? But it seemed fatal to say he had bought it. Moreover, he still needed it. The work wasn't quite over yet. And this time the risk would be the greatest ever. For, if he wasn't actually suspected, Hood would quite likely keep an eye on his movements. He would call it routine.

When lunchtime came—lunchtime was after the one, about twenty past—he went to get his hat. His diary said: 'Commander Legge. Berkeley. 1.30 p.m.'

Going briskly out of the building, police and commission-aires touched their caps to him.

Announcers were the cream of the place, weren't they?

May the third dawned a beautiful day for Marjorie Bisham, wife of the famous announcer. It was gravely sad, she felt, that all days were not inevitably beautiful for everybody in all countries. It was not, for instance, beautiful for everyone in Poland, or Russia, or England even, largely remote though it was to many of the more harrowing possibilities of war.

It seemed selfish to think about your husband's birthday, and to go about the garden gathering flowers and singing.

It was not a very beautiful day for Mr Jonas Wintle, however. He didn't see daylight until three in the afternoon, if you excluded the artificial daylight used in the studios.

Yet there was in his life now a light which kept him going

at all hours. The light was changing him, and it was Annabella, and she was to come home with him for their days off. Moreover, the Bishams were expecting them to dinner. It was old Bisham's birthday, or something of the sort, and there was a bit of a dinner, and afterwards people were coming in to dance. It would probably be thoroughly browning off, but Annabella would be there, and there would be sure to be plenty of hootch. Further, he might make another attempt to persuade Ernest Bisham to use his influence and get him made an announcer. At seven that morning Ernest Bisham had been rather preoccupied. He'd been late as hell and made everyone as annoyed as they dared to be. This dinner date would be a splendid opportunity. Jonas had been rehearsing his voice with Annabella, and she declared it was very much better. She said: 'It's resonant, Jonas, with just that touch of nasal trouble you want.'

To Annabella, May the third did happen to be a beautiful day. But since she had first set eyes on Jonas, all her days had become strangely beautiful. True, he was nothing very much to look at, and when you'd discovered some of the things he'd done in the war, and suffered, you could scarcely believe it. It seemed impertinent to want to try and improve him. Yet the truth was, whatever he'd done, he was still only a boy and had grown up before his time. The first thing she did was to make him brush his hair differently so that it didn't fall all over his eyes. Then she made him get rid of his shapeless flannel suit and get a pair of blue corduroy trousers. '*Not* brown ones, Jonas! Be different!' Everyone else, she said, wore brown ones at the BBC. 'Now,' she said, proudly surveying him, 'now you'll be able to hold your own with Mr Mundy!' And, indeed, he had almost at once transmitted a complicated disc programme about Brahms for Mr Mundy to the theme tune of 'How Lovely Are Thy Dwellings Fair'. Mr Mundy had flung his arms heavenwards and logged a glowing report about Mr Wintle which, reaching Mr Black, had almost caused Mr Black to have a stroke, for he'd been looking after Transatlantic Call at the time, and there too everything had actually gone without a hitch. Annabella's motherly attitude had at first irritated Jonas, for it savoured too much of what was dished out at home. However, he discovered other qualities in Annabella, remote from the maternal. There was something so calmly glamorous about her, and soothing. The way she kept her yellow hair so tidily in that net, and the way her long arms worked about above that cutting machine, and the calm way she told Mr Peat, 'Well, if *you* don't ever have a bath, I *do*, that's all,' and off she'd sweep dressed in her blue dungarees. All the girls she worked with looked rather like her, but none was quite so magnificent as Annabella.

Today, preparing to leave, she felt very gay. She threw everything into a blue leather case and got her red hat. It was the size of a muffin and she shoved it on the back of her head. Then she went to say good-bye to a friend in the Control Room, and 'phoned another farewell to a friend up in glamorous Studio Bookings. Jonas rang down from the Disc Library saying that he was searching through tiers of discs for something Mr Black wanted, and said, 'Must do everything I can for him, he's been so decent; invalided out of the Navy, you know, that's why he's a bit out of sorts at times,' to her extreme astonishment. 'Hurry,' she called. 'I'll meet you in the reception hall.'

'Righto . . .'

'I hope you realize I'm not bringing an evening dress, Jonas?'

'Nobody dresses for anything till after the war,' he said briefly, and rang off.

She went to the front and waited for him. It was thronged with sailors and airmen and Commandos coming to do a broadcast. Both lifts were working overtime and small boys were dashing about with messages. A tall Indian wearing a sort of fez was singing 'Pale Hands I Loved' in a rather aggressive manner, as if he was rehearsing. Three of his male secretaries made a chorus and looked rather yellow and respectful. Everyone seemed pleased.

'Here we are,' said Jonas suddenly. He was carting a huge brown suitcase.

He said 'Hallo' to the Indians, who he thought were a much nicer race than was generally realized.

They got a carriage to themselves. At Waterloo he stared about, hoping to see Ernest Bisham, but there was no sign of him. Perhaps he was in already, and of course he would travel first class. Jonas said he would travel first class the moment he started reading the daily bulletins. He asked her if she thought announcing was more than just reading out loud, or whether it was better to be one of the chaps who wrote it all. Then he suddenly startled her by saying he'd been browned off by the idea of marriage for some time, but now he thought it was 'quite a logical process to contemplate. Don't you?'

She turned pink.

'If that's a proposal, I'd rather you put it in more romantic terms—'

'No,' he chattered, interrupting. 'But you know what I mean. I mean, it's fatal for *some* people to marry. You can see that everywhere.'

'*Is* it?'

'It's fatal to marry a skinny woman, for instance, don't you think?'

'I haven't thought about it,' she stared.

'I think the whole point about marriage,' he said, pulling out fags for them both, 'is to be able to have a snooze on Sunday mornings and read the papers in bed. And who wants to lean up against a skinny lizzy?'

The train rattled along.

'I don't know why *you've* got to do the leaning,' she complained tritely. 'What about me leaning on you? You're not so plump yourself.' Later, she swayed about with the train and said quaintly: 'I hope your mother likes me. I'm not exactly out of the top drawer.' She said her mother and father ran a milk-round near Epping, and she gave her young, jerky laugh and her mouth shot open and showed red. She leaned her head back and said the Bisham affair was scaring her stiff. A little before Woking, after a great deal of chatter, she said: 'Well, I suppose we're practically engaged? Or what's the line?'

'Oh, I asked you to marry me in the mixer yesterday.'

'Oh, was that what it was?'

'And you accepted. During Jack Benny half-hour. I'll come down to Epping, of course.'

She laughed.

'Dad'll receive you in the dairy in his shirt sleeves!'

'Father's nearly always in his shirt sleeves,' he answered her solemnly. 'He's all right, but he likes water weasels and things.' He warned: 'Be careful of our gin. I think it's a bit phony. Somebody came the other day and went away quite squiffy . . .'

They jumped out onto the platform and started looking for Ernest Bisham, in case he actually was on the same train. But there was no sign of him. The platform smelt of May blossom mingled with fish from scores of crates stacked up outside the waiting-room. It was hot.

Marjorie Bisham often wondered how cooks withstood the heat of kitchens during spring and summer days. Perhaps the fact that they had to, contributed to their somewhat caustic front on cooking occasions. Mrs Leeman was in a singularly caustic mood about something, at any rate. Perhaps she didn't like the idea of the mistress cooking the pheasant and making the trifle. It was very uncomfortable knowing that Mrs Leeman was standing about all the time, with her arms akimbo and that expression on her face. Mrs Leeman exuded an aura of the hypercritical, as opposed to the hypersensitive. She didn't have to speak, or even look. Her presence in the smoky kitchen was more than enough. The kitchen smelt of pheasant and stuffing and roasting potatoes and boiling cauliflower. The trifle reeked strongly of wartime sherry. It was vinegarish.

Mrs Bisham had spent most of the day in and out of the kitchen. She had bent over the kitchen table for hours slicing up bits of apple, Mrs Leeman saying coldly that she didn't hold with the habit of putting apple into every blessed thing. And when Mrs Bisham started putting sliced onion into everything, she said she didn't hold with that either, because of "alitosis, madam'. She said, 'Oh!' whenever madam said how she cooked this and that, and she looked very bored when Mrs Bisham's eyeblack started to run from the stinging onion-vapour. Mrs Bisham had had to go into the garden with tears streaming down both sides of her large nose.

Mrs Bisham was in fact having a tremendous day, according to *her* ideas. And then, in the middle of it all, Leeman had answered the door to a most extraordinary visitor. It had given Mrs Leeman 'a turn'. Leeman came into the kitchen and said a 'tec had called on madam.

Mrs Leeman turned pale.

'*What . . .?*'

'Oh, pipe down! I recognized him at once,' said her husband, speaking calmly, but visibly moved all the same. 'It's Hood, from the Yard.'

'What does *he* want . . .?'

'He forgot to tell me,' said Leeman sarcastically, but he crept along to the hall to listen.

But they'd gone into the garden.

Leeman hung about, feeling quite certain Hood would send for him. He didn't know why he felt it, he just did.

But he was wrong. Hood didn't send for him. Hood sunned himself for hours in the garden with madam. He seemed quite taken with her.

'I'm sorry to miss your husband,' Mr Hood said, regretting to have to lie. He knew Mr Bisham would not be here yet. As a matter of fact, quite against his will, he was having Mr Bisham watched. They'd insisted, at the meeting. Well, there was no harm in it, perhaps.

The truth was his brain was being teased in a persistent and most extraordinary manner. It was this revolver business.

Mrs Bisham was charming. She answered everything and was kindness itself. She offered to show him the house and everything. He hesitated at first, because he knew Leeman was watching. He was very interested in Leeman. Leeman's fingerprints might be a good idea. Was he a man with the revolver habit? And what about Mrs Leeman? Mrs Bisham spoke fairly well of them both. Dunkirk, eh? H'm . . .! When Mrs Bisham did show him the house a rather convenient incident cropped up. She was called to the kitchen just as they reached the room she called 'my husband's den'. When her footsteps faded away, he stood listening for the other footsteps. They came all right, too. Leeman certainly seemed interested. He must have a bit of a think about Leeman. Leeman, Leeman? It didn't touch any chords in his memory, but . . . He turned and peeped inside Mr Bisham's room. It was inevitable that his eyes should alight on the new green safe. It was rather a big one, wasn't it?

At about the same time on this hot spring afternoon, Commander Bryan Legge, VC, ex-pugilist, ex-politician, was standing in the study of his home in St John's Wood. He was cleaning a revolver. It was a hefty Service revolver, and bullets the size of one's thumb were sprawled on the table. In marked contrast to it, there lay on the table a blood red diamond attached to a chain no thicker than a spider's web. Seeing it lying around there, the Commander seized it with clumsy fingers and shoved it into his trousers pocket. Then he went on humming and cleaning his pistol. He had no particular use for a pistol, he'd just got the revolver habit.

Commander Legge was supposed to have broadcast last evening after the six o'clock news. In common with others, he had had a vague notion that you just went along to the BBC, with what you wanted to say written down on the back of an envelope, and you met one of those announcer chaps, who took you to a studio. A red light went on, or perhaps it was a green one, and then you started. If you said anything rude, some unseen hand cut you off until you got back on the tracks again.

He'd looked forward to the broadcast very much. Commander Legge was retired, and fabulously rich, and he spent many of his days trying to persuade the Admiralty to give him something worth while to do. They did now and then, and on this occasion they'd rung him up suddenly and said the BBC wanted somebody to give a talk about these new aircraft carriers. It sounded a novelty and so he said he would be very pleased. He sat down at once and seized a few old envelopes and started writing his views about the new carriers. He was so carried away he used up about forty envelopes, some of them income tax length, and chased about the house looking for more.

He had had a dull time recently, the only excitement being that he had at last concluded a deal over the Maybee diamond, now perhaps the most sought after diamond in the world, by those still in a position to search after diamonds. He didn't really want it; he wanted to say he'd got it, and quite likely he would sell it at a loss before long, when he was bored with it. When the new excitement of a broadcast cropped up, he shoved the diamond in his trousers pocket and forgot it. And he remembered how, when he was in the Mediterranean, he'd heard that chap Ernest Bisham's voice booming aristocratically out over the ether during a pretty exciting engagement. And he'd thought again what a wonderful thing the radio was. There was a man placidly sitting in a London studio—and here was his voice and personality dancing about in the gunfire above the blue water. One day he'd meet Bisham and tell him he'd heard him reading out the football scores one Saturday when all the guns in the ship were plastering the daylights out of the enemy! It might amuse him! And the first thing he did after the Admiralty telephoned him, not knowing any better, was to ring up Ernest Bisham. However, he'd sounded pretty passable and they'd fixed a lunch date. Bisham had congratulated him on his purchase of the Maybee diamond, it was in the papers that morning. In fact, Bisham had mentioned it on the air. Nice of him, Legge supposed, not knowing how decisions were reached about what should comprise the news.

When he had finished covering the backs of envelopes, the Commander grabbed a telephone in his impulsive manner. Another of his crazes was telephones. He had one in almost every room.

He got through to the BBC and started to harangue them in his peppery manner. He had the knack of flying into a temper at the least sign of being crossed, and now here were chaps telling him which department he had to speak to, it was nothing to do with Mr Bisham, and telling him envelopes were no good at all, things had to be typed, and things had to be no longer than three minutes, and things had to be recorded first. '*Recorded?*' roared the Commander, and stood, an old yachting cap on the back of his white head, glowering into the telephone. A tinny voice told him, in effect, he must come up and make a gramophone record of his talk, and that it must be censored. He roared: 'I shall come up in person at six o'clock, or you can get somebody else!' However, at six-twenty or so, he heard them put out another talk, about the habits of seagulls, and he roared upstairs to his wife, 'Am I to be outdone by a damned seagull?' and rushed to a telephone again. This time he was told he could do the talk straight into the microphone if he insisted, but it would have to be censored, and it would have to be no longer than three minutes. Feeling that he had won on points, he stumped upstairs to tell his wife.

Mrs Legge was in bed. She slept during the day and played cards with her husband and one or two friends during the night. In wartime all their friends were fighting somewhere or other, so she spent a lot of time in her bedroom. She rarely listened to the radio. She said she thought there should be two broadcasting stations in England, rival concerns, then we might get something good now and again. She only liked 'Marching On', and because of the music links. She was an astute old woman and favoured bed-caps. She was a withered-looking person, rather Chinese in appearance, from so much travelling. She had always been jogged around on ships, or in rickshaws, or on bony mules, and it was a relief to be able to spend the rest of her days in bed. She had a house fairly full of strange servants, none of them English, and all having to report to the police at regular intervals. The house itself was rather like a vast pagoda.

CHAPTER XIX

THE slightly eccentric figure of Commander Legge was quite a usual sight in any studio. There had been many worse; novelists, for instance, who were all very curious.

And he arrived in a very usual way, hurried and aggressive through nervousness, and abundantly curious.

He was met and taken to the talks department, during which brief journey he learnt that the Home News Talks department was a separate entity to the news department, and to the announcers, and to the Sunday Postscript, and even to Home Talks, and to a wealth of other departments and programmes. Startled and a little at sea, for he had thought the whole affair was rolled up into one, he allowed himself to be conducted to a thin gentleman who stood in a small room surrounded by other thin gentlemen and three secretaries, one and all using telephones and coping with questions concerning censorship, release dates, forthcoming talks and dispatches from the fronts. Commander Legge was invited to produce his script, and he pulled out of his pockets his wad of old envelopes. There was a curious stillness for several seconds.

The next half hour was a confusion of noise and argument. In spite of the Commander's roaring, his envelopes were taken from him, patched up into shorthand, rattled down on a typewriter, and dictated to the Admiralty on the telephone for censorship. He demanded to see Mr Bisham, who he still thought was 'head of the firm', and he was suddenly hurried along to a studio and offered a glass of water. This seemed to be the crowning insult. '*Water?*' he bellowed, like a cornered bull. He declared he never drank anything less than Napoleon brandy, and never would, and he again demanded to see Mr

Bisham. 'Mr Bisham is through the wall,' said the thinnest gentleman firmly.

'Through the wall?'

'But we're on Point Nine, so you will be able to hear the news coming through on this loudspeaker, and you will hear your cue. I'll wave my hand for you to begin. But you can watch for the red light, if you like.'

The Commander thumped into the chair facing the microphone. As he did so, six pips were to be heard coming from the loudspeaker in the corner. Mr Ernest Bisham could be heard saying it was the six o'clock news, and that he was the person who was reading it.

The thin gentleman sat on a high chair and craned his neck upwards to watch for the red light. A cue sheet pinned in front of him said: 'And now to end the news, here's Commander Edward Legge, VC, who's going to talk about the new aircraft carrier mentioned for the first time in Parliament two days ago. Commander Legge is a veteran of the Battle of Jutland, when he won the Victoria Cross. In this war he has seen service in Africa and the Mediterranean, where he was temporarily blinded during an engagement with the enemy. Commander Legge has since recovered the use of his sight.'

Commander Legge's script began with determination:

'I may as well say at once I can see perfectly well or I shouldn't be sitting here. I never used glasses and I never will. Well, the first time I saw one of these aircraft carriers was about a month or so ago. As a matter of fact it was the day Mr Churchill returned from his trip to . . .'

The typescript in front of the Commander was slightly blurred, his eyesight being erratic only when he was unusually excited.

Listening to the Commander, in his own studio, Mr Bisham sat waiting to say:

'You have been listening to Commander Edward Legge, VC,

who has been talking about the new aircraft carrier now being used by the Royal Navy. And that is the end of the news.'

As he waited, a pencilled note was put in front of him which said that Commander Legge was anxious to meet him.

And when at last he was free to meet him, he took him along to the Duty Room, where the Duty Receptionist gave him a mahogany coloured whisky and soda. Left to themselves, it was not long before the Commander's wide conversational powers brought the topic round to the subject of his own life. A vain man, thought Mr Bisham. Unusual in a VC. But an interesting man; he didn't exactly pose. He was tough, and he was brave, but he was inordinately full of the idea that he was so much tougher and braver than the next man. That there were sporting instincts mixed up in this attitude was undeniable. But on the whole Mr Bisham found it difficult to like the Commander. He boasted too much. He talked too much altogether. He didn't know an audience could tire. All the same, he had his moments, had he not? And it was a great moment when he put his hand casually into his left-hand trousers pocket and produced the Maybee diamond. That was a pose, of course. To cart a hundred thousand pounds around like that. And it was a sort of challenge.

Mr Bisham had never seen such a wonderful sight as the diamond lying in his hand.

Suddenly tense, he turned again to study its present owner. There was something of the eccentric, little doubt, but he was a man to reckon with for all that, perhaps because of it. There he sat, with his hairy wrists, his dusty uniform and his old yachting cap, and with his fair skin and his sea-green eyes so full of challenge, boast and attack. By comparison with such toughness, Mr Bisham felt flabby.

Discussing their proposed lunch date on the morrow, May the third, the Commander insisted on Mr Bisham coming along to his house in St John's Wood. 'I want to show you some of my cups.' Thinking quickly, Mr Bisham said he would accept the invitation, but he must catch the three-eighteen at Waterloo.

'I shall expect you about one,' said the Commander. He put the diamond back in his trousers pocket.

Accepting, Mr Bisham remarked that it seemed a very unsafe place for such a valuable diamond.

The Commander looked even more challenging, and said conceitedly:

'I'd like to meet the man who'd take a diamond off me!' He said he always carried a new gem about with him for at least a month, 'just to get the feel of it'. He started a long conversation about the various purchases he had made in his day, diamonds, yachts, 'planes and cars.

That night, Mr Bisham slept rather fitfully in his bunk. His mind was over-active. He intended this to be his last little journey, and he intended it to be successful. He had an appointment with Mr Leveson soon too, who was soon going to Russia. Mr Leveson was staying at the Dorchester. Yes, for Marjorie's sake, he was going to give up his little hobby. And he could feel he had done a little extra something for the war; he had indeed given of himself.

In the darkness, he saw the diamond, blood red.

Sometimes he saw it lying on Marjorie's bosom.

Throughout the seven and eight it seemed to be lying on the papers before him. He was not reading the one, but he had told Marjorie about the lunch engagement with Commander Legge, and he would catch the three-eighteen.

Today was his birthday party.

It had started to rain.

Mr Bisham had bought himself a new mackintosh for the spring. It had an exceptionally high collar and hid most of his face. Looking at himself in the mirror, he had seen something pleasingly dramatic about the effect created by the addition of a low-brimmed slouch hat pulled well down over the forehead.

You could really only see a pair of eyes.

He wore his tight fitting gloves and went out into the rain, thinking: 'I shall soon see if I'm being followed.' He called a taxi.

He had had a strong feeling lately that he was being followed by a young man in a grey trilby hat. He peered back through the small window, but there was nothing following him. His taxi made for Baker Street and turned right. There was nothing following him.

Yet, had he but known it, there was a small police car sitting round the corner from Broadcasting House. In it sat a young man in a trilby hat named Detective Inspector Hanbury, attentively listening to 'a selection of gramophone records, chosen by Mr Ernest Bisham, who is here to announce them'. The young man in the trilby hat was not to know that, due to an unusual error, it had not been announced that he was listening only to a recording.

Mr Bisham, unobserved, bowled along towards St John's Wood in the rain, thinking:

'I shall be at the house at a quarter to one. At that moment the Commander will be getting my telephone message saying I can't come, and that I'm going to write and explain—pressure of duties, you know.' He might possibly be in a position to hear the telephone ringing. What sort of a house was it? Something of a fortress, no doubt. Yet the Commander was too conceited to feel he needed any fortification but himself! It would probably not be too difficult, and it made a change doing a daylight job. It might be exciting.

Mr Bisham was not of the order of cat-burglars which planned in advance to the minutest detail. That was for a very different type of mind as well as motive, and it implied accomplices. To work alone was to think alone, and he believed so greatly in chance. And yet, while he thought what was to be would be, he also persistently thought Fate played a fair game with anyone who was brave enough to play daringly with her. He was bearing these things in mind as he sat back in the taxi and saw the rain splashing the pavements. It had started out such a beautiful day, by all accounts, and now it had turned to a deluge. It was May rain and would be wonderful for Marjorie's flowers, he thought.

When he reached St John's Wood he stopped the taxi and dismissed it. It was raining over-heavily and had grown rather dark. The taxi splashed away and he asked a woman for the street where the Commander's house was, and when she went scurrying off in the rain he hurried towards the broad street with the lime trees. All the houses were big here, and they stood back behind large, hidden gardens and stone walls.

Commander Legge's house was large and Oriental. Red, white and sprawling, it stood between the cold care of two huge poplars. The pagoda effect was largely robbed by modernism, and rain slithered down the dirty windows and brown walls in frustrated attempts to get down the leave-choked guttering. Thick tentacles of ugly ivy clung under most of the windows and choked the place of any delicacy or beauty. Mr Bisham kept his hat well down and his collar well up and without hesitation darted through the broken gate to the wall of the house. The wet streets were deserted and the only sound was the melancholy sound of the rain and the purposeful sound of his own footsteps on the gravel. He moved quickly round the blind side of the house, avoiding an angular front window. He came to another window and peeped through. Commander Legge was pottering about in there—he was cleaning a pair of pistols. Mr Bisham stood back against the wall and waited. After a little while, the Commander left the room, taking a pistol with him. Mr Bisham at once tried the window. It slid upwards silently. As it did so he heard the telephone ringing. He climbed quickly into the room and closed the window after him.

Mr Bisham was thinking that things might have turned out a better gamble if he had accepted the Commander's invitation to lunch and decided upon his tactics then; but the fine point still remained—could you rob a man who had asked you to his house like that? It would be biting the hand that fed you, and it would hardly be the act of a gentleman, least of all an announcer. No, things looked a bit tricky this time, but he felt queerly confident. Yet, remembering how confident he had felt just before Bardner's self-locking door had closed upon him, he remained keyed up and alert. There was something tremendously stimulating, like a drug, to be standing, a man in a mackintosh, in a strange room in a strange house. It was quite desperately thrilling. A clock was ticking creakily. (There was always a clock.) The furniture was heavy and they went in for stuffed birds in glass cases, red tablecloths with tassels, a Buddha and a painted Chinese screen. And there were rows of the Commander's silver cups on the high black mantelpiece. In the firegrate was a huge spreading fern. Marjorie liked a fire until May was out, if it was only a wooden one. There was no sign of the Maybee diamond. Needless to say, it would be in the old boy's left-hand trousers pocket. It was a good place for it, wasn't it? Probably better than a safe, really. All the same, he'd have to disgorge it; it was promised to Russia. Who else lived in the house? There didn't appear to be a sight or a sound of anyone. Eerie, but satisfactory. He tip-toed across to the half-open door. Through the crack, he saw the Commander standing at the telephone in the hall. He wore the same old uniform as yesterday, his yachting cap on in the house and pulled skew-whiff over his white hair. He bawled into the telephone in the deafening way he had. 'What? Can't he? Well, damn him, then; I'd got hold of a chicken, curried chicken. Never mind, never mind . . .!' Without further hesitation, Mr Bisham left the study and moved quickly up behind him. 'Touch the wall with the palms of your hands,' he said in an urgent whisper. The Commander's hands went up after only a fractional pause, and Mr Bisham reached for the revolver lying beside the telephone. It wasn't loaded, but he tossed it onto a chair. It was an old rocking chair and he saw the chair swinging gently to and fro. You noticed everything at such times. Then he frisked him. He took care to start at his top pockets so it should not appear he must have known where the diamond was. He found it in the left-hand trousers pocket and put it in his own left-hand trousers pocket.

Commander Legge stood stock-still, listening to the sound of the mackintosh. In the shadowy mirror almost opposite he saw only a pair of eyes. He kept his hands up in the air rather as if he was too old to keep them really upright. In his utter astonishment his mouth had fallen wide open. The last time anyone had dared to do this to him had been in Singapore, when a damned native had hustled him for his wallet. But the native had made the mistake of underestimating his elbow power, and he'd come too close altogether! A sharp jab from the elbows and the fellow had been quickly disarmed, and well, what he'd done to him then was nobody's business! A man wasn't a VC for nothing.

But this chap seemed to know his onions, he was keeping well back. He'd got the Maybee diamond too; well, he needn't think he was going to get away with that!

Commander Legge peeped at him in the mirror there, by the grandfather clock. He seemed to be a big chap. He was all dripping mackintosh and hat. All you could see was the shadow of his eyes. And all you could feel was outraged indignation and a damned gun sticking into your back. Was it a gun? It was devilish to know it just might be his thumbnail . . .

He decided to play for time. Discretion was the better part of valour.

Where the hell was everyone? The house was chock full of servants; where the devil were they?

Mr Bisham decided it was time to back away again, and that it would be best to return to the study where he knew there was an exit. No more self-locking doors for him!

'Count ten before you do anything silly,' he whispered to Commander Legge—and he dived for the study.

But he hadn't got through the window before Legge plunged through the door after him and took a pot at him. The bullet smashed the window-pane above his head into a thousand pieces. There was no time to wonder where he had found a gun, and he darted under cover of the ledge towards the greenhouse. It seemed the safest thing to do. But as he went two bullets shattered the greenhouse roof.

He scrambled into the greenhouse, looking for the exit on the other side.

CHAPTER XX

COMMANDER LEGGE congratulated himself on his gun habit. If it was convenient to have a telephone in every room, it was even more convenient to have a gun in every drawer. And in the hall chest of drawers there were two six-chambered revolvers. He darted round to the far end of the conservatory, letting fly as he went. He drilled a few holes in the boarding where he guessed the man might be crouching. Then he took cover beneath the far door and took two pots through the window-pane above his head. There was a shower of glass and he got a brief glimpse of the mackintoshed figure crouching within. Screeching pigeons and sparrows flew up in the air and two colossal reports answered him.

Mr Bisham took care to aim above the Commander's head. He was no murderer, but there seemed to be every point in making the Commander think he was. It was bluff, and by it alone could he hope to cover his retreat and make a get-away. He let fly again, and then started to slither backwards along the greenhouse floor on his haunches. Then he twisted over onto his knees, keeping as flat as possible, and started to make for the door by which he had entered.

Commander Legge, swearing like a trooper, kept down under cover of the wooden skirting and took three more pots through the lowest glass panel. He splintered a flower-pot and another pane, and in the distance voices started to clamour excitedly.

Mr Bisham pulled his collar up and his hat down and came to the conclusion that the Commander's eyesight wasn't as good as it had once been. He fired again and ran out of the green-house. Seeing strange figures approaching from garden and road, he dived for the nearest house window. It happened to be the one he had entered and left once already. As he clambered

186

through it Commander Legge popped up and saw him. He took another pot at him. He missed again but split the window into fragments. In a shower of glass, Mr Bisham fell head over heels into the room and knocked over a globe of the world. Two maids were now in the room, but they let out feminine cries of terror and Mr Bisham darted past them. He rushed through the hall, keeping his collar well up, and found himself bounding at a Chinese butler with a pigtail. He dodged him and dashed up the steep staircase. As he did so, Commander Legge, having rushed round the front of the house and in by the front door, came roaring into the hall like a maniac. Mr Bisham plunged up the stairs just as two bullets shattered the chandelier above his head. There was a shower of crystals from it as if it was raining jewellery. He turned and took a pot at a picture above the Commander's head. Both slid to the floor. Mr Bisham then became aware of an elderly woman in a dressing-gown who was on the landing taking careful aim at him with a double-barrelled gun. Fascinated by this apparition, he stared at her stupidly. Then he dived at her.

It was Mrs Legge, and she fired a second too late.

There was a roar like a five hundred pound bomb hitting an arsenal. But she fell flat on her back, and suddenly there was no sign of the man in the mackintosh. He vanished through a bedroom door in a cloud of acrid smoke, and locked it.

Commander Legge told himself he hadn't had such excitement since Jutland. He had reloaded and was standing in front of the bedroom door roaring out: 'Stand back, everyone,' and he let fly at the lock.

The house re-echoed to the shattering aftermath. Pictures and plaster fell to the floor. Mrs Legge got up off the floor and started to reload her twelve-bore. The whole thing made her think there was a bit of life in the place after all. Imagine if you were married to a civil servant!

The stairs and the hall were now thronged with figures. The

staff had appeared like magic. The baker, postman and milkman had appeared. Two small boys had appeared, holding scooters.

Several passers-by had dropped in, telling themselves they'd often heard the Legges were 'unorthodox'.

The only people who didn't seem to be there were the police, but they had been telephoned for.

When the door at last flew open, the Legges both roared out:

'Stand back and keep low—he's armed!' But both rushed into the room without a thought for themselves or their own safety.

The window was wide open in there.

They rushed to it.

'There he goes!' shouted Commander Legge excitedly. 'And he's got my diamond, the Maybee diamond!' He took careful aim at the figure running across the garden in the rain. The figure reached the distant wall.

But Mrs Legge, taking careful aim herself, jogged him at the psychological moment.

The net result was a white cat and two chimney pots belonging to the house opposite. All three slid noisily down the slippery tiles and crashed into the street.

The figure in the mackintosh got over the wall and disappeared from sight. They heard his footsteps pattering swiftly along the distant road.

Cursing, the Legges rushed for the nearest of their telephones to communicate with Scotland Yard. Where were the police, damn them? They were always at your elbow when you were doing a spot of speeding, but they were never about when they were really wanted.

Mr Bisham came safely into the main road and dropped into a brisk walk. He felt pleased and safe as he hopped into another taxi and said, still slightly breathless: 'Charming weather? Waterloo, if you please, my friend . . .' It had been an exhilarating adventure; bullets whizzing about, people shouting and converging from all directions; altogether a mighty close shave! But his luck had held and this was his last job. It was a fitting and worthy finish. He was satisfied he had not been watched or followed when he left Broadcasting House, and he was satisfied he was not being followed now. The truly magnificent Maybee diamond was now in his own left-hand trousers pocket. Tonight, Leveson was coming to the little birthday dinner party Marjorie had planned, and he would be given the parcel of jewels. Leveson was a dull old stick, but he was an old acquaintance, if not exactly friend, and he was going to Russia tomorrow night, by submarine, on a special Admiralty mission. He had already agreed to take 'a brown paper parcel, not exceeding twenty pounds in weight', and of course it would not be anything like that; and it would be addressed simply, 'To The Russian Government In Moscow'. Leveson had asked few questions; he knew Bisham, and he also knew the Russian Government. Further, he promised Bisham lifelong secrecy. Leveson was a man whose bald head contained more secrets than the heads of a hundred men added together. They would all die quietly and unobtrusively with him. 'Only a matter of some twenty-four hours or so,' thought Mr Bisham, jogging up and down restfully in the taxi and suddenly became aware, to his mortification, that both his mackintosh and his trousers were badly torn in a quite impossible place. He screwed himself round, trying to estimate the true extent of the damage, as the taxi bounded up the incline into Waterloo station. And who should open the door for him but Lord Sudbury! Fortunately, Lord Sudbury always concentrated on the matter in hand, and the matter of the moment was just to grab anybody's taxi; it didn't matter at all whether he'd met the present occupant before or not, life was full of bally coincidences of that sort. Mr Bisham, nevertheless, kept his back view in the direction of the station hotel, and his front view in the direction of his lordship. His lordship looked ruddy and stooping, and as if he had just returned from examining his crops in some southern part of the country. He had on a little green hat with a pheasant's feather in it, and chamois gloves. He blared: 'Have you done with this thing?' meaning the taxi and went on: 'Ah, it's you, how do! They haven't caught the scoundrel,' he said at once, 'they call the Man In The Mask, yet! I don't know how that feller Hood spends his time, I'm sure! I wonder if he ever thinks of the taxpayer,' his lordship proceeded to grumble at some length.

'I don't suppose they ever will catch him,' said Mr Bisham in a burst of confidence, but partly for something to say. He became aware that his lordship was staring at him strangely.

'What the devil have you done to your face?' enquired Lord Sudbury sharply. He stared at it.

Mr Bisham had been just about to enquire after Bardner. He felt a little conscience-stricken on behalf of Bardner, and would not like to think he had got him the sack.

'My face, Lord Sudbury?' he said, startled, and forgetting Bardner's existence.

'It looks as if it is covered in soot, sir!' Lord Sudbury sounded as if there was quite enough wrong with our announcers as it was, without having to see their sooty faces into the bargain. 'If you'll forgive my mentioning it!'

There was then the picture of ruddy Lord Sudbury, sitting forward in the departing taxi, looking in continued astonishment up and down one of England's leading announcers, who was standing rather apologetically with one hand held curiously behind his back, and with a sooty face, and with a wet mackintosh which appeared to be daubed with plaster or paint. In the folds of his hat there were strange fragments of glass and chandelier crystals.

'Mad!' muttered Lord Sudbury to himself. 'Stark mad! Altogether too much glass and paint at Broadcasting House! I suppose the fellow's been indulging in one of those BBC quarrels . . .!'

Ernest Bisham then became aware that he was cutting an

exceptionally curious figure and that people were staring at him.

He turned, holding his torn trousers, and hurried into the station hotel. He couldn't possibly go home like this.

Immediately he got into the hotel, another voice hailed him. One always met simply everyone at Waterloo.

And it would have to be Bess!

She exclaimed at once, and at the top of her voice:

'Ernest! Good gracious!' and demanded to know if he had been run over by a taxi or a bus, seeming inclined to favour the latter.

He told himself, as he had done on many former occasions, that there was just that something about his sister's aura which so readily caused him to feel—and appear—so irritated with her. It was in her aura, which was the colour of khaki, and in her masculine face, which was the colour of sunburned chalk, and it was in her intonations and her masculine manner. And then she had this knack of always appearing at the wrong moment, as now, when it was difficult to keep either dignity or temper. All he wanted, he said, was the temporary use of a room, and, he said, putting it badly, the temporary use of the hotel housekeeper, with her needle and thread and clothes brush.

He said so at high speed to the only official apparently available, a very old gentleman with no jacket and a long white beard.

But the old gentleman appeared to be foreign.

'Don't I make myself clear?' Mr Bisham said to him with vanishing patience. The old gentleman wasn't foreign, but merely a product of wartime. 'I want a room for a few minutes, perhaps an hour. And the use of your housekeeper . . . That is—'

'Here,' Bess interrupted, in her parade ground voice, 'let me have a go at him.'

She was satisfied that both men were a little dazed, the one through honourable age, and the other through having been run over in the skiddy road by a bus. She explained stolidly: 'We want a room, please. My brother has been run over by an omnibus . . .'

'I have not been run over by an omnibus!' Why did she always say 'omnibus', when everybody else said plain 'bus'? 'Leave me to handle this, Bess.'

'You're not capable of handling anything in your present condition. Nobody would dream you're . . . who you are, Ernest. You haven't been drinking?' she suddenly wondered. 'You used not to,' and it was suddenly possible to see her deducing hideous scenes at Tredgarth, Marjorie appearing with black eyes at breakfast, and the public never dreaming of the true character of their favourite announcer. 'You must get cleaned up,' she said, 'and your clothes mended. Then we'll have lunch and catch the next train.'

The aged hotel official started to tick over.

Oh, the lady and gentleman wanted a room? Well, then, he'd go and find the receptionist.

'That will be something,' said Miss Bisham tritely.

He shuffled slowly along the red carpet.

In the train, Ernest sat resolutely behind his *Evening Standard*. He offered no explanation to Bess as to his odd appearance; one didn't, to sisters. She seemed to think he had had a tumble, and that was good enough. For the rest, she sat in her khaki, with her grey, bobbed hair looking mannish, and with her legs crossed. She wished him 'many happy returns of the day, I haven't got a thing for you, I thought of a tie, but no coupons,' enquired after Marjorie and marriage with her usual suspicion. 'I 'phoned her from Ipswich. She sounded rather quiet. Is she?'

'Quiet . . .?'

'Has she got a cold, perhaps?'

'Don't think so.'

'Well, perhaps it was the line.'

'Perhaps.'

She said: 'Who's coming to dinner?' and when he said he hadn't the faintest idea, she sniffed and said: 'Typical!' She was thoroughly *au fait* with invasion developments and details, and dark about them, completely confident and full of post-war plans—worldly and personal. Indeed, the trend of her conversation really seemed to have left the war; the war was rather like sand which still clung to her fingers, but which had almost run safely through.

'And how's the old BBC?' she wondered chattily. 'Any excitements lately? But of course you're really rather a dull crowd up there, aren't you?'

CHAPTER XXI

ALL the same, her remarks about the end of the war had made him thoughtful; what of his own future, with Marjorie?

When he stood alone in his study, the diamond in his hand, he felt a premonition of gladness that his exotic escapades were indeed over, and that something strange and indefinable, unallied to fear, had cured him, if cured was the word. Also, he thought he knew what it was. It was something that would be rather difficult to put into words, or even clear thoughts; it was something to do with Marjorie; something to do with having been obliged to lie to her. Indeed, there was a strange new feeling about her, a new tension. Just now, coming in with Bess, he had felt positively shy of Marjorie. Shy of your wife? Why? It wasn't anything Bess had said— and she had said a great deal about the incident at Waterloo, 'and there he was, my dear, and I made him sprawl over the housekeeper's knee, he simply refused to take off his trousers—being who he is, I suppose!' Marjorie took to the idea of an accident, with due sympathy and concern for him, and so there was another lie. And Marjorie had said Hood had been on the prowl and seemed to be interested in Leeman— and so there was another lie, in essence, for he had had to allow Leeman to reside in shadows of suspicion which really belonged to himself.

He put the Maybee diamond in the safe and relocked it. He suddenly longed for the morrow, when jewels and gems would belong to the murky past. He would sell the safe . . .

As he straightened his back, Bess came striding in.

There was a truly astounding incident.

She was curiously flushed.

'Ernest!' she cried. And she suddenly gave him one of her

rare kisses, rather like a woodpecker. 'My dear—why didn't you tell me? And I suppose you hope it will be a boy . . .!'

He stood stunned.

She didn't stay; news of this kind always sent Bess Bisham to a telephone without delay. Coupons would no longer present the slightest difficulty. They would be found somewhere and somehow. Meanwhile, she would rush about the house pulling open strange cupboards and drawers in search of long-forgotten garments and enormous knitting needles.

When he found the use of his legs, Bess was to be heard thumping about up in the spare room.

He stood on the landing and called:

'Marjorie . . .?'

His immaculate voice sounded strangely hoarse. He felt ridiculously and intensely shy and suddenly knew what was the matter with him. Love was a queer thing, especially when it got you after forty.

'Marjorie, my dear?' He called her again.

His voice echoed through their gingerbread house.

She had fled down the garden.

She hadn't meant to tell Bess. She hadn't meant to tell anyone until she'd told Ernest. But, a little faintness . . . And you couldn't possibly hide anything from Bess.

When he found her, she was bending over the new chicken coop. She had taken to rearing chickens, on the advice of Shorter, who declared it would help see the local hospital through eggs next winter, 'if handled right', and, trying desperately hard to 'handle it right', so that Ernest wouldn't see the rush of colour to her face, she gave the chickens fresh food and water. They were streaky yellow and brown, with white little beaks.

He came up to her and started looking a little pink and ponderous.

She looked rather large, bending down, and he had the naïve thought that their child would be rather large too, when it bent down forty years from now; it would be sure to be a girl and go in for odd colours, like Marjorie did. Marjorie was in a long flowing red dress; it matched the flowering currant at the door of the greenhouse there. Her hat was the colour of the newly painted green water barrel. After a bit she looked up and gave him a bright smile. He smiled.

She noticed the quaint frequency with which he embraced her throughout the rest of the afternoon and the early evening, not even minding Bess's presence. He seemed to think that this procedure was required of him, and urgently; and as she was in love with him, it was, of course. He seemed to think she should now sit down more than she should stand up, and that Lucas should not bound at her, and that she should not bump into things. He politely moved chairs, saying: 'Careful, my dear!' and frowning anxiously. He was rather hot and red. Just before going down to receive their guests, he kissed her again, and in consequence had to go and wipe her lipstick from his face. Before going, he turned to her and said quaintly:

'I don't think I realized quite how fond of you I really am, my dear. Until today.'

He meant, of course, that he was in love with her. She knew that. Men were scared of the word 'love' and preferred to say 'fond'. They dodged 'dearest' as much as possible, and often even 'darling', and said instead, 'My dear', like an announcer!

Her eyes sparkled.

'Dear Ernest . . .!'

And the evening sparkled as well as any evening of their lives so far, notwithstanding the dourness of bald Mr Leveson, who was politely stiff and inarticulate in technique, and to whom Bess talked continuously in a loud voice upon all subjects throughout dinner. The three Misses de Freece, looking very tall and smiling, sat in a thin row, saying it was wonderful to have anything to eat at all when one thought of the European countries. They had several new guesses when the war would now end, making it much nearer than usual. Annabella and Jonas sat saying very little and holding hands under the table in a chaste, old-fashioned way. There was nothing abandoned about the love-products of this war; it was old lace and lavender; there had been nothing new to learn, either about love, or about sex. After dinner quite a lot of people, described as 'strays', were 'dropping in for a drink and a dance', including Mr and Mrs Wintle, who didn't drink or dance, but who liked to be neighbourly whilst declining to eat other people's dinners in wartime. Sitting at the head of his table, and watching Marjorie at the other end, Mr Ernest Bisham felt that things were all too good to be true. And, very suddenly, to the tune of his favourite modern song, it came startlingly to his senses that they were! He had just said good-bye to the Misses de Freece, who didn't care to be about too late in the blackout. He closed the front door on their torchlight and there was the distant strain of 'When I Look At You, I Look At An Angel', which Annabella had put on the radiogram; they were dancing in the hall-lounge. He had the uncomfortable sensation of not being alone in the curtained lobby by the front door there—and suddenly there was a second sensation. Something was sticking sharply into the pit of his back.

'Count ten before you do anything silly,' Leeman said softly, but quite pleasantly. He suggested: 'Shall we go up to your study by the back way, Mr Bisham?'

Marjorie's laugh rang out. There was the quaint sound of Bess and Mr Leveson discussing the 'Victory Polka'.

Things were getting merry.

Mr Bisham's sense of the ludicrous did not desert him as he walked silently ahead up the stairs. Leeman's footsteps creaked behind him. Where was Mrs Leeman? Gone, no doubt. This was no doubt carefully arranged. Leeman probably had a record—or had he merely been attracted by the new safe?—and the sight of Hood today might have given him swift-moving ideas. How much did he know? Did he know anything at all? He couldn't. Yet there was the uncanny feeling that he did. Had he really got the gun habit? Or was it bluff? This was indeed ironic! The tables turned and the biter bit! But, to be sporting, it was entirely justifiable and deserved. Alas, that it should have to be at such a time, when, tomorrow, it would have been too late. He tried not to think of exposure and shame, of Marjorie and their child, who, he thought, would be called Daisy. She would be a lady announcer called Daisy Bisham reading it. Now was the time to keep calm. Calm? Bess, the family name, Marjorie and Daisy; their joint future in the happy peace days which were round the corner . . .

'That's the ticket,' Leeman said. 'Go right across the room, near the wall. You can drop your hands, I know where your gun is!' He grinned and locked the door with a quick movement. He stood with his back to the door and the gun raised, looking yellow and grinning.

Mr Bisham, feeling slightly embarrassed, sat on the arm of a chair and pulled out a cigarette.

To his acute discomfort, he became aware that the safe was standing wide open. On the table in front of it, his parcel for Leveson was also lying open. The Maybee diamond, amongst the former possessions of Lady Stewker, Mrs Mansfield and Lord Sudbury, were glinting attractively in the firelight.

Leeman said:

'So I looked at it this way, Mr Bisham. I totted up the rewards offered for recovery of the missing jewels, and for apprehension of the Man In The Mask, and I thought of the pleasure to be got in seeing him unmasked! And it is a pleasure, not to say a surprise! I couldn't believe it at first—'

'Shall we get to the point?' suggested Mr Bisham. He sat with his arms folded, the smoke from his cigarette curling up his back. 'My guests, you know! I rather fancy that our time is, of necessity, limited,' he hinted. It was meant as a warning to Leeman, who seemed commendably calm and sure; but it was also a voicing of his own fears; Marjorie or one of the others might come and look for him any moment. Of course, he realized Leeman held all the cards, and had only to expose him . . .

'I think we're all right for five minutes,' Leeman said. He kept the revolver poised. 'If anybody comes before we're finished, I shall have to ask you to say something tactful through the door!'

Mr Bisham thought:

'When *I* point a gun—it's sheer bluff. It is with most people . . . What about you?'

He tried to measure this delicate problem while Leeman talked. He'd started to talk rapidly, all his cards, as it were, tumbling excitedly onto the table at once. He was more excited than he probably wanted to show. That was a fine point. He looked sallow and lean, but his cheekbones were slightly tinged with colour. His hair was greasy and sleek and excessively unattractive. Mr Bisham tried to guess his strength. He was thin, but he looked wiry. He was evidently an expert safebreaker, and that probably meant he'd done time, his complexion indicated that, so probably he was pretty tough in a scrap. Mr Bisham peeped down at his own ever-growing paunch, regretting it anew. All the same, if Leeman got at all close, or off his guard, it might be a good thing to chance it? Yes, about the only hope of salvation would be to lay Leeman flat and keep him like that until Leveson was safely out of the country tomorrow night. If Leeman tried any nonsense about exposure then, he would just be laughed at, without the necessary evidence. The only alternative, which Leeman was now verbally inviting, was, alas, quite out of the question. The man seemed to think that announcers were millionaires!

'I haven't got that amount of money, my friend,' Mr Bisham apologized ruefully, and got up from the arm of the chair with a casual movement.

'Keep over there, please.'

'With pleasure . . .!'

'Well, it's my only offer. And I reckon it's quite a sporting one, Mr Bisham? But, after all, I don't bear you any malice; I've no wish to get you or anybody else seven years—I know what it means! But I have to think of the money, and you know what reward they're offering. I can't afford to ignore it, and that's the truth.' His little black eyes gleamed and he seemed almost to plead, in a quaintly childish way: 'Mrs Leeman and I always wanted a hotel in Bognor.'

'Bognor,' thought Mr Bisham.

'It's very wet down there,' he heard himself criticizing stupidly. He was trying to decide whether Leeman really would decide to shoot if he rushed him. He certainly looked a nasty piece of work.

A door opened downstairs.

'It's for you to say the word, Mr Bisham,' Leeman's voice almost pleaded. 'And to show how much I respect your word, I'd take a cheque. The Man In The Mask has a reputation for being a sport.'

Mr Bisham thought:

'Well, there's one solution!'

But he knew he could never sink to a solution like that. It was a question of honour.

During the pause, he strained his ears to hear if anyone was coming up the stairs.

But the door shut again.

'Well?' said Leeman.

'Sorry,' said Mr Bisham, stubbing out his cigarette in the duck-egg ashtray Seal had given him years before. 'I suppose I could easily give you a dud cheque, my friend! But it's not my way of doing business!'

'I'll drop it to five thousand pounds, then. Half down and—'

'I have not got that amount of money.'

'You must have,' exploded Leeman, turning aggressive. 'In your position!' There was an unsatisfactory pause and he went on: 'Very well. But you can't say I haven't given you a sporting chance.' He shrugged. 'I take the jewels to Inspector Hood. And I say where I got them from.'

'Be careful! He may not believe you!'

'I've thought of that. But having been down here *I*'ve got a perfect alibi—'

Suddenly Mr Bisham made up his mind.

With guns, he decided, Leeman was too much of the pleader to be anything but bluffing.

Having positively decided this, he strode quickly and rather weightily across the room and, unimpeded, except by a warning snarl, gave Leeman a straight right across the jaw.

Unfortunately, when he stepped back, he did not observe the little red footstool Marjorie had bought for his comfort from Heal's. He fell flat on his back with a heavy, breathtaking thud.

Leeman made no second error of judgment. He knew he never had any inclination for what he called 'swinging jobs', and now that his bluff had failed so surprisingly he stuffed the revolver back into his pocket and picked up a small black chair. He was against robbery with violence too, with its unpleasant sentence if and when caught, but, for once, he felt he was working on the side of justice. He wanted the evidence and he meant to get the reward it would bring. Mrs Leeman would be at the station by now, waiting for him. He'd given the man every chance.

He brought the chair down on Mr Bisham's head with plenty of force and without feeling too squeamish about it.

As he did so, portly Mr Bisham made a dive for his legs and seized them in a muscular grip.

He fell to the floor, knocking over a small table. There was a loud crash of smashing brandy glasses.

Bess Bisham gave a slight start. She thought she heard a crash upstairs, but she wasn't sure. Mr Leveson didn't appear to have heard anything. He danced stiffly with her to the vocal refrain entitled 'How's Your Love Life?' It seemed a little unseemly, but Mr Leveson wore a thin, polite smile on his pale, studious face. He was bald at the front of his domed head, and two beads of sweat rose and swelled and rivalled each other in size. It was a hot May night, and without being able to open any windows or doors because of the black-out wartime dancing was hardly a pleasure for the aging. Soon, however, all doors and windows would be flung open to the spring and summer nights, and the scent of tobacco plants would seep excitingly in again. Mr Leveson started to say that he must be getting back to London and the Dorchester. He was leaving at midnight on the morrow and still had much to do. He had an Admiralty car, which he drove himself; their beautiful chauffeurs embarrassed him. She took him to the sofa, where Marjorie gave him a drink. He turned to Marjorie and asked where Ernest was. Marjorie, startled, realized that Ernest had been missing for some little time. Just then, Bess thought she heard another crash upstairs. What on earth was going on? Where was Ernest, anyway? Neglecting his guests like this! She crossed the dance floor and started up the stairs. As she reached the top, she heard a door open and shut and somebody, she thought, hurrying down the back stairs. She marched to Ernest's door and opened it.

'Ernest . . .!'

He was sitting dejectedly in his armchair. The room was in complete chaos and there was a large lump on the left side of his forehead.

He thought:

'Well, the game's up. I suppose it was bound to beat me in the end.' He remembered how sure he had always been that you never got caught out if your motive was clear and you had no fear. That was wrong, then? He felt his head painfully and wondered if he was going to be sick.

He interrupted Bess's flood of enquiry with a vague:

'Oh, I had a . . . fall.'

She cried:

'A fall? *Another? Have* you taken to secret drinking, Ernest?' she again demanded sternly. 'Just look at the room! What on earth is that lump on your head?'

'I've just told you.'

'How could you fall, up here? At your age—'

'I suppose a man can slip.' Slip was indeed the word.

'Slip? On a thick pile carpet?' She stared round the room. She had never seen such chaos, and Ernest so tidy and methodical.

'Please spare me all these questions and get me something for my head.' He invented, with an eye to the inevitable discovery of the Leemans' absence: 'If you must know, I've had a row with Leeman. He was . . . insolent. He's left.'

She mouthed his words.

'Insolent? *Left?* He *struck* you?'

'Well, he tried to . . . that is to say, he wanted some money. Oh, what does it matter? I fell over the damn table. Get me something for my head and for goodness sake don't say anything to Marjorie. I mean, about Leeman. I can't have her upset.'

'Upset? She's been wondering where on earth you've been all this time. Ignoring your guests . . .' She strode out for a cold compress, calling over her shoulder: 'And Mr Leveson's going . . .'

He thought, staring at the empty safe:

'My whole world is going. It goes with Leveson.'

Going, going—gone.

He buried his face in his hands.

CHAPTER XXII

WHEN everyone had gone, he sat alone with Lucas by the dying fire. Bess and Marjorie had gone up to bed.

He regarded himself as a man who had already been sentenced, but who had been granted, as a boon, this one night of sanctity and freedom. Honour was still intact; he would go upstairs in a moment or two, and in Marjorie's expression there would still be that trust, respect and contentment. She would no doubt give him another cold compress, and they would talk of Daisy and their plans for her. He was sure it would be a girl, and they must plan for her. Perhaps she would be the first lady to read the Home News!

Their plans!

What could those plans be now?

He was not due on duty on the morrow until the nine o'clock news, which he was to read, and she would be looking forward to his company until about seven, when he would have to catch his train. That was what she would be contemplating now. But what would, in fact, happen? Leeman's train would by now be running into London. He was evidently determined on contacting Hood at Scotland Yard, and nobody else. Probably he would contact him tonight, and then, some time tomorrow morning, well, there would be a ring at the front door.

In the evening papers, all of them, there would be, perhaps, headlines which would oust the war. It would give the gentle reader a change of diet—and a spicy one.

And at nine, when Big Ben was striking, Marjorie might be sitting here listening to the news, which, this awful time, would have to say, in another voice . . .

*

He lit a cigar and got up.

He went into the night-scented garden.

The sky was a fading black, turning greyer and somehow higher; stars had begun to peep in the East. Gradually, it would turn to dim light in the small hours, blushing, finally, through seeping dew, into another beautiful day.

When it at last dawned, Inspector Hood sat up on his elbow in bed.

The telephone was ringing.

He hadn't been in bed long, having been at work on another case outside London, a tasty affair of a woman found dead in a wood. She was wrapped up in a sack and had a silk handkerchief stuffed down her tonsils. There had been one or two irritations to complicate things, notably another assinine example of carelessness on the part of his young man Hanbury. Young Hanbury had fallen down again in precisely the same way he had fallen down only yesterday, when he'd detailed him to watch every movement of Ernest Bisham and trail him. In this murder case, Hanbury had gone and lost the trail of a suspect, as yesterday he had altogether failed to see Bisham come out of Broadcasting House. However, it was certain, was it not? Bisham could not have been at Commander Legge's house in Hampstead at the time of the astounding latest exploit of the Man In The Mask? For he was on the air then. Hanbury was safe about that, one presumed? At any rate it was confirmed in the *Radio Times;* Hanbury had produced a copy. Or ought one to check up even on that? What a very queer thing, though— yet another 'coincidence'—once again the victim had had very recent dealings with Mr Ernest Bisham, the announcer! Nor had one forgotten the very unsatisfactory item of the revolver and the three flattened bullets. Most unsatisfactory! Mr Bisham possibly didn't think so, but . . .

The telephone shrilled again and he put out a hand for it. The alarm clock said five to six, which was almost Mrs Hood's getting-up time. She was snoring tunefully; nothing but an actual alarm clock woke her.

'Hullo?' he said.

It was Hanbury and he was at the Yard. Well, he was a worker, anyway, even if he was a bit of a bungler at trailing people. Lots of the lads were bad at that, it required a sort of flair, and perhaps Hanbury would improve.

Suddenly Mr Hood sat bolt upright in bed.

'Say that again,' he said.

'It's a fact, Mr Hood. Every one of the missing jewels. In a brown paper parcel. It says on it "For The Russian Government, In Moscow", in an unidentified handwriting. Leeman won't open his mouth until you come, but he says he doesn't flatter himself *he's* the Man In The Mask. He's pretty cocky.'

'Have they checked up on him yet?' got out Mr Hood hoarsely.

'Yes. He's quite well known to us, but this kind of thing's right out of his class, I'm sure of that.'

'I'll be right along,' said Hood, and rang off.

Mrs Hood, used to this kind of thing, stirred in her sleep and said automatically:

'Who'd be a policeman's wife!'

The alarm clock went off as her husband scrambled out of bed, and he said: 'I don't know about that—we sometimes have our moments!' He stumbled past the cot containing Mrs Hood's dolls and went to the bathroom. He frowned all through breakfast and hardly listened to his wife's animated conversation, which was always about broadcasting at this time of the morning. She again demanded that she should be taken to Broadcasting House, 'to get a glimpse of Ernest Bisham in the flesh', the height of her ambition; only allow her that and she would die happy. Mr Hood looked blank. Why, what was so different about him, then? He was an announcer, admitted, but he was a man. And perhaps (it just occurred to him) he was a man who didn't think quite so highly of announcing as Mrs Hood did. His frown deepened. What sort of a man *was* he? His wife was certainly a delightful, homely creature; their home was beautiful; it was peaceful and happy in atmosphere. It was impossible to think anything dark about Ernest Bisham. Yet why did his name have to keep cropping up in this peculiar way? What was behind the mystery? Next, he frowned and thought: 'The Russian Government In Moscow? Unidentified handwriting?' Was there a political solution to the mystery? Goodness knows, he would much prefer the Russians to have the jewels than their original owners, but that was hardly the point. Mrs Hood sat chattering at the table with her black hair in curlers. She saw her husband frowning more than usual and she said didn't he like his ersatz egg? 'I don't know that I do, and I don't know that I don't,' he said, chewing it.

'It all depends how it's made. I always put plenty of fat with it—when I've got it. If you do that, it tastes like prewar.' She said not to take too much sugar in his tea, or it wouldn't last the week. And she said not to have any marmalade at all, as he had too much yesterday. She said men had no rationing sense, and she said: 'I hope you're going to be back to lunch, dear? I've got a rabbit from Agnes in the country.'

'A rabbit,' he said absent-mindedly, as she brushed his bowler hat by the door. Country, he thought. He had a wonder if he might not be back in the country by lunchtime, with a warrant for somebody's arrest. Leeman had come up from the country. Leeman was a cracksman, and there was the memory of a large green safe in a certain study. There was also the knowledge that Leeman could not have been in Hampstead at one o'clock yesterday.

He felt so perplexed he almost forgot to say good-bye to the canary.

'And you haven't kissed me,' Mrs Hood complained, shaping her lips like a spout.

He kissed her and explained:

'A certain case is getting me down, I'm afraid. However, it may be nearer the end than I dare to hope.'

'But shall you be back to lunch, dear?'

'I dunno.'

'Try.'

'I'll try,' he promised, going out of the front door. 'I'll ring up presently.'

'And don't forget you promised to take me over to Broadcasting House—'

'Oh, some day.'

'Oh, you said Mr Bisham said any day, dear! You said he was charming!'

'We'll see,' he said, and going out into Shepherd's Bush he wondered whether it mightn't be even sooner than he anticipated that he, at least, might not be seeing that august personality again. He was charming all right.

In Shepherd's Bush, the new day was getting ready. Buses were lining up at their starting point, and on the green, coatless gentlemen in mufflers were letting their restive dogs off their leads.

In about twenty minutes he was back at the Yard.

He stood staring at the missing gems, and from them to Leeman—and back again.

Leeman had said his say and he sat on a wooden chair in Hood's office with a cigarette hanging from his mouth, and with his thin hands hanging between his knees. A pale grin touched his features, and he took no notice of the police officer standing at the door. Policemen had no fears for him this time; he'd found the missing property, and he'd discovered the identity of the Man In The Mask—or so he believed. It was a good day's work altogether, and when the reward was paid over he and Mrs Leeman would retire to Bognor. No more prison life for him. He felt sorry for Mr Bisham, but he'd given him his chance and if the man was too vain, or too mean, to take it, that was his affair.

He glanced across at Hood, who seemed in quite a stew about something or other. What was he sweating himself for? The whole thing was plain as a pikestaff.

Hood sat down at his broad desk and suddenly said:

'Lock him up,' and stared sourly.

The police officer moved forward and Leeman jumped to his feet.

'What . . .!'

'Oh, only on suspicion,' Mr Hood explained, bored. 'I mean, of course,' he explained sourly, 'on suspicion of having robbed Mr Ernest Bisham, the announcer, at his country place.'

Leeman had turned livid.

'*Robbed* him? But I've already explained—'

'I don't know that it's particularly legal, Leeman, to open a safe like that. And you haven't offered any suggestion that you knew beforehand what *was* in Mr Bisham's safe. What would you have done if there'd been nothing but money in it? . . . You come up here and bring me some interesting little trinkets, admitted, but which trinkets seem to belong to the Russian Government! Mr Bisham will no doubt explain why he holds them, and when they're due for dispatch! I don't see that it should concern you at all!' He waved a hand. 'Take him away. I'm afraid we shall have to hold you until I've had time to look more closely into it. I can't be sure, at this stage, whether you've robbed Mr Bisham—or the Russian Government.'

Leeman rolled his eyes in anger and bawled:

'Can't you see what's in front of your eyes? Mr Bisham is the Man In The Mask!'

Mr Hood shook his head regretfully.

'I'm afraid announcers aren't quite so romantic as all that!' He put on his pipe. 'There's one little point you ought to know, Leeman. Mr Bisham has as good an alibi as you. When Commander Legge was being robbed yesterday in Hampstead of that little beauty,' he pointed at the Maybee diamond, 'Mr Ernest Bisham was deep inside Broadcasting House . . . broadcasting!'

'But—'

'How it got into Mr Bisham's safe is a knotty little point I've still got to solve.' He nodded to the officer. 'Take him away and give him a nice cup of tea. We're always considerate to our guests here at the Yard!'

As he was being led protestingly away, young Hanbury's red head appeared round the door.

'Get on to the BBC,' said Hood thoughtfully, 'and find out if Mr Ernest Bisham is expected in town today.'

'What—the announcer . . .?'

'Yes,' said Hood drily. 'The announcer! Don't say you're after his autograph too?'

'No, sir . . .'

'And if he is expected—what time.'

Hanbury looked at him. But Hood's face was expressionless. He was staring at the jewels, and at the handwriting on the brown paper. 'Nobody asks for my autograph,' was all Hood commented, and Hanbury went out.

Hanbury was feeling very thoughtful himself, and it was about a very uncomfortable little matter connected with the dramatic theme—Could The BBC Possibly Make A Mistake?

For Detective Inspector Hanbury had made a bad howler over the little matter of trailing Mr Bisham yesterday. Hood knew that, of course, and had given him a warning and a dressing down, but he didn't know the true extent of the error, for he had only just discovered it himself. In a way, it was a forgivable mistake, except that Hood never forgave anything in that line. But it was a fact that the *Radio Times* had printed—rather, misprinted—the information that Mr Ernest Bisham was 'here in the studio to announce a selection of his favourite gramophone records, chosen by himself'; in addition, it had been announced over the air like that. In consequence, Hanbury had sat outside Broadcasting House in his police car, listening to his radio set, confident that his quarry was safely within and need not be watched for thirty minutes. Whereas, the awful

truth was that Mr Bisham, well, might have been anywhere—
even in Hampstead. And in a few moments it would be his
painful duty to tell his chief he had not checked up his facts in
advance—if he had the nerve to tell him. Was it *really* necessary
to tell him, he wondered. Could it possibly be . . . postponed
until a bit later, when the Chief Inspector was less worried,
when they saw how things shaped? The jewels were here, after
all; a solution to the mystery must be very near, it was probably
something to do with Leeman. On the other hand . . .

He dialled Welbeck 4468.

Thinking hopefully, he stood listening to the burring sound.
A seductive feminine voice said:

'BBC . . . BBC . . .'

By the time he had returned to Mr Hood's room, he had made
up his mind. It was clearly his duty to confess to Hood at once
and risk his renewed wrath. He would tell Hood the news that
Mr Bisham was expected at Broadcasting House at about eight
fifteen tonight, for the nine o'clock news, and then he would
get it over.

He knocked at the door.

Chief Inspector Hood, however, was gone.

Another clue, his secretary told him, had just cropped up
in the murder case; he'd probably be back in the late afternoon.

'A short reprieve,' thought Hanbury to himself.

He went out, chewing his nails and pondering weakly:

'Shall I tell him? . . . Or shan't I?'

CHAPTER XXIII

MR. ERNEST BISHAM, the famous announcer, showed his pass and walked into Broadcasting House for what he considered the last time. It had been a day of torturing stress, and it had almost been a relief to say good-bye to Bess and to Marjorie (and to Daisy). He did not pretend to know the cause of the delay in arresting him; no doubt they were waiting until he reached London. Alighting at Waterloo had been an anxious and distressing moment. Passing the barrier, all the faces there seemed to be watching him and waiting for him; he could feel in advance a hand on his shoulder. Yet as he whistled nervously his favourite tune, he safely reached the taxi rank. 'They'll be waiting for me at Broadcasting House, then,' he decided, and he sat back in the taxi and painfully shut his eyes. The bump on his forehead had gone down a good deal, but it was crimson and yellow and blue. The picture of Marjorie flooded back, as she tended it. It was quite true that motherhood increased a woman's beauty and softened her. She'd said, so sweetly: 'Good-bye, Ernest, dear. Bess and I will be listening at nine.' Even her voice was softer. Even Bess seemed to be affected for the better. There was the good-bye picture of them both together on the sofa, with Lucas chewing Bess's copious knitting. 'No more falling about, for goodness sake,' had been Bess's crisp good-bye. 'Remember, you need dignity now, Ernest. You're not merely an announcer—you're almost a father!' He'd walked quickly out of their gingerbread house. In his pocket was a letter which would feebly and desperately try and explain to Marjorie and the jury the simple but no doubt astonishing truth that announcing was an over-glamourized pastime. You couldn't compare it to memorizing *Macbeth*, and, *'how can I put it, Marjorie, it just didn't seem* worthy *enough, or in any way a big enough contribution to the war effort. It's just reading out loud, you see, my dear, and I thought I wanted to do something bigger than that, so many people are taking such unbelievable risks, to help bring the war to a happy conclusion and, well, frankly, being a cat-burglar seemed to be the only thing I could do, and I'd had my training.'* Later in the letter which was a very long one, written on BBC notepaper, it said: *'But then I fell in love with you, my dear, and quite a long time after our marriage. And all at once it dawned on me that it didn't really matter what job we did, all of us, so long as we did something honest, and did it well. And then suddenly I thought of Daisy. She might be quite proud to know that her father had actually announced the signing of the Armistice on Victory Night. Then I knew, positively, Marjorie and Bess, I was not ashamed of being an announcer, after all. I was proud of it. Being a cat-burglar, even for Russia, seemed unnecessary, when there were many more intelligent and less humiliating ways of helping her.'* And he put: *'I really did it, mistakenly, for you, my dear. It was our daughter who really put a final stop to it.'* Once, he put, thinking of his daughter: *'At least I've never been a journalist.'* He had a new and desperate anxiety for wanting her to be proud of his record.

He apologized to Marjorie for assuming their child would be a girl, but he said he 'couldn't help feeling it would be'. He put: 'I must not say *it*, must I?' and went on to suggest 'a choice of names for *her*'. He thought Maisie was nice, or Prunella, or Leslie, or even Bess, if you used it in full—Elizabeth. 'But, Marjorie, let's call her Daisy. I always wanted a daughter called that. Marjorie can be her second name.' Anything could do for any third name, except Seal. Elizabeth, no doubt.

Thinking, rather pleased, about all these points, he entered Home Presentation. Only one person remarked on the colourful bruise on his forehead, blandly assuming that old Bisham must have had one of those rows with the Home News Talks editor. Otherwise, everything and everybody was quite as usual and he hung up his hat. A lady announcer, in a green jersey, was eating a spam sandwich and polishing her nails at the same time. There was the smell of spam and the smell of peardrops. A fellow announcer, who was so good looking he looked ill, was telephoning his wife in aristocratic tones and going: 'Oh, well, let her come, then, Sweetie, the poor little thing.' His striped back view kept going: 'Oh, well, let her come, then, Sweetie, the poor little thing.'

Mr Bisham moved along beside the bed and washed his hands in the wash-basin. Then he took a towel and dried his hands preparatory to going up to the news room.

As he did so, a messenger knocked and put his head in the door. Mr Bisham had an immediate presentiment and his heart had already started to thump when the man said:

'Mr Bisham? Two people to see you at the Reception Desk, sir.' He waited.

He swallowed.

He tried to say: 'I'm about to go on the air,' but no sound came. It was like his first audition.

'Two people,' his voice came.

'From Scotland Yard,' the man said, and vanished.

Somebody made a quip, but nobody else said anything and he threw his towel down and went unhurriedly out into the corridor. In the corridor there was a strong smell of fried fish coming from the canteen. Figures were hurrying to and fro, there was a show going on in the Mixer, the red light was on. An elderly cleaner in a brown overall was sweeping up fag ends, and the Brains Trust, flushed, were leaving Studio B3 with much animated conversation, the Question Master looking hungry but pleased. Mr Bisham was trembling. He put on a cigarette in the familiar way; the case Marjorie had given him, the lighter Bess had given him. He decided:

'May as well get it over. There are others to read the news tonight. And my voice has gone.'

A burst of music came from the Disc Room. Sir Henry Wood.

He would go and face the music and then send a message.

He felt very sad and wished he could have read aloud to Marjorie for the last time.

There was the customary crowd and sense of bustle at the Reception Desk. The messenger had referred to two people, but he was aware only of Chief Inspector Hood, in the throng, looking just as he had looked that last time, in the Drawing Room. Now, wearing the same baffling expression, a fusion of the whimsical and the shrewd, he sat on the leather seat underneath the new photographs of the workers in the Corporation, producers and script writers busy in studios; he was the man who held his Destiny in his hands; Marjorie's happiness, Daisy's. Hood was not looking at the photographs, though. He was not looking sentimental, either, and he was looking at him.

Scarcely conscious of what he was doing, he went up to Hood, shook hands with a smile and sat down beside him. He glanced at his watch from sheer habit. He should normally be up in the news room in four minutes' time. Messengers and messenger boys hurried to and fro all round them; men and women came and went. The exotic ladies beyond the wire of the Reception Desk dealt with telephones and a succession of anxious people waiting to sign passes. There was the stir and din of many voices, and in the hub of it he and Hood sat looking at each other—smiling shyly. He then became aware that on Hood's knee rested a familiar-looking parcel addressed to the Russian Government in Moscow, in painfully familiar handwriting.

'I need hardly say,' Hood's voice was saying pleasantly—no doubt it was etiquette to be social even on these delicate occasions—'I feel very sorry to . . . interrupt you at such a moment, Mr Bisham!' He gave a polite glance up at the clock there, beyond the policemen at the gate. 'Indeed, I shouldn't have been at all surprised if you'd sent and said you, er, couldn't come!'

Mr Bisham continued smiling rather brilliantly, but once again his world-famous voice had deserted him.

He cleared his throat.

'Er . . .'

'But,' went on the inspector, smiling, still himself, 'I would, of course, have waited.'

'Of course,' Mr Bisham got out, overloudly this time, as if his voice had been glued before and was now suddenly unstuck.

'And I daresay you know why I've come,' Mr Hood said next, and dropped his eyes to the parcel.

Mr Bisham dropped his eyes too.

He heard somebody say excitedly:

'There, Doris! Over there! . . . That's Ernest Bisham, the announcer . . .!'

Deeply sad, he lifted his eyes again; but to see, astoundingly, the Inspector suddenly and calmly pass across the parcel, and to hear him say, even more astoundingly:

'But I felt it important to return you your very valuable property, Mr Bisham, for—er—Russia; and to say you've nothing further to worry about—we've got Leeman safely under lock and key, and I've got a very strong kind of feeling,' he seemed to be suggesting, 'we shan't have any more trouble with the Man In The Mask?'

Their eyes met.

Yes, there was something exceedingly whimsical about the Inspector's eyes, wasn't there? Particularly when he went on to say: 'Ah, I'm not saying *Leeman* was the Man In The Mask'; and when he got to his feet and said, with little better than schoolboy artifice:

'But where are my manners, Mr Bisham! I've taken the very great liberty of bringing along an admirer of yours who *very* much wanted to meet you! May I present—Mrs Hood?'

It was an electric moment, perhaps the most electric and exotic of his life.

Yet, as their two secret minds remained sealed and inartic-ulate, it also seemed to be the most outwardly ordinary and simple moment, Mrs Hood, wearing a feathery hat, blushing and saying shyly: 'Pleased to meet you, Mr Bisham, I'm *sure* . . .!' and the Inspector's laugh. He laughed and declared: 'Why, my dear, I daresay Mr Bisham doesn't find his job nearly so glamorous as some others, say, the Man In The Mask, eh, Mr Bisham? A job's just a job, as I soon found out myself—once you've found out all you wanted to about it?'

'Yes . . .'

'Everything's so much a question of *proof*,' was the Inspector's obscure concluding remark. 'Well, my dear,' he said, 'we mustn't make Mr Bisham late! There are twenty million people waiting, so I believe, not to mention a very charming lady I recently had the pleasure to meet . . .!'

Mr Bisham walked up to the news room in a daze. The parcel was in his hand and his mind was trying to concentrate on Mr Leveson and the Dorchester. Realizing that there would be time enough for that until midnight, he tried to focus his bewildered mind onto realities. Words came back. 'Everything's so much a question of *proof*.' And: 'I'm not saying *Leeman* was the Man In The Mask!' A voice (his own) told him: 'There goes . . . no policeman—but a patriot!' It said: 'He thinks more of Russia than a Sudbury or a Stewker! Than a reward or a conviction!'

Another voice said:

'Truly our British policemen are wonderful!'

That patriot's sole return was to have brought a moment's exotic happiness to his wife. Indeed, to two wives. And to a child who wasn't born yet. One day she might walk up these very stairs.

Even the news room seemed a Paradise tonight, and the Duty Editor St Peter himself at the Pearly Gate!

In the studio, waiting to play a recording of 'An American Soldier's First Visit to Piccadilly', Jonas Wintle found Ernest

Bisham in the friendliest of moods, notwithstanding an unpleasant bruise on the left side of his forehead. It was clearly the time to tackle him about the possibility of becoming an announcer, surely one of the most colourful of professions, and very fitting for a newly married man.

And in a drawing-room down in Surrey, amongst the pine trees there, was another Paradise. For Marjorie had just told Bess she thought she had reached her nearest approach to earthly happiness. She agreed with Bess that Ernest was, perhaps, inclined to be a little stolid, even dull, but he was the man of her dreams.

If ever her happiness could reach a higher level, it could only be at such moments as when Big Ben chimed the hour, and she waited, as she was waiting now, to hear the voice like velvet she knew so well, saying that it was the nine o'clock news—and saying who it was reading it!

THE END

THE ALARM BELL

HE put on his old mackintosh because it was early and a bit chill, though not chill enough for an overcoat. In any case, he hadn't got much of an overcoat; also, in any case, it looked as if it might turn to rain presently—it usually did nowadays. He put his huge hands into the oddly small pockets of his rather shapeless mackintosh and went out as usual into dingy Shepherd's Bush. There were no signs of any shepherds, or of any bushes, but there were a few trees knocking around and he'd often thought it would make a fairly nice walk if he made a detour and cut through the green to work round by that way. But as a matter of fact he never had made such a detour before, because he had never been early before. He liked to read with his breakfast (well, he liked to read all the time, really—a spot of Shakespeare or something)—and he felt it was quite bad enough having to go to work at all, without leaving too early and going in for detours. Prolonging the agony, so to speak!

He gave a sort of chuckling grunt at the thought of all the tedious work which was involved in living, a sort of cynical *brmph!* and feeling good-humoured all the same, decided to make the detour for once, and so he went slowly and silently past the Shepherd's Bush Palace, the barrack-like pub at the far corner there, with no name on it, and across the green. The green was more brown than green from people sitting on it last summer, but there were plenty of autumn leaves and bare-looking trees, and dogs were up to their larks and trying to kid themselves they were in the heart of the country.

He moved lightly and silently for such a huge man, and his enormous hands were out of sight deep in his little mackintosh pockets right up to the thick, hairy wrists. He went on towards his work and on the way came to the dreary little street of red

houses—'family houses', he always thought of such dwellings—
which the milkman hadn't reached yet, and where one or two
collarless figures were leaving once again for collarless destina-
tions. There was the tumbling, waking noise of London, and
there was the smell of distant trains (the District line) and the
rattle of them, and then very suddenly the bell went off.

Trrrrrrr.

It came from the small house with the dirty green blinds.
He'd been deep, deep in thought (as anyone was entitled to
be—there was such a vast amount to think about in life), but
without knowing what it was he was thinking about so deeply
(as anyone was entitled to do), and what with the insistent
suddenness of the bell, he got deeper and deeper yet in thought;
people often did that, in the street or anywhere else—actors or
composers, for instance, though he was neither—that was how
people got run over by a bus. All the same, what with the bell
and the unusual morning detour, who can say but that the
Randall family might not still be alive today? But the bell of
their family alarm clock had gone off, and clearly at the psychological moment, and the next thing he saw of his hands was
when they were softly sliding up the unlatched window—people
really ought to go in for latches and locks more than they did.

He was a huge, quiet man in a mackintosh, and he stood
there at the strange window in the strange, empty street. He
softly pushed aside the faded green blind and stared in. It was
practically pitch-dark in there.

He didn't, of course, know who was in, if anyone, or who lived
here, or anything, any more than he knew when a policeman
or somebody might not come along the street. He didn't *know*
there was a family living here, but he supposed there must be
someone, since an alarm clock had gone off to wake someone
up and send that someone off to work once more. Alarm clocks
did go off freakishly, to be sure; they were temperamental things,
and if you wound them up carefully and set them for seven

o'clock tomorrow, quite likely, if they felt like it, they mightn't
go off until next Palm Sunday in the middle of the afternoon.
That was why his eyes were trying to pierce the depth of gloom
in the room, to see if there *was* someone who ought to be getting
up to go to work.

Well, if there was, they wouldn't have to go to work today—
they wouldn't have to go to work at all any more! How lovely
for them! It was to be hoped they said their prayers properly
last night, after setting the alarm bell.

He slipped silently into the dark room and quietly dropped
the blind back to the window behind him so that he was shielded
from the street again. The room smelt fuggy and cheap and
suddenly he heard someone breathing. It was all at once
intensely exciting. His huge hands started to grope, gently. They
had been hanging down, waiting. But they started to grope
towards the breathing. He ran his hands along, it was a long,
thin mound and it felt like a man—fairly young, the throat was.

It was soon over. It was tame. It wasn't a bit exciting. The young
man, if that was what it was, slumped back in the bed and
certainly wasn't breathing now. But then, suddenly, it was
exciting again. Very. Hang it, there was another person in the
bed! She suddenly shot up and let out a shrill:

'*Who's there? Is someone there?*' in tones of terror and alarm.
Then she started to shriek: '*Bob—?*' But fortunately she was
near, and he soon put a stop to that. All the same, she had
plenty of kick in her, and before he had finished with her he
heard a distinct and expressive thud on the floor above his
head, like a person just hopping quickly out of bed.

He didn't know it, of course, but it was Mr Randall, head of
the house.

Mr Randall sat on the edge of his untidy bed staring at his
pale, flabby feet. He slept in his day shirt and his white hair
stood up on end. He looked tasty! Old and muscular, tattooed,

and with white bristles all over his chin and fag ends all over the bed-table. He stared at his feet, but he was really trying to see through them, and through the floor, down to Vera and Bob. He thought she'd let out a yell of alarm, but on second thought she and Bob had only been married a week, it was probably just that. And she was always yelling at Bob anyway, apart from that; why the silly boy ever went and married such a creature, goodness only knew. But there you were; he was a Randall, and they never did know how to pick a woman! Widowerhood was by far the best; the last two years had been sheer heaven—he could smoke in bed again!

'You all right down there?' he called down vaguely, and vaguely wondered about burglars. But nobody called out again and she never said anything more, so he supposed it was marriage larks. And then he did hear some sort of movement down there somewhere—it sounded as if it was coming from Uncle George's room. Scuffling about or something. Let's hope somebody would have energy to bring up a spot of tea.

Mr Randall lit another fag and went on sitting on the edge of his bed, waiting to hear a step on the stairs which ought to mean tea.

He thought about Uncle George down there and wondered if that lazy man was thinking about him in connection with a cup of tea.

Uncle George wasn't! He was thinking about something much more pressing!

When the alarm clock by his bed had gone off, he first started thinking it was an alarm bell of some kind and meant some awful sort of danger. This was because he wasn't properly awake and had been horribly drunk last night again. First of all he thought the bell meant fire, and then his befuddled and drowsy brain decided it meant approaching murder. He tossed and turned in his semi-sleep, flinging his scraggy arms about, his blue-striped pyjamas buttonless about the chest, hating bells and, of course, murder; and his brain started up that conversation he'd had with a drunken crony about how it was that strangely queer tragedies sometimes happened to people *for no apparent reason*.

Why *did* certain things happen, things which one could never explain? For instance, in the blitzes, you heard about whole families who were wiped out overnight—and never a hint that they'd deserved it, or anything like that. And then the film, *The Bridge of San Luis Rey*—those people, just happening to be on it when it bust like that? What was the reason for that?

Uncle George then suddenly woke up. There had been a cry of some sort a moment or two ago, and he thought with rising resentment that it was Vera expecting him to get the tea again.

He got up, on an impulse, intending not to get the tea today—well, not at first (he had to remember he never paid any rent)—but to bawl at Vera through her door. Why shouldn't she get it? Or Bob? Or Sid, the lodger in the basement?—he was one of the family now, even if he was a sardine salesman and told interminable stories which everyone had heard before.

He thought angrily about Vera and buttonless pyjamas and sardines, and went to his door. He opened it, and then he stood there transfixed.

He saw the most incredibly horrible sight he had ever seen in his life. There were two eyes looking at him out of a huge mackintosh. But that wasn't all. While the eyes were looking at him (thin, trembling *him*), two enormous hands belonging to, and coming out of, the mackintosh, via two hairy wrists, *had got Sid*. They were dropping Sid, as if just about bored with him now, and Sid was grey and had newly arranged white eyeballs instead of eyes, and his tongue (which had talked so much) was bleeding on the wrong side of his teeth. It was like a huge, terrifying cat dropping one little mouse because it has suddenly seen a nice, long, trembling, thin one that has lost even the power to squeak.

And, indeed, that was exactly how it was. When Uncle George *was* ready to squeak, he found it impossible, on account of the intensely unpleasant pressure at his Adam's Apple. And as the pressure increased still more, Uncle George saw Sid, dead, and then, through the open door there, Vera and Bob, dead. That was three. *I'm the fourth, then*, Uncle George thought, aghast, and also thought of the *News of the World*, Sunday—imagine missing it! His head began to swim, and his thoughts started to send a frantic, telepathic warning upstairs to the old man. But his head started to burst and something awful was happening to the strength in his knees.

Old Mr Randall finished his latest fag and began to feel extremely irritated. What was the use of alarm clocks if folks just kept on wallowing in bed? He sat on the edge of the bed and looked like an angry old bull, for he had worked down at the docks all his life and was tough even if he was old. He decided that if he didn't hear a creak on the stairs before very long he'd start bringing the house down. He could hear the milkman getting nearer and nearer with his bottles, so they couldn't pretend there wasn't any milk—that was an old one, that was.

Mr Randall was just going to start roaring when he did hear a slight creak on the stairs. He felt a bit better tempered. Then there was a gentle knock on the door, which was unusual, and he growled, 'Oh, come in,' and turned away for his old dressing gown at the foot of the bed, in case Vera (who was a first class prude, considering the way she'd lived before she was married) made out she was shocked. Then, after hearing the door open softly, he was astounded to feel Vera's hands getting at his throat from the back. Then, suddenly, they were too strong for Vera's hands, there was a mass of hair at the wrists, and there was an unaccustomed smell of a mackintosh.

He plunged violently up off the edge of the bed and heaved his assailant across to the opposite wall. But it didn't do any good, there was iron here at his throat, and so he heaved and plunged back again and the table and lamp and fag ends fell to the floor with a crash. The brown room began to spin. The man in the mackintosh had worked his iron hands round to a frontal position, and the two gasping figures heaved desperately to and fro and fell out of the bedroom doorway and struggled frantically on the little landing there to the tune of approaching milk bottles. Then they started to tumble together down the narrow stairs, snapping the bannister rail. At the foot of the stairs, Mr Randall, who had had his day, was almost exhausted and breathless and had started to go a bit green.

The man in the mackintosh finally dumped him by the back door and then hurriedly went through the little house to the front door. He let himself out and went into the street. Except for the milkman's horse and cart, it was empty. There was no sign of the milkman, so he leaned up against the fence to get his breath back. It had been pretty terrific. He stood taking in great gusts of air.

The milkman had opened the back door in the way the Randall family always asked him to, and started to shove the milk bottles in. Then he saw Mr Randall.

Then he saw Sid, the lodger.

Then he saw Uncle George Randall.

Then he saw Vera and Bob Randall.

He went green as green and his mouth fell open and looked as if it would never shut again, any more than his eyes would.

He raced round into the street. The only person he saw in the distance was a man in a mackintosh going off to work. He tore up to him and gasped out that five people had been strangled at Number Twenty-Two, the house with green blinds, and to fetch a policeman at once while he went back and watched the house. Then he ran back.

The man in the mackintosh, startled, started to look for a policeman at once. He found one suddenly and agitatedly told him what the milkman had said. He gave the address of the house with green blinds and the policeman said cautiously, as if he never believed things straight off:

'Murder?' and moved away fairly quickly.

The man in the mackintosh watched him go. He felt upset, disliking melodrama, except in fiction. He had started, curiously, to think about bells. Why bells? But there, why did you think about anything at any given moment? Bells.

Good heavens, that reminded him, look at the time! What on earth was he doing this morning? He had made quite a detour. It was silly—he never would again. Quite apart from being late for work, imagine starting an already sordid day by being told by a milkman that a whole family had been wiped out overnight by a murderer! Why *did* such incredible things happen, he asked himself as he mingled with the crowd. Why, surely, only because madness was responsible for the ugliness and evil in this world. It was said the police had a positive theory that it was possible for a man to commit murder and not even know he'd done it. But surely that was going a bit far, even for madness!

Reaching his work, he dismissed the whole incident from his mind. It was nothing to do with him and there had been quite enough murder in recent years.

He heard the bell ring where he worked, and he was a sad man and it made something stir very vaguely in his head. But he smiled to himself and thought a bit whimsically about Shakespeare, whom he loved. He smiled and thought, *The bell invites me!* And he thought, dramatically:

Hear it not, Duncan! For, it is a knell that summons thee to Heaven! Or—to Hell!

THE END

Also available

Mr Bowling Buys a Newspaper

Donald Henderson

'I have a book called Mr Bowling Buys a Newspaper *which I have read half a dozen times and have bought right and left to give away. I think it is one of the most fascinating books written in the last ten years and I don't know anybody in my limited circle who doesn't agree with me.'*

RAYMOND CHANDLER

Mr Bowling is getting away with murder. On each occasion he buys a newspaper to see whether anyone suspects him. But there is a war on, and the clues he leaves are going unnoticed. Which is a shame, because Mr Bowling is not a conventional serial killer: he wants to get caught so that his torment can end. How many more newspapers must he buy before the police finally catch up with him?

'Henderson pursues a grim little theme with lively perception and ingenuity. His manner is brief, deliberately undertoned, and for the most part curiously effective.'

TIMES LITERARY SUPPLEMENT

Also available

Below the Clock

J. V. Turner

'One of the very few exponents of the art of the thud-and-blunder thriller who can stand comparison with the late Edgar Wallace.'

Many highly dramatic and historic scenes have been enacted below the clock of Big Ben, but none more sensational than on that April afternoon when, before the eyes of a chamber crowded to capacity for the Budget Speech, the Chancellor fell headlong to the floor with a resounding crash. For the first time a murder had been committed in the House of Commons itself – and Amos Petrie faced the toughest case of his career.

In *Below the Clock*, John Victor Turner—a journalist who as David Hume had become known as 'the new Edgar Wallace' for creating Britain's first hardboiled detective series—returned to classic Golden Age writing with an ingenious whodunit set at the heart of the establishment, a novel that did the unthinkable by turning Parliament into a crime scene and all its Members into murder suspects.

'He knows his underworld inside out.'